IF ONLY

IF ONLY

A Novel
by
Vigdis Hjorth

Translated
by Charlotte Barslund

VERSO
London • New York

This translation has been published with the financial support of NORLA

This English-language edition published by Verso 2024
Originally published as *Om bare*
© Cappelen Damm 2001
Translation © Charlotte Barslund 2024
Permission to reproduce Henrik Nordbrandt's 'Homecoming'
courtesy of Alfabet © Inger Christensen and Gyldendal

1 3 5 7 9 10 8 6 4 2

Verso
UK: 6 Meard Street, London W1F 0EG
US: 388 Atlantic Avenue, Brooklyn, NY 11217
versobooks.com

Verso is the imprint of New Left Books

ISBN-13: 978-1-83976-888-0
ISBN-13: 978-1-83976-890-3 (US EBK)
ISBN-13: 978-1-83976-889-7 (UK EBK)

British Library Cataloguing in Publication Data
A catalogue record for this book is available from the British Library

Library of Congress Cataloging-in-Publication Data

Names: Hjorth, Vigdis, author. | Barslund, Charlotte, translator.
Title: If only / a novel by Vigdis Hjorth ; translated by Charlotte
  Barslund.
Other titles: Om bare. English
Description: London ; New York : Verso, 2024.
Identifiers: LCCN 2024003496 (print) | LCCN 2024003497 (ebook) | ISBN
  9781839768880 (paperback) | ISBN 9781839768903 (ebook)
Subjects: LCGFT: Novels.
Classification: LCC PT8951.18.J58 O413 2024 (print) | LCC PT8951.18.J58
  (ebook) | DDC 839.823/74 – dc23/eng/20240202
LC record available at https://lccn.loc.gov/2024003496
LC ebook record available at https://lccn.loc.gov/2024003497

Typeset in Electra by Biblichor Ltd, Scotland
Printed and bound by CPI Group (UK) Ltd, Croydon, CR0 4YY

If Only

A NOVEL

Vigdis Hjorth

Your parents
became someone else's parents
and your siblings, neighbours.
The neighbours
became someone else's neighbours
and live
in other cities.
They come home in other cities
just like you do.
And they recognise you
just as little
as you recognise them.

Henrik Nordbrandt, 'Homecoming'

I

A long, long time ago when I was nineteen, I was at a railway station in another country. I felt so alone, so wretched. I remember asking myself: What's going to happen to me? What am I going to do, where will I be twenty years from now?

The curtain rises and here I am!

In a café at a railway station once more, twenty years later, yes, it's me!

I write in my diary, I raise my glass. Secret signals to the girl I was twenty years ago. I lean back and tentatively smile, I act as if she were watching me.

And I remember her as she sat there all alone, wretched, lost. I try to resurrect her in my mind. Call out to her, get her attention in order to comfort her.

What seemed mortifying then, doesn't seem so now. The pain she felt then filled her with shame, which she had no need to feel and I'm not ashamed now because I understand the secret of the unhappy girl.

1

I can remember the smell of the railway, the café. I can remember the words which had left her with that shame. They were ridiculous, too ridiculous for her, for me, to take the pain they caused seriously. They hurt, but I also felt ashamed at the pain, I collapsed under the weight of my own pain. Poor, poor girl.

Why wasn't I with you back then? Why couldn't I go to you, sit down next to you, hug you and console you?

I, your mature self, was many years away. At a railway station twenty years too late.

II

A relatively young woman, aged thirty. She married in her early twenties, had two children. She writes radio plays and edits a magazine on the same subject. It is winter. January and minus 14°C, white, frosty mist around the parked car, around the spruces, the mailbox on its post, but higher up the sky is blue, clear, the sun has come back. She has written in her diary that she is waiting for the heartbreak that will turn her into her true self. She has an impending sense of doom or possibly her own death.

Her children are at school and at nursery. When she stops writing, the house is very quiet. She gets up and wanders around. There is a debate in the newspaper. A young, male dramatist has attacked more senior ones and the seniors have responded. The issue will be discussed at a seminar at which she has been invited to speak. February, melting snow drips from the roofs. She knows what she is going to say, that is not what is troubling her or why she is so restless. It is the arrival of spring itself.

A reporter from a radio station is present at the seminar. The angry young man is the first speaker. He says he is no longer angry. It might be because his most recent play has been well received, he says. Or because the weather has been good lately, he says.

It is March now, spring is coming. But anyway, he is no longer angry.

Any comments? the radio journalist asks the panellists in turn, but what can they say? If the young man is no longer angry, there is nothing to discuss. Nothing to argue against, nothing to defend. Only the final panellist, a small man with close-cropped hair who is sitting on the far left, the Brecht translator Arnold Bush, wishes to respond. He completely disagrees, he says.

He completely disagrees? The audience pricks up its ears, the radio journalist rushes over to him.

'The weather hasn't been that good lately. Certainly not up north in Trondheim where I live.'

In the evening they drink. Arnold Bush tries to stroke some woman's hand, the woman snatches it back, startled. He is bold, Ida thinks to herself. Some go to bed, others stay behind. The last ones end up around a small table. There aren't enough chairs so Ida perches on the armrest of Arnold Bush's chair. Some participants have accommodation in an annex a short walk from the main building, they need a separate key to get in and agree to leave together. When they get up to leave, when he gets up to leave, Ida says: You don't need to go, you can sleep in my room. So he sits down.

Later, when they finally retire, he follows her up the stairs, he took me seriously, she thinks. He is of slim build, he has a diamond stud in one ear, he might be gay, they can sleep top to tail. She undresses and gets into the bed. He undresses, fetches a glass of water from the bathroom and gets into the bed, his head at the same end as hers, he takes out his contact lenses and puts them in the glass.

'Mind you don't drink it,' he says.

She turns out the light. He touches her as if they are going to make love. They try to make love, but he hasn't come by the time dawn breaks.

'Aren't you married?' he says.

'Yes.'

'Me too.'

'I thought you were gay,' she says.

'I have a three-year-old son,' he says, he sounds offended.

She is giving the first presentation that morning so they get up. Her body feels strangely light. While she is in the bathroom, she wonders if he will be there when she comes out, he is, it makes her happy, he stands naked on the floor and he has a scar that reaches from his armpit to his shoulder.

'What's that?'

'A scar. They don't call me Scarnold for nothing.'

I bet he says that to all the girls, she thinks to herself. They leave her room and walk downstairs. She continues onwards to the auditorium, he turns left so that people won't see them arrive together, she realises. He sits in the audience while she speaks, then he disappears, but returns after the next presentation in a clean shirt. A young man talks about writing with his body, writing with his penis. Arnold Bush holds up a pale hand and is given the floor. He gets up and stands with his lips pressed together. He waits until there is silence, until everyone is looking at him, he waits too long before he speaks and his voice is too soft so everyone has to strain to hear what he is saying, it is as if he can't be bothered to raise his voice, as if it is not worth it, as if he is bored by the whole thing.

'I have', he drawls, 'during this seminar had confirmed something I have long suspected. That Norwegian dramatists are better off than we – and they themselves – think. In contrast to my university colleagues and I who view writing as a challenge, who struggle to write, the dramatists enjoy writing, they say. And not only that. I've also just learned that it brings them to orgasm.'

She couldn't get over it. An orgasm. While she was in the room. Something he hadn't managed last night. He wanted to get a laugh. And the audience laughs. Leaning slightly forwards in a clean, pale-yellow shirt, he shows his true colours. Even this early on it is clear what kind of man he is.

Later that day, the day of departure, he is walking along the waterfront with another participant. She runs down to join them and taps him on the back.

'I need a word with you,' she says.

The other man nods and disappears.

'Do you regret last night?' Arnold wants to know.

No, that's not it. They walk fifty metres along the water-front before they turn and walk fifty metres back. He is a decade older than her and his career is going well, he will be made a professor soon. Hers has barely begun.

'We're both married,' he says. 'This affects people other than us.'

That's still not it. He has misunderstood. It was just because. She needs nothing. It is time to leave; up by the hotel the other seminar participants are ready with their suitcases and bags. Ida and Arnold hug each other politely by way of goodbye and walk up to join them. They say goodbye, they shake hands, they hug everybody – except each other. He is going home to Trondheim and is catch-ing a bus to the airport. She is going home to Oslo and is catching the train. Most people fall asleep on the train, but not Ida. Not because she has a guilty conscience. She has done this before. She is heading for a divorce, she has known it for a long time. But what she didn't know then was what the future held for her, what had only just started.

You can be aware of your capacity for love before you meet your beloved. Sense your potential for passion before you experience passion itself. You can know it as a child, as a latent possibility: I am able to love deeply. Even if you never meet him, you still comprehend something about love. The spirit sleeps in stones, it slumbers in plants. It awakens in animals, she is about to become an animal.

Her husband picks up her from the station, she doesn't feel guilty, rather she feels strangely elated. She doesn't think about him in the days that follow. Then a brown envelope arrives from the University of Trondheim with a handwritten A. Bush above the university logo. A poetry collection by Göran Sonnevi, *The Impossible*. She is delighted. She reads it and writes back to thank him for it. She thought, not at the time, but often later on, that he had gone to the bookshop and asked for it or found it himself on a shelf, placed it on the counter, paid for it, decided what he would write on the title page: *If better poetry has been written in modern times / then I have yet to read it / in the darkness / in the shadows of shadows* – as if to say that not only Sonnevi, but also the sender is of a lyrical nature, he can even be regarded as an artist – he put it in an envelope, wrote A. Bush with a red pen above the university logo, looked up her address, a call to directory enquiries, she assumes, bought a stamp, licked it and dropped the envelope into a post box; the title of the collection, however, *The Impossible*, is telling her not to get her hopes up. She dreams explicit sexual dreams, they have a cinematic feel to them, as if disconnected from her, but she enjoys them nonetheless and after her pleasure someone is killed for what she has done.

I set things in motion, she writes in her diary, and then I run away as if they have nothing to do with me, I'm still trembling, one day something terrible will happen.

His letter arrives three days after her thank-you note. Four handwritten pages on German drama, about his work as a translator, about this and that, about the sun that sets in the fjord while he sits on the terrace with a glass of wine as he writes. His wife is away. Kjersti is away, he writes. She replies, not as lengthy a reply as his. He is older than her, a well-established academic. He critiques contemporary drama. She writes it, she has only just begun. She is a little intimidated by him. She writes that. She mentions the age gap. She doesn't enter into a discussion about Goethe and Schopenhauer.

Easter comes. She goes skiing with her family. She goes for walks, lost in thought, along the lake in the darkness. She stands by the hotel window, watching her husband. He is outside talking to a woman, it is agony, she is losing him now, he knows she doesn't love him and he is distancing himself from her. She must divorce him before it happens, before he leaves her. She skis right up to the glacier on her own, then returns to the illuminated hotel via the lake in the twilight. Where are the children? They are with their father. He is standing with them outside. He is talking to mothers who stand with their children between their legs on the slope. Her body is warm, the air is chilly, the mountains are cold, the only sound is her breathing. A dark shadow on the other track is heading towards the hotel, she skis back slowly in order to make it last longer. Back to dinner, children, music, the other guests. Only wine helps, wine helps. She inhales the darkness as she leans over her ski poles: What is going to happen to me? What is he doing now? He is in the lobby with hoarfrost in his holiday stubble, dark, talking to other women who appreciate him, who find him attractive. Their smiles say: I will be nice to you. My arms are warm. I will give you what she doesn't, which everyone can see she isn't giving you, which you need and long for. She is in the process of leaving him and braces herself for the loss, that is what is going on here. She is rehearsing losing him so that she will know what to do, so that it won't take her by surprise. This is what it means: You will lose him, he will kiss someone else. He will direct his energy, all of his enormous, positive energy at someone else. She dreams that he is unfaithful to her, it is horrible. But it is also agony when he talks about the weather, about the food, when he chats to strangers, and she has to walk away. His language is unbearable, that is the worst, but that is who he is. When they get home there is a letter from A. Bush in their mailbox, she picks up their post and sorts it. Over Easter he has read an article she wrote for *The Journal*, which she edits, and discussed it with his mother-in-law. His mother-in-law is a librarian, he writes. His mother-in-law is there. He is sitting with a glass of wine, watching the sun sink into the sea this time as well. Kjersti has gone away again. He mentions Kjersti. He mentions her age because Ida brought up the subject. Kjersti is twenty-five, he writes. He is thirty-nine, how strange to think that she is older now than he was when they first met. Thirty-nine and hearing the thundering of old age across the steppes, he writes, it is pretty. Would it be possible, he finishes off, or impossible for them, the two of them, to one day watch the sun go down in the sea together?

She reads it under a streetlight near the forest. She puts his letter with the others in an envelope behind the books on the bookcase in her study. She writes back, not as lengthy a reply as his, but longer than the last one. It is April now. Yes, I think that might be possible, she writes. He replies that he will be in Oslo in late May, on the twenty-fifth, he is the external examiner for first-year German students, and he asks if they can meet.

Was it Constitution Day in May that year? Did she dress up the children and join them in the parade? Did they have a festive meal with the family, did she go to the children's school and take part in the egg and spoon race? Yes, we can meet, she writes as the date approaches, we can meet 'as if nothing has happened'. She doesn't hear back and grows increasingly nervous, has she ruined it before it has even started, has she wrecked it already? The days pass, it is getting closer, she hears nothing. She doesn't think he is being very kind, she can't call what happened at the seminar love. Why is her body filled with such trembling anticipation and why does she want to cry? She writes to him that they can meet 'as if everything, as if everything has happened'. Four days pass before he replies, four desperate, nerve-racking days before she receives two letters. One in reply to her first and one in reply to her second, though both are written, she gathers, right after he received her second one, in which she wrote that they could meet as if everything had happened. They can meet as if nothing has happened, he writes in the first one, and see if they hear the ringing bells of nothingness. Or they can meet as if everything has happened, he writes in his second letter, and gives her his office number for her to ring. She writes it down in a place where no one will find it. She is to call on Tuesday, he writes, between 2 p.m. and 3 p.m. She can't sleep the night before Tuesday. She will ring him at 2:30 p.m. on the dot. She visits a friend to make the time pass more quickly, she takes the children. Her children play with her friend's children in the garden, they sit underneath the trees, drinking coffee. Having something to do is essential, talking to someone about other things.

'Can I borrow your phone?'

She enters the darkness of the house, her hand is shaking.

'Hello,' he says, he has been expecting her.

She says that he can decide the time and place. She doesn't mind either way.

He tells her what he needs to do first and when approximately he thinks he might be done. How about Herregårdskroen, Thursday, six o'clock, is that any good? It is.

'I'm looking forward to it,' he says.

He is looking forward to it. She wants to say: Me too, but can't get the words out. He is looking forward to it, he just said so. A man has just said that he is looking forward to it. She returns to the garden. She has never felt like this before, she is in love. Can't you see that I'm completely transformed? Can't you see that I'm in love? Does Mummy look strange to you?

'No.'

'Does Mummy look like herself?'

The child studies her face. 'Have you hurt yourself?'

'No. Why?'

'There,' the child says, tapping the skin over her eye.

She arrives first. She sits on a low wall, waiting. A man of slim build wearing a light yellow T-shirt, black jeans, a black suit jacket hooked onto a finger over his shoulder. Is that what he looks like? Pale, no hair. They greet each other. He is not her type. They drink beer. They talk about relationships, about the past, he has been married twice. It is hot. It is bright. He is skinny.

They wander around looking for a place to eat. They find a restaurant. He has read an interview with her in the latest issue of *The Journal*, an amusing interview. It made him a little scared, he says. She understands. She pretends she doesn't, but she does, she knows she does. He is not scared now, she is the one who is trembling now. Suddenly he touches her cheek, she turns in surprise, and he smiles, it is the ringing bells of nothingness.

It is spring in Oslo. They have paid the bill, they have gone outside. She doesn't say goodbye. She doesn't say that it is time for her to go home. He has a bottle of wine back at his hotel room, he says, she doesn't say no.

The bottle is already open. He had a glass before he went out. He pours wine into two glasses and places one on the table next to her. 'Mind you don't drink it,' he says with a smile to remind her of what he said that first night at the seminar when he put his contact lenses in a glass of water. She smiles and drinks her wine and he sits down next to her on the sofa and again he touches her cheek and then he kisses her. They undress, they have sex. He comes. He rolls onto his side and smiles: 'I need a break,' he says. They drink more wine. He calls her Kjersti once, but it doesn't matter. He laughs as he says: 'You're not supposed to do that, are you?' He asks about her husband, about her marriage, she is honest. She is heading for a divorce. He, for his part, says: 'I can't handle another breakup.'

Maybe they sleep before they wake up or maybe they don't. She has an early meeting at the radio station. She told her husband she was staying over at a friend's house. His bald head peeks out under the duvet, he opens his heavy eyes as she kisses him, he is so unfamiliar. They agree that she will ring him in the afternoon, it is his last full day in Oslo. He is leaving tomorrow morning, tonight he is having dinner with a friend and he will be staying over there.

'It's serious,' he says gravely.

She smiles, she is not scared. She doesn't walk, she runs through the city.

She calls his hotel as they have agreed, he is not there. She calls early in the afternoon as they have agreed, they tell her that he is in his room, but no one answers, he doesn't pick up the phone. She keeps calling, eventually in hysterics. She knows it: he has chickened out. She keeps ringing for an hour, terrified that she will never see him again. She finds his letters, almost thirty pages in total, and tears them into pieces so small that they can't be glued back together and puts them in an envelope and writes his name on the outside in order to send them to him. This is what I do with your letters, with your love. When you don't pick up the phone. She stops calling, she has given up, what she needs to do now is to surrender, calm down. He calls her fifteen minutes later. His voice is intimate and her anger evaporates. There must have been a problem with the phone, he says, he is lying.

'I got so angry. I thought you were just like every other man, a coward, that you had lost your nerve.'

He says that he got scared when she told him about the state of her marriage, that she wanted a divorce. That he might be just one piece in that puzzle, he says. He can't handle another breakup, he says. Yes, he is scared. They agree to meet in two hours. Before he goes to see his old friend and his wife and has dinner with them, where he will also stay over, it has been arranged a long time ago. At

Herregårdskroen where they met yesterday. She waits by the wall. He turns up wearing black jeans, a black T-shirt, a black suit jacket, black briefcase, black sunglasses, he is her type. She has the envelope with his torn-up letters in her bag, she doesn't want to give it to him. They hug, you look nice, he says. They share a bottle of wine and stroll through the park to the taxi rank, among the trees when no one is watching them, he pulls her close.

'I've missed you,' he says.

I've missed you, he says. They share a taxi, stopping at her destination first; in order not to have to go home, in order to be able to carry on drinking, she has arranged to see a friend. When the taxi pulls up in front of the house, they kiss. Quickly because the taxi driver is there, because he has another fare and it is late. She enters her friend's garden, it hurts after just four paces, even after just one. She drinks, she talks, but it is no use, she paces the living room in circles, shaking from a longing so intense that she feels she is burning up. I have to tell him that I love him. I love him. She looks up his friend's number, calls it and asks to speak to him in order to tell him that she loves him. A woman picks up the phone, his friend's wife.

'Could I speak to Arnold Bush, please?'

He comes to the phone. He sounds reserved. He is with friends who know his wife, who might get suspicious. Is she one of those women who might cause trouble, who can't control herself?

'I'm calling to tell you that I love you.'

Sure. That's great. See you. See you. He doesn't know that it is the first time she says that word, love. Once she has rung off, it gets worse, intolerable. She decides to throw out his letters, she drinks in order to get so drunk that she can summon up the courage to throw his torn-up letters into a rubbish bin on her way home.

Later in their story, one time when she was angry, upset, as she often was during the first year they knew each other, she told him to throw away her letters to him. To hurt him. She thought it was the worst thing she could ask him to do because she believed her letters meant just as much to him as his letters did to her, that they were irreplaceable. She regretted having thrown hers out. She wouldn't have done it if she hadn't been drunk, she drank to get the courage to bin them, something inside her wanting to destroy everything before it had even started, as if she already suspected the price it would exact. She asked him to throw away her letters, but never thought that he would. He kept them at his office. He was sober when he was at his office, he wouldn't throw them away sober. Later, much further into their story when they were together, she asked him if he really had thrown them, and he said that he had.

'Because you asked me to.'

He had thrown away the most precious evidence of their unique story and he said it without blushing. He hadn't been where she had been. He wasn't where she was. Perhaps they were never in the same place at the same time.

Where were her children? Did she feed them? Take them to nursery school? Did she attend parents' evenings? She doesn't remember, she remembers only one name. She carried children or pushed buggies with children around while she thought of one name. In the forest, by the lakes, bare-legged on the dusty road, she thought of only one name. She would lie in the grass, gazing at the sky while they climbed around her and on top of her, thinking of one name only. At the school's summer assembly in the sports hall, the children on a small stage singing *A dream is a wish your heart makes*. Her little boy right at the front, to the far left, with his hair sticking up and big anxious eyes. Perhaps you shall go to the ball. She is overcome with emotion. Her husband puts his arm around her. All the time this one name. Everything she sees, everything she hears, including her own darling, anxious child, makes her think of him, of Arnold, with infinite tenderness, as if he is the one who is needy, anxious, helpless, as if he were the child. The urge to hug him and cling to him and carry and comfort and love him is almost unbearable. There is no release from this urge. Will the whole summer be like this, will she have to feel like this all summer?

He writes to her later that night, after she has called him and told him that she loves him, used the word for the first time. When his hosts have gone to bed and he is alone in the guest bedroom and regrets his dismissive tone which sprung from his fear. She imagines the window open into the night, fruit trees blossoming and stars in the sky. He misses her. He thinks about her. The letter in the mailbox transforms her unbearable, destructive longing into dizzy joy, which lasts a day or two before it slowly morphs into unease. She writes back quickly so that he has time to reply before the unease sets in. She repeats her own sentences in her head over and over while she does the laundry, mixes cordial, butters toast. Three days, then her unease arrives and mushrooms overnight, but the next morning her hope lights up along with the dawn and sustains her until the post arrives, if there is no letter she won't sleep that night, she cries for no reason, she turns away, squirming, there is no rest anywhere but in his presence, in his voice, in his writing. On a piece of squared paper torn from a notebook he has scribbled in haste that they, Kjersti, Berthold and I, in that order, are going on holiday to Nøtterøy, 'so we will be closer to each other than usual', and some lines from a Paal Brekke poem she doesn't know and has never been able to find since. He could ease her unrest, he doesn't. He could have written: We will meet in August, but he doesn't, he never makes any promises, it is a matter of principle, he promises nothing, then he can't ever be blamed. He is gone, perhaps she will never see him again. She writes a desperate, accusatory letter, she can't help herself.

Heavy summer, everything drips, everything hangs, the sun sags. She gets used to her unease, it mutates into desire, a heady, intoxicating desire, which gives her a new spring

19

in her step. She can't eat for desire, she smells of desire so strongly that men and dogs turn when she passes them in the street. Her husband approaches her carefully and in the dark. In daylight he looks at her anxiously. *He* doesn't come to her. Not because he doesn't love her, but because he can't. Because he has responsibilities, he has a wife and a child who need him. Because he is scared that a relationship with Ida might mean more pain than happiness, as is always the case with great love. The great love disappears, the lesser love remains, say the books he reads. She tells herself that she hasn't been abandoned because his love is too small, but because it is too great. She feels it, she knows it. She has his love and that makes all the difference. She is enveloped by love although she hasn't seen him or heard from him all summer, she walks around like a loved woman. Her beloved loves her, she radiates his love. Because she is so loved, she is able to give out love, caresses, she thinks, talks, breathes eroticism, wrapped in his love, she walks with sashaying, bouncy steps and if she spots any slim-built, bald men with his unique gait and guarded eyes, she will sit down as close to them as she can, meet their gaze, hold it and try to sniff out their scent. They smile back, they look at her, they spend money on her, drinks arrive at her table if she is on her own, but she rarely is, it is the holidays, she is travelling with her husband and children. She sees nothing but him, she sees him in all men, and because he isn't available to answer her questions, she asks them of others. Because she can't write to him, she writes to others. She sits on stones in the forest and writes because she has no opportunity to respond to his love anywhere but in her thoughts, she responds to it via other people, her husband, other men, whispering pent-up words into the ears of others with such passion that they blush and some whisper back words they have rehearsed long ago, intended for women other than her, pressing their bodies against hers, there is so much unrequited love, so many unhappy people who yearn, who will never end up together, so many who love in secret.

'You're so handsome,' she says.

'You're so strong,' she says, few have been told that they are handsome, strong; brimming with love, she walks through airports, stands on escalators, takes the tram, walks down the streets.

If only it could have stayed this way. If only this state could be frozen and preserved for ever, if only she could have gone through her life consumed by his imagined love and then met him twenty years later. Met her beloved with his wife and the child who has grown up in the intervening years. They stop for a moment, not sure if they recognise each other. He doesn't know if Ida is really Ida, but he is even more unsure if he is still the man he was. And she feels it disappear. If he looks at her for a long time, it disappears, and if she hears them talk, if she sees him address his wife, his son, it disappears and so she leaves, she just waves, she turns and leaves, and everything has to begin anew.

There must be a letter from him at home which she will get on their return. He loves her, anything else is unthinkable. The question is whether he dares, whether he is strong enough. He has never been loved like this before, he can't have been, it is the first and the last time. If only he can believe it. He must feel safe, she must make him feel safe, what if he never finds the courage.

There is a letter for her when they come home, she picks up and sorts the post. It is long, but composed; when she isn't composed, he is, the tone is paternal, as if he isn't besotted, as if only she is, as if that is not unusual, as if he is used to women swooning around him. She has no reason to blame him, he writes. He has never promised her anything. He mentions his wife, he mentions his child. But I have thought about you every day, all summer, he writes. Pushing you away and pulling you back again. As if it is an honour, as if she ought to be grateful. He has thought of her every day? He has thought of her constantly, every second, even at night, go on, admit it, if you do not dare, we have no chance.

They meet twice during the autumn. He has work in Oslo or is passing through and stays in a hotel. He writes to tell her that he is coming to Oslo, nothing more. She has to ask, suggest, plead, take responsibility. He makes sure never to promise, never to ask, never to plan, perhaps he has convinced himself that they meet almost by chance? She writes: Can we meet? She writes: I want to see you! She writes: Tell me when and where and I'll be there! He writes back late, at the last minute, when and where, and there is always a but, he might be late, he writes, his plans might change, something might come up, he writes, she knows he will come, he can't help himself, he pretends that there is a but, he adds a but to keep her on the rack. Sometimes she writes back in uncontrolled capitals: THEN DON'T COME, YOU BASTARD! STAY AT HOME, COWARD! The ensuing silence is unbearable, no sign of life, that is her punishment, she repents desperately and is scared that she has ruined it for ever and begs his forgiveness and apologises: I love you! she writes. Love, love you! she writes. Forgive me! she writes. Please, Arnold! she begs.

And so it continues. The day arrives, the hour arrives and he arrives. Don't be angry! Don't ask for anything! Baby steps! There he is!

Here he is. He is actually here. She is in the cloakroom at Tostrupkjelleren. She has popped in to see if he is already there, he isn't. She is about to go outside to wait when he comes down the steps. More than three months have passed since they last saw each other. His coat flaps behind him. His head is bare. His gaze shy. His hands in his pockets. Now he takes them out. Pale, refined hands and olive-green eyes under lines and wrinkles. His coat flaps behind him. She loves him. She doesn't know what to say. He doesn't say anything, he feels the same way. She wants to throw herself at him to get it over with. Cling to him and bite him for all the times she has been drunk while he was away, all the men she tried to sleep with in order to exorcise him, all the misery he brings, sink her teeth into him and never let go. They nod cautiously to one another. They don't hug, they don't smile. Everything there was between them, although it wasn't very much, is still there, and yet everything has gone, every time they have to start afresh. He drinks beer, she doesn't drink, she is driving, it isn't difficult to stay sober, she is already full to the brim. After a beer he talks about trivial things, how can he? The seminar he is going to, the other participants. They step outside into the dark autumn. It is raining. The wind is blowing, causing his coat to flap behind him, he hasn't buttoned it, his hands are in his trouser pockets. For years to come she will feel a pang in her chest whenever she sees a man's light-coloured trench coat. They go to a hotel and make love, it is simple. Two or three times, it gets easier every time. He drinks whisky.

'What can I get you to drink?' he asks.

She needs nothing. She is driving, tomorrow she will go to Spain with her husband to the place where they stayed when they still got on, in the hope that they might do so again. Leave behind the pain which is bound to follow, but which is impossible to imagine as long as they are together. He pees without closing the bathroom door. He sits naked in the chair under the lamp in the hotel room and smiles. She sits on his lap and rides him like no one has ridden him before, she thinks. He has a broken toenail, like old people in care homes, it needs clipping. I can't be with a man with such a toenail, she thinks, relieved. They go to bed. They have sex. They talk, she drinks from his glass. She leaves first, she is going to Spain tomorrow. He gets up with her and gets dressed alongside her. She stands in the bathroom. He enters behind her and rests his head on her shoulder. Their eyes meet in the mirror. This is what the two of them look like. A picture of a double tragedy. She tries to smile. She always tries to smile. He walks her to her car. He peers through the windows and asks what is in the bag on the back seat. Why does he want to know, so nosy, so suspicious. It is a pair of shoes. She had left them behind at another man's house and stopped by on her way here to pick them up. They kiss. She is leaving tomorrow. He has to walk back to the hotel on his own. She can tell from the kiss that he is the one prolonging it although they are now out in the open, where they can be seen. A broken toenail, she must remember that. It is easy to leave when he doesn't want to let her go. To smile when he doesn't smile, to hold back. She sounds the horn and raises her hand to wave goodbye. Goodbye! Perhaps we'll meet again! He stands on the pavement in the rain. She travels to the smell of thyme, to sunshine. His naked head, his heavy reptile gaze, alone back to the hotel.

It never occurs to her that he can call someone else. That he has women he can call at night and ask them to come over. So he doesn't have to be alone. So he doesn't have to feel the feelings that arrived when the two of them parted, which only the presence of another can ease. Another one to have sex with in the bed where she just lay. He can't cope with any more breakups and tries to stop himself from falling in love so the breakup becomes inevitable, in order to forget her quickly, but how quickly can you forget if another woman enters the room, lies down in the bed, will he forget or be reminded of her? Is that what he did? What difference does it make now? Did he feel the way she felt? Was it for him the way it was for her? What difference does it make now? She never asked. Perhaps he would have given her an honest answer. Or perhaps he wouldn't.

In the sun all men look like him, slim-built with olive eyes and crooked noses. They smoke Gauloises like he does. She feels the fabric of her dress against her legs, a gust of wind. She feels the leather insole of her shoe against the sole of her foot. She feels the straps of her bra, the knicker elastic against her hip, thigh against thigh, the fabric of the seat pad, the table under her elbow, the glass against her lips. She can feel the moon's yearning for water, the hot core of the Earth, the will of the stars, she is magnetic and electric and feverish.

In a market she spots a silver sailor in an old box of knickknacks. A two-centimetre-long silver sailor with a scarf around his neck and a cap. When she was a little girl she used to pretend that she had a sailor brother who would come to her rescue when she was in trouble, it is a sign. She wants to glue it to a card and write something on the card and send it to him. Arnold, my sailor! It lies in her hand. Her hand is in the pocket of her dress. Her dress pocket tickles her thigh. She will send her husband off to do something, then sit in a café and drink beer and write the card in the sunshine, sit down with him in the sunshine. She finds a stamp and an envelope and posts it before her husband comes. Back home it is October. No one is as lucky, as happy as she. In the evenings they drink wine in the garden and watch the boats in silence. Her eyes are shining, she can see it in the wine glass, in the wine cooler. She thinks of one thing only. They make love in their hotel room. Afterwards he gets up to open the window. He stands by the window and raises his arm towards the hasp. She has shared the same bed as him for almost a decade. This is what he looks like. It is unbelievable, he is too big. He has too much hair. It's over, cut it off with a pair of scissors. He comes back and sits down next to her on the bed, she shifts in order not to be so close to him. He moves nearer to her, leaning towards her as if she is his woman, it is like sitting too close to someone on a bus. It is not something she has decided, it just happens.

They meet once that same autumn. It is November. At Gamle Major in Majorstua. It is more complicated than usual. She has written to him that she is getting a divorce. It really is happening and it hangs over them. She is not stupid enough to have written: It has nothing to do with you. It would have happened anyway. That is the truth. But even so. She goes with him to his hotel. She has an early meeting with the radio station the following morning. She has told her husband she is out with a girlfriend and that she is staying over at her place to have a short commute to her meeting the next day. It is a hideous, modern hotel, a small, hideous room. Nothing remarkable happens, it isn't like the last time because she has written to tell him she is getting a divorce. It is the first thing he mentions when he arrives, he asks if it is a certainty. Because if it is, they are finished. He can't cope with another breakup and if she gets divorced, she will want something different, someone different, someone who isn't married. They drink too much. Perhaps that is why she doesn't remember it very clearly. She has lost a lot of weight. He is still asleep when she gets up and she dresses in the darkness. She kisses him quickly on the cheek and leaves and feels the pain before the door closes behind her as she walks down the corridor through the empty reception, the hideous hotel in a hideous part of town. It is late October or is it November already? It is dark outside, it is raining, it rains constantly. She takes a taxi to the radio station. He is still asleep, he is catching a noon plane to Hamburg. During her meeting, it is now eight-thirty, he is probably still in the hotel room, she steps out and asks to use their telephone. In an empty office, there are people in the adjacent office and no door, she bends down and cups her hand over her mouth: 'It's me.'

'Yes?' He sounds curt as if he is saying: What do you want?

'Are you asleep?' she asks.

'Not anymore,' he says, then there is silence.

'What is it?' he wants to know.

She gets very scared.

'Nothing.'

They hang up. The pain. Here it comes.

They don't articulate it more precisely because they haven't found the right words yet.

'Don't fall in love with me, you'll suffer.'

'I want to suffer!'

'You don't know me. I can be bad.'

'I'm not scared!'

'I'm cursed. I have to torture every woman who falls in love with me. Do you understand? I torment them.'

'What do you mean by cursed?'

'You'll soon find out. Being cursed means you can't change.'

'What do you mean you can't change?'

'I'm cursed, I tell you, I can't stop.'

It takes her a long time to even think the words, to voice them to herself. Longer still to say them out loud, to others, she shapes them like a question: Have you ever thought about . . . How do you think it would be if . . . To say them to those they concern the most is impossible. Shout it out during an argument. Divorce. So the word exists in the house, in the space between them. In the morning he brings her a tray of coffee, hot milk, the newspaper before he takes the children to nursery, to school, so that she can work undisturbed. In the evening when they have put the children to bed, she sits on the floor in front of his chair, he strokes her hair. She reads. He watches television. He is not a bad man. He is trustworthy. There is no nonsense with him. He is a decent man. He treats her, and everything that relates to her, with respect. You should always marry a man you can divorce. Someone who will take care of the children before and after the divorce. A capable, decent man who will survive and find someone else to be with, who won't throw himself out of the window or end up on the streets when you leave him. Don't exaggerate your importance, Ida. He'll be fine without you. What should she say, what reasons can she give? I want this because? I don't love him. I don't love you. She has known it all along because you can know your capacity for love before you meet the man you will love. Because you don't love me. Because he doesn't love her. Because he doesn't know who she is. Because he doesn't see her. Isn't capable of seeing her or doesn't want to or doesn't dare. Because he is afraid of her. Because he couldn't handle seeing her as she really is. He would lose his balance, stumble, and he doesn't want to, he can't be tripped up, so what happens now?

He saved her. It is true though he doesn't know it and she is grateful for that. He led her into the world, into the daylight. Coffee in the morning and a child who needs looking after. Grounded her. So she survived. She said yes to him in order to survive. Because he smiles, is easy-going, doesn't ask questions. Because he doesn't grow, he is nailed too solidly together for that. He chews and the inside of her brain creaks. His voice on the phone makes her brain ache: Oh, that's nice! Long time no see. Great. Absolutely. Excellent!

She wants to punch him in the face to make it split! Is she destroying him slowly without him noticing, steamrolling him without him noticing, pushing him nearer the precipice without him noticing? I have to get out of here. Out of here. Her daughter clings to her at night, why is she so on edge, something is wrong. Does he go to their daughter's room at night? When he comes home late from parties she can't be bothered to go to. She hears him come in, but he doesn't come to her in the double bed, what does he do? She tiptoes downstairs, he is asleep in front of the telly. Something is definitely wrong. She is listless. She wanders around, overwhelmed, she cries for no reason. She hasn't heard from Arnold. It is dreadful and she can't stop herself from writing: You're just like all the others! A coward! You light matches, you start fires, but then you run away so you don't get your fingers burned! One, two or three encounters a year whenever you fancy a quick fuck and want to feel like Casanova and then home to the security of your wife and child, your ego boosted and another notch on your bedpost, YOU TOTAL SHIT!

And she sends her letter while she feels angry, before she can change her mind, just to breathe more easily for an hour or two.

He has got his fingers burned, he replies. Yes, he got scared, he replies. He can't handle another breakup, he writes. And about this, he writes, he has been honest right from the start.

That is true. It makes no difference. It has to end. She will never write to him ever again! Then he'll be sorry. Fuck him.

Her sister is a student at the University of Trondheim. At the Department of English, which is next to the Department of German where Arnold Bush works. Her sister often sees him in the corridors when he is going to the lavatory, he goes to the lavatory a lot, does he have a UTI? Ida calls her sister. Have you seen him, she asks. Going to and from the loo? She can see him every day, perhaps she is flirting with him, perhaps she is sleeping with him, who knows, who can know, it feels as if there is something her sister isn't telling, doesn't it? He turns up in his long leather coat, her sister says, Ida has never seen the leather coat. It hangs next to the light-coloured movie director's trench in the hallway, in the house where they live, he and his wife, Kjersti, aged twenty-five, and the child, their son Berthold. And her outerwear hangs next to the leather coat, the director's coat, her coat and her jacket so close to his without them even thinking about it. His wife doesn't slip inside his coat to sniff it, she doesn't caress it tenderly, because she doesn't know the man with whom she lives. She shares a bed with him as if it is nothing special, and she isn't grateful for the hours she spends in the same room as him. She lies naked in the double bed beside him and if he falls asleep first, his wife can hear his restless breathing. But he probably isn't asleep, he is probably holding her, wanting to make love to her the way they always do it, the way they usually do it so she comes before he does, and no man can watch and listen to a woman coming without feeling tenderness for her, feeling affection for her, and being aroused later when he recalls it. He has had seven orgasms with Ida. Kjersti lies naked alongside him every night, they lie naked every single night or most nights. They share a bottle of wine on the sofa on a Saturday evening and his wife doesn't think, she has no idea that somewhere in the world is a woman who wants nothing more than to sit next to Arnold on a sofa. His wife is close to him without even being aware of it when she gets up and walks past him to fetch another bottle.

'It's Ida. Have you seen him?'

It is Sunday. It is cold. It is December. It is bad. She thinks about him all the time. She has got the children into their coats, they are going out for some reason. They are waiting in the hallway when the phone rings. Her sister asks if this is a good time.

'Has something happened?'

Yesterday there was a party in the German Department and Arnold left with a student and spent the night with that student, her sister knows this because she shares a flat with Åse who knows the student, whose name is Tone. Then Ida's husband appears and she has to ring off. This is jealousy. What she feels now makes it impossible for her to move her lips, her body, every limb is rigid, she will never smile again. Something has broken and can't be mended. Unbearable anxiety trades places with unbearable pain. Love is a surgeon. It cuts you with a knife. It slices off lumps of flesh. She may as well die. He won't be sorry. He is doing it with *another*. He could be doing it with Ida, but he is doing it with *another*. He will do it with Mette, with Dorthe, with Ingunn and more names she will never know. He could have had Ida, he chooses *another*. They walk to the cold car and put on their seat belts. They may look like a family, two adults in the front and two young children in the back, on a Sunday, in the car, going somewhere. He has done it with Tone. In Tone's bed, which smells of Tone. Undressed himself and undressed Tone and entered Tone's body. They were probably going out for a family dinner. She can't eat. She can't speak. She is able to drink red wine. The moment they get back home, she runs downstairs to the basement and calls her sister.

'What does she look like? Is she pretty? Is she dark-haired? Is she fat? Is she stupid? Say something! Help me!'

A pretty, dark-haired woman underneath him in her bed with bedlinen that smells of her, her perfume and night cream and other seductive potions in the bathroom where he goes to pee, his tongue in her mouth, circling her tongue. And he comes inside her and he cries out and maybe he says that he loves her, the way women like to be told, perhaps he really does love her, no, that is impossible.

He asks her if she has a bottle of wine they can share before he has to go home and she does and they drink it while they sit next to each other, shoulder to shoulder, naked in the bed where they have made love and been intimate. And the next day or one of the following days, *whenever she wants to*, Tone can make her way to the Department of German and expect to bump into him. She can knock on his door and he will call out: Come in! And they will sit, face to face, in his office and maybe they will do it on the sofa, he probably has a sofa in his office and maybe they will do it again, every day in his office if Tone wants to, she probably does, and he is unable to say no. She can't stop herself from writing to him: SHAGGER, SLEEPING WITH YOUR STUDENTS, YOU ABSOLUTE SHIT, I NEVER WANT TO SEE YOU AGAIN! In large uncontrolled capitals. She drives to the post box and posts the letter before she has second thoughts and changes her mind. It is true, it is like a scalpel to the body, it cuts, if it doesn't pass, if the pain doesn't subside, she will kill herself, that's why people do it, you can't blame them. Will she ever feel happy again? If only she could forget it, if only it were possible to forget about it for just a second or an hour, a whole day, but all she has to do to bring it back is think about him. And at the same time, in the middle of the pain: It's because he's missing me. In the middle of her pain: She's a substitute. And: He's careless. He's wrecking his marriage. People might find out and gossip about it, and his wife will hear and they will divorce. In the middle of her pain: Consciously or subconsciously, he's doing this to come to me.

She didn't know then, and she should count herself lucky that she didn't, that it wasn't just the one night or two. But many nights, affairs, trips to other cities and hotel breaks and coffee in bed and at the office. Over coffee at his office he says in a reproachful voice to Tone that she mustn't talk to anyone about something that isn't a relationship. Tone must have said something to someone because rumours are rife about the relationship – which isn't a relationship – and have travelled all the way to Oslo. He is thinking about the letter from Ida. He's married, he says, and he's her lecturer, and what they have together, this non-relationship, must end.

And Tone thinks of Åse because she hasn't talked to anyone but her, and Åse says that she only told Jorunn, and Jorunn says that she only told Ida, her sister in Oslo, who is infatuated with Arnold. So it must be Ida who has called or written to Arnold because she is one of those women who can't control themselves. And so Arnold summons Tone to his office and talks to her in a professorial voice and tells her that their non-relationship must end. And Tone feels upset and somehow this is all Jorunn's fault. And it is serious. Because what if the vice chancellor found out, Arnold Bush says reproachfully. There might be consequences. Arnold Bush doesn't want a reputation for being somebody who sleeps with his students. He doesn't want to be the kind of person he is, so please could you all shut up.

He writes in a measured letter to Ida that he doesn't have to explain himself to her. Yes, I went to a party and no, I didn't go home alone, he writes so she can really imagine it for herself. Besides, my student is a grown-up, he writes, she is thirty-four years old. It is not what Ida thinks. Ida has been invited to a seminar on alternative theatre in Trondheim. It must have been advertised in *Adresseavisen*, the Trondheim newspaper, or he might have seen the leaflet, which says that she will be on the panel, because he concludes his letter with: I see you're coming to Trondheim. I will be in Bergen and Kjersti in Stavanger. Fuck you, Arnold. As if she would contact him against his will. Intrude on him. Or his wife. Track down his wife and tell her about his infidelity. Break up the happy family. Take revenge, be the homewrecker. As if she would be that stupid. As if she thinks she can win that way. As if she has no self-respect, as if she doesn't think she can be loved without begging and threatening.

She calls her sister and asks her if she has seen him in the corridors. But Jorunn doesn't respond as usual, she hesitates, she sounds awkward. And some days later, Ida receives a letter where Jorunn writes that she wants nothing to do with this, and that is entirely understandable, but the upshot is that Ida is now all alone with it. And she has no choice. It is a matter of life and death, she can't choose to make it stop. He is not worth it, dump him, do something else, Jorunn implies between the lines, but Ida can't choose to make it go away. It is a matter of life and death.

She arrives at Trondheim in the evening, close to tears. Everyone who sees her must think: That woman is miserable. It doesn't matter. Why should she be ashamed of loving? Her voice trembles when she speaks. She has recorded a message on her answering machine in that trembling voice, which he can hear if he calls, how unhappy she is. She doesn't contribute to the discussion. When she realises that nobody there knows him, knows who he is, can tell her anything about him or report back to him about her, she loses interest. A woman she knows from earlier comments in the ladies: 'You look so sad, Ida.'

Ida nods: 'My heart is broken.'

Trondheim is grey. Drizzling rain. She goes for a walk in the rain, to get raindrops on her face. They feel good, like tears. On the seafront a man stops her and says:

'It's Ida, isn't it?'

His hood is up so she can't see his face. It turns out to be Erik Grøver from a study group a long time ago. He looks miserable. Yes, he is miserable. The wretched can sniff each other out miles away. They walk together in the rain, in the darkness along the Trondheim seafront, roads she has never walked before, paths through a forest that smells of moisture, of rotting leaves and rain, as he pushes a pram in front of him. He has his child on Wednesday afternoons. His child is asleep in the pram. When Erik was seven his parents divorced and the children had to choose where they wanted to live. His big brother chose their mother as did his big sister, which left their father on his own so Erik had to choose him. When he visited his mother, every other week-end and every Wednesday afternoon, when he had been yearning and looking forward to going there, his mother never seemed to have yearned, anticipated, looked forward to him coming, the things Erik liked were never in the fridge, and his mother would often go out. That is his torment.

Ida loves Arnold, that is hers.

'Are you sure', Erik asks, 'that it's the real thing?'

Trondheim in the rain. She walks with Erik in the darkness. Dinner with the seminar participants on the last day. Ida sleeps with a man as payback for the student Arnold slept with. In order to rid herself of her distress, to forget it for a moment, she drinks and goes with a man to his hotel room, she sleeps with him in the hotel bed. She screams from pleasure, her lust insatiable because of Arnold and his student, Tone. She has forgotten the case for her contact lenses and so puts them in a glass of water, which she places on the bedside table before they go to sleep. The man returns from the bathroom and reaches for the glass. Now it is her turn to say: Mind you don't drink it.

Except she can't use the cherished remark at a moment like this. The man picks up the glass and drinks her new contact lenses costing fifteen hundred kroner, she stands paralysed, watching him, and when he puts down the glass, she screams: You just drank my contact lenses! That's it, I never want to see you again!

She runs to her own room and she never sees him again, besides, he is married as most of them are. Ida, that's enough! Ida, you have to stop now! Where is your self-respect, Ida? You have to do something, take action. Who am I, we ask ourselves, if you respond timidly, you will have a different life to the person who responds to that question with courage. Who are you, Ida? It is time to choose.

He sits in his chair in front of the television. The one he often sits in, in his usual way, his legs slightly apart, slumped, the children are asleep. She snuggles up to him, moving from her chair to his, she sits on his lap and he is pleased and puts his arms around her. Now?

They are in bed having made love and she is on the verge of tears, he senses it.

'What is it? What's the matter?'

Now?

They are alone in the car, they have taken the children to something or other, the mood is oppressive. Now? They go for a walk, she suggests that they go for a walk that evening and they walk in the darkness, it is snowing, and she is trying to say it, but he misunderstands or she isn't clear enough, and yet clear enough for him to get angry and refuse to listen anymore, and he walks four metres in front of her all the way home.

You will probably think that by doing what I'm doing now, I'm inflicting great pain on you and the children, irreparable damage, yet I am sure that I am doing the right thing. For me, but also for you, also for the children. It is inevitable. Now? He stands by the kitchen counter, making himself a sandwich. If you're going to leave me, then do it clearly and with a single blow. Now?

She can't. They undress and go to bed and make love and she starts to cry, and he realises that there is a problem, but not the gravity of the situation, or he understands the gravity and that is why he has stopped asking questions. She hasn't told him about her passion because it is not about that. But she has talked about her passion to her sister, to her friends, to the wife of one of his brothers, she was drunk, late one night she told his best friend. She has talked because she can't stop herself from talking, out of the abundance of the heart the mouth speaks, dear God, let him come to me! Do you, do any of you think he'll come to me? Say yes! She sets traps for herself, hoping she will fall into one of them and lose control and it won't be pretty. She travels to New York to be able to send Arnold a postcard from there, sending him a postcard from Oslo would seem odd, she travels to New York, a postcard from New York isn't weird. She travels in order to leave her thoughts behind, to think of something else, but it is no use, she thinks the same thoughts, perhaps she travels only so that she can think them in peace, she has no other thoughts and when the children, her husband aren't near she can surrender to her thoughts without inhibition, her chest is pounding as if she were by the stage at a rock concert, as if she were standing close to a plane taking off, as if the floor were vibrating, perhaps it is a plane, she is at the airport, she drinks wine on the plane, it helps, she drafts the text for the postcard. She flies to New York to find a postcard and send it to Arnold Bush. She stays with a Norwegian writer and her husband and their children, she has said she is making the trip to see some plays. She finds a postcard, Frida Kahlo's self-portrait with her lover Diego's face painted on her forehead. She goes to the Grand Central Oyster Bar and orders oysters and champagne in order to write about it to Arnold on the card, 'Greetings from The Oyster Bar, Grand Central Station, New York, where I'm eating oysters and drinking champagne.' She finds a clairvoyant in Greenwich Village who says that her energy is low, but it will get better. Her love life is mediocre, but it will get better. She sees a ring, the clairvoyant says, perhaps it's a wedding ring, say yes! She sees an enemy with the initial T, perhaps it's Tone the student, and another enemy starting with the letter O, who can it be? If she gives her more dollars, she will keep talking.

She goes to a Chinese restaurant and the message in her fortune cookie says that her future depends on today, that her actions today will determine her future happiness or unhappiness. Her future depends on the present, it is important to do the right thing. Which is exactly what she keeps telling herself!

Her heart is racing. She finds a shop that sells crystals and buys a crystal to calm her nerves, one to heal a broken heart and one to increase her allure. That evening she has dinner out with her hosts and thinks that her friend's husband looks like Arnold, slim-built with a crooked nose, and when his wife has gone back to relieve the babysitter she starts seducing him, when they get back they have sex in the guest bedroom next to the room where his wife is asleep. She puts out tripwires, soon she will trip herself up. She runs overconfident laps in Central Park with Frank Sinatra in her headphones. *If you can make it here, you'll make it anywhere.* She samples Arnold's aftershave on the back of her hand in a department store on Fifth Avenue and has to sit down. Wow. She gets some on her leather watchstrap and the scent lingers. She starts to cry. She can't stand it, it is unbearable. She loves him across the ocean. What is she doing, what does she think she is doing? She checks into a hotel in order to be alone, but can't handle being alone, she drinks in order to sleep but is woken by a terrible dream: there is a man in her bed. She is facing the wall, she doesn't know who he is. Dear God, please let it be *him.* She turns over carefully, it is not *him.* She almost had him. And then she lost him. So close and yet so far away. She is losing. She can't stop losing and she will lose him. She takes the elastic out of her hair and gives it to the man. It has a loose thread and comes apart in her hand before he can take it. It is raining. It is dark outside the window. There is a crazy woman outside, screaming. She is the madwoman who is standing in the rain, screaming.

'You've taken everything from me,' her husband says to her.

The aftermath, the shame and the fear, it is degrading.
Choose him again, Ida. It's the only option. Or go.
Say yes to him again and stay with him. Or go.
She doesn't love him, and now she knows what love is.
So she has to go.

There is no letter waiting for her when she comes home. She cries that night when they make love and she tells her husband that she wants a divorce. He doesn't believe her, he thinks it will blow over. The next day, in the light of day. He says nothing, he doesn't ask, the next day, in the light of day. The next evening she cries again when they make love, and he says: 'What is it?'

She says she wants a divorce. He doesn't believe her. He thinks it will blow over. Tomorrow, in the light of day. At the breakfast table, when he brings the tray with coffee and the newspaper, the children, all of it. He knows her, he knows what she is like.

It is Sunday.

They have had breakfast.

The children have gone to watch TV in the living room.

It is dark outside, it is almost Christmas.

'About what you said last night?' he begins.

She doesn't have to say anything. He can tell from looking at her. He doesn't ask if she means it. He might even know why, perhaps he has thought along the same lines. He is no fool. He is different, in the sense of wanting different things. There is nothing he can do. She won't be deflected. Perhaps he thinks that she will turn, change her mind. But he knows her. She has made some progress.

His whole life, everything he has imagined, has been upended. He is sinking. It is dark, it is December. She is making it dark.

She is invited to a seminar in Trondheim. In May. On modern German drama. In May. Arnold Bush will be on the panel. It is late December, time passes slowly. In May. Go through with it, get through it, survive until May.

Strange processes in her mind transform the pain into energy and action. If she pauses for a moment, she can feel it. Her husband is slumped in his TV chair. She finds a house not far away, not too expensive, she makes an appointment with the bank. She fills in applications, places them in front of him and he signs them. She divides up cutlery, china, their books into two when the children have gone to bed, they will tell them soon. They agree on the date, in the afternoon. She is nervous right from the morning, she will be the one to tell them. It is her decision, her fault that they are harming them. The children won't be able to sleep that night. They won't be able to fall asleep. They won't be happy for a long time. They will be sad and tearful for a long time. Down. She is dragging them down. She is inflicting this pain on them. It has to be done, it is necessary. Focus on a single point and walk towards it as if on a tightrope. Don't look down or to the side. Your friends must go home now. Why? Because we need to talk. Daddy and me and you.

They suspect it, they know it, but it can't happen! Her daughter has beseeched her all autumn: You're not splitting up, are you!? You're not splitting up, are you!? If you do, I'll die! And Ida has replied: 'Oh, no. Of course not.'

Their daughter has lit candles all autumn, on the piano, on the chest in the hall, on the dining table, on the windowsill, as if it were a special occasion, a party, a birthday, Christmas. She comes to her in the morning in baggy pyjamas, with messy bed hair. She's had a bad dream, they were in a boat on the ocean and a storm came and Mummy fell overboard and nearly drowned.

'Oh, dear.'

'But then a dwarf turned up and saved you.'

The dwarf, that is *him*.

Their children's friends go home and they eat dinner in silence. There is pudding today. She can't do it. He has to do it. So she can see what she is doing, what she *wants*. It sounds so brutal. Now she has to say that it isn't true. There is silence for a while because nobody believes it. They look at them, waiting for them to deny it, but they don't. Her husband starts to cry so it must be true, Daddy's crying. Their son screams and runs to the door.

'I'm going to kill myself,' he says. 'I'm going to kill myself. If you split up, I'm going to kill myself!' Their daughter says nothing. Her face is dark: they really are splitting up. They were always going to. She knew it all along.

Nobody will have to move. You won't lose either of us, it's important. You will live with Daddy just as much as you will live with Mummy. Mummy will move into a house down the road. Not yet, in a little while. Once you have grown used to the idea. You can pick the colour of your bedroom. Why don't we go there to have a look at it?

They put on their outdoor clothes. Thick, slightly too big puffer jackets in which it's hard to move. Puffer jackets with room to grow and home-knitted hats. Mittens with string looped through the jacket sleeves. Two small people between them down the road in the darkness, hand in hand in a slow file down the snowy road in the darkness. The younger one's boots are too big. To the house where for the last few weeks she has gone every night once the children were in bed, when they had fallen asleep while her husband sat in front of the television, to knock down, throw out, renovate, make it ready for this day, and the days that would follow, the future.

Today she doesn't understand how she did it, where all that energy came from, now she remembers only fragments, as if she acted under a spell.

Her family doesn't want her to go through with it, but what can they say. Her family is worried. What will become of her without him? He saved her originally. They know it, they saw it. They hope for the best, what else can they do. The unpredictability makes them anxious. Will she be able to take care of herself? And the children? But what can they say.

'Think about the children,' they say. 'It's not just about you, Ida. You're responsible for people other than yourself now.'

Her daughter with her pink glasses. The school's Christmas assembly in the church. It takes place in the morning so just a few parents, mothers, are present. The children enter in two rows from either side of the sacristy in white gowns, concentrating hard on not tripping with the candle in their hand. Her daughter looks around. Is my mum here?

'I'm here, darling,' she whispers. She moves her lips, she holds up her hand to show her where she is, but her daughter doesn't see her, instead she keeps looking around. Where's my mum? She has to be here!

Here I am, darling! Here!

Then her daughter spots her. She beams with joy. She loves her mother so much. Children love their mother, they depend utterly on her. Her daughter smiles. She is going to pull it off. She will show her mum. Her mum is here! One by one the children proceed up to the big candle, which has been lit. They reach their own candle into the flame and light it. As they do so they say: Today we light a candle. And then, holding the lit candle before they

48

turn and resume their place in the uneven queue: We light a candle for the hungry.

They light candles for the homeless. They light candles for the poor, the unemployed. Ida's daughter walks up, bends over the candle, the light reflects in the lenses of her glasses, she looks at Ida:

'Today I light a candle,' she says, lights the candle and smiles as the golden flame flickers across her face: 'We light a candle for the lonely.'

She so desperately wanted children in order not to be a child herself but a mother. No longer a daughter but a mother, and the children grounded her, stopped her from floating up into the air or imploding because she didn't know who she was. How can someone who was never whole know where the missing piece lies? She counts the glasses and packs half. She asks him which frying pan he wants. He nods silently in response to all her suggestions. She counts, divides and packs, she carries her desk and chairs from one house to the other through the forest until late at night, she has superhuman strength. Her husband sits in his armchair in front of the television. The children are asleep.

'Do you want this one or that one?'

He turns to her. The tears are streaming down his cheeks, it is the first time in a long time that he has looked at her.

'Not now, Ida,' he says. 'The king is dead.'

The date is in the history books. She got divorced when King Olav died. Young and old walk with tea lights and flowers to the Palace Gardens in the winter darkness, it looks like the scene of a tragedy. She will meet him in May. She is calmer. There is a great deal to keep track of, not to forget. There is the lawyer, the deeds to the house, many bills to pay, but one of her plays will shortly be performed and she is translating another, she reviews, she edits *The Journal*, she will manage. She does it for him. She can't forget him. One day he will come. She writes to him for the first time in a long time. Her writing is calm, she is another person now and in another place. She writes from far away, as if it is the past and she sees it clearly, and somehow it is true: I would have jumped into the deep end with you, she writes.

His reply is also calm, for him it may indeed be a long time ago: I didn't want to jump into the deep end with you. I'm scared of the deep.

He is being honest, she realises, and she can handle his fear of the deep, she can work with it. But in the same letter he writes something else, an issue she has suspected in him, but hoped wasn't there, something she might not be able to live with. Uptown girl meets underdog, he writes. Uptown girl, that's her, Ida. The underdog, that's him, Arnold Bush, a senior university lecturer. He doesn't know enough about her yet, that is the problem. He is guessing. He is speculating. He can sense her strength, the one she is slowly discovering. The fearlessness, the independence she doesn't yet have, but is in the process of developing, he can sense it and he may not be able to handle it, if he can't be the teacher, what is he?

'Why do you need me?' he asks her, much later.

'I don't need you,' she says. 'I love you.'

Uptown girl? She writes back along with a line from a Pär Lagerkvist poem she cuts out of a book and glues onto the letter: Beloved! Leave me without words.

Beloved! Leave me without words. She won't hear from him now. This is goodbye, but she will see him in May. Then all will become clear. She makes curtains and hangs them. She paints walls. She assembles beds for the children and bookcases and a desk. She thinks: He will see it all eventually. One day he will come and then he will see it all, the yellow living room, the blue kitchen. He will come, she has plenty of time, right up to May.

The children sleep at her place for the first time. She never leaves them, they sleep in their new bedrooms on the same night that she sleeps in her house for the first time. Nothing could have been any different, yet it still hurts to write it now. It is a Saturday. Their father comes with them and says good night to them with her and stays for a while in the living room with Ida, so the children can fall asleep listening to their talking, their voices, their parents' voices. Then he leaves. Walks alone up the road in the darkness to *his* house and sleeps there, alone, for the first time, in the big bed. He has bought a new bed, it is the first time she thinks about him, how that night must have been for him. How could she? How can people, and yet they do it all the time. If it hadn't been a necessity, she wouldn't have had the strength. They are asleep. The children are sleeping. They are not pretending. They don't lie wakeful in the darkness, yearning. She has been in to listen to their breathing. Seen their arms flung out, their open mouths and pale eyelids. They are asleep in her house. The road was long. She doesn't know when she set out on it. It is so quiet. She is alone, there is no one to ask, no one who knows anything. She has a bottle of sparkling wine, perhaps it is wrong to open it. She runs a bath and lies in her own bath tub and empties the bottle so she trembles a little the following day, that is the appropriate response to her situation.

He calls her new number and hangs up. She knows that it is him and he knows that she knows. He can't make contact, she wrote: Leave me, but do it without words. He calls, she picks up and says: 'Hello.'

There is no voice on the other end, only a presence, then he hangs up or she does. Sometimes they wait for a long time as they hold their breath. She also wrote 'beloved'. Beloved! Leave me without words. Not many have called him their beloved. Her telephone rings and there is no one on the other end when she picks up.

'Hello!' she says, thinking: now he hears my voice, that's what he wants to hear. 'Hello!' she whispers, over and over, then he hangs up. That is a sign. He is coming.

She gets more signs, she notices them when the children are with their father and she is alone, it looks like madness. In *Adresseavisen*, his newspaper, there are horoscopes every Saturday. She goes to the Narvesen newsstand at the railway station on Saturday mornings to buy it and read his horoscope, the forecast under his star sign because she knows that he reads it, to find out how he is. One Saturday it says under Capricorn, his star sign: Go on, jump into the deep end! What are you afraid of? After all, you're wearing a life jacket.

Jump into the deep end, it says. Which he had written was exactly what he didn't dare. He was scared of the deep, he wrote, but now it says so in the paper: Jump! Jump, Arnold! After all, she is waiting for him with open arms! But what does the bit about the life jacket mean? She calls the newspaper to find out who writes their horoscope and learns that the astrologer is called Wendy Manters and she calls Wendy Manters who lives in London and asks her what the bit about the life jacket means. She turns on the radio in the car while she waits for the lights to change, and hears the poem 'The Wind and the Blue Sailor' on a request programme as a message to a much loved woman from an anonymous listener in Sarpsborg. It has to be Arnold,

Arnold my sailor, he is currently in Sarpsborg and can think of nothing but Ida, except she has asked him to leave her, when he finally leaves her, without words. So he can't write, which is what he wants to do, and he can't call, so instead he sends her the sailor poem via a request programme on the radio. What is he doing in Sarpsborg? Did he stop by Oslo on his way there? Who did he meet? It will be May soon. She finds a four-leaf clover in the grass and a ten-øre coin on the pavement, portents of good luck!

The nights are long and filled with disturbing dreams. What if she will be on her own for ever? The sea is stormy, she is drowning, a boat appears, she waves to it, but it sails on. Even though the man in the boat sees her, he sails on, leaving her to drown. She has a dream where she lives in a derelict house, it is in ruins. The sink has been smashed as has the lavatory. Yet there are guests whom she must serve, converse with. It means she is letting too many people into her bedroom. She lets in too many people when she really ought to be alone, clearing up and mending. The lavatory is blocked, it overflows with waste. She is bleeding from her arm, from her groin. There are wounds to her body, boils on her face. She is drowning in stinking water and sewage. Her legs sink into the mud, she tries to keep her head above the foul-smelling sewer. She is trying to reach a temple on the shore. A woman walks between the columns, Ida can see her back, she is tall and wearing a Greek tunic with one shoulder bared, then she starts to turn and she may well have a ruined face. All that is missing is that this woman who looks so beautiful, so elegant from behind, turns and shows Ida her ruined and terrifying face. She turns, she looks at Ida, her face is beautiful, composed. A wise, mature face. An ethereal, insightful face. She looks at Ida with turquoise, almond-shaped eyes. It is a greeting from the place where she is headed.

Sometimes at night she feels a sudden paralysing pain and hates him. He could ease her pain, her longing. He could have written an ordinary letter, but he doesn't. He could have asked: How are you? Rather than hang up. He could have said: I love you. But I'm married. What are we going to do about our love?

But he doesn't.

Sometimes her daughter comes to her bedroom at night. She can't sleep and wants to get into her mother's bed.

'No,' Ida says so it doesn't become a habit, so it won't be a problem when *he* arrives. It is a horrible thought. Her daughter is six years old, she comes downstairs crying and wants to sleep beside Mummy, but Mummy says no. So brutal, so foolish. She walks her back upstairs and lies next to her and leaves, with those big eyes hanging on hers. Then she doesn't even do that. She just shakes her head when her daughter appears in the doorway at night. She says: No! Go back to bed! And the child lingers in the doorway, crying silently.

'Go upstairs to bed,' she says sternly and hears, after a while, little pyjama footsteps up the stairs. On one occasion she doesn't hear them and gets up to find her daughter lying on one of the bottom steps with open, dark, wet eyes and her thumb in her mouth. It is horrible to look back on, but unless she is completely honest with herself, she won't learn anything. Her daughter comes down at night, she knows she will be rejected and no longer comes into Ida's bedroom. She lingers in the doorway or outside the door, her presence, her sobbing breath wakes Ida up, but she turns to the wall and ignores her. Poor child, poor child. She has asked her daughter now, long afterwards, if she remembers it, and she doesn't remember it, it was that bad.

'I was mad back then,' Ida says, 'mad from being in love.'

When the children are not with her, she works and she walks. She walks to the shops, to the swimming pool, to the library, to and from everything while she talks to herself, composing the speech she will make when they get married. How can you express the inexpressible so that those who don't understand will understand? There is no one outside, it is dark. She is talking to herself. One word in, one word out. Things he probably doesn't remember. That he was an external examiner when she took a German exam during her first year at university, a long time ago. He was sitting at a table outside the door when she had gone in for her oral and done well, she was the last student, and she had thought that he was attractive and wanted to tell him so, but didn't dare. She will say in her speech what she had thought back then, the very first time they met. And she will include the contact lens incident because it was funny. The way he had said: Mind you don't drink it! On their first night together. And perhaps she might mention how, whether to console herself or as revenge, she had later been with a man in a hotel room in Trondheim, a man who accidentally drank the water in the glass with her contact lenses because she didn't want to say: Mind you don't drink it! Because it was Arnold's remark from their first night together. Except he might think she makes a habit of it, going with men to hotel rooms, and he might get jealous and angry and make a scene on their wedding day. He must never be in any doubt. Not for a second. That her desire is directed only at him. That her love is directed only at him and that it will last, that she will be faithful and never leave him. He must be convinced, one hundred per cent, that if he gives in, gives himself to her, then he will be safe for ever. She will make it happen.

What if he dies before 12 May? She prays to God that he lives until 12 May. If he dies before 12 May, she will be left suspended in the same emotionally unresolved state she is in now, only worse; without the prospect of it ever ending. Waiting, longing, while the object, the only thing that could assuage her longing, is gone, dead. Her fear of his dying was stronger back when they didn't have a relationship than later on, when they were together, lived together, were each other's closest confidante. Then there were times when she would fantasise about his death because it was the only way she could be free of him and of her love of him, which took up so much space, so much energy, which was so painful, it made her so vulnerable, it put her through ordeals she would never have thought she was capable of enduring and surviving. A friend of hers from Sweden once said: You should be with a man who makes you feel like a queen! And Ida had thought: Yes, that's true.

But it is not that simple, oh no.

Dear God. Please don't let him die before 12 May. She throws coins into fountains and wells. What about foreign policy, government crises, earthquakes? No. Does anything else exist? No. Children? Work? Dear God, let me breathe normally again, please stop this pounding in my heart. No, please don't take away the only thing that matters, without this pounding in my heart, this all-consuming longing, I am nothing, I will be numb, life is meaningless, what will I think about then, what will I wait for, what will I replace it with? Dear God, fewer palpitations please, no, I misspoke, I'm talking crazy. So the days pass as May approaches, in the evenings, at night when the children aren't there or when they are asleep, it happens that instead of hope and longing, she feels a profound sadness, she is consumed by sadness, exploding with or erased by sadness. She collapses in pain, it feels like falling and being in freefall, a kind of endless agony which presses equally hard from the inside and the outside at the same time.

If she has ever felt anything remotely like it, it was one time in Copenhagen. She had gone there so as not to be at home when her first play was broadcast on the radio, so as not to read the reviews the following day, she had gone to visit a friend of her husband's in Copenhagen. And because she was staying with her husband's friend, she couldn't flirt with men when she went out in the evenings. But one night in a bar she found herself standing next to a woman and this woman suddenly touched her arm and Ida let her touch her arm and the woman caressed her cheek and Ida let her caress her cheek. The woman kissed her and she responded, she went with the woman to an archway and let herself be touched, and she in turn touched this random woman in Copenhagen. The next day her hand was trembling, she trembled at the thought, she felt aroused at the thought. The ground was shaking beneath her, the city was shaking, the houses shook on the cobblestones, something terrible was about to happen. Disaster is looming, she can sense it, it already exists within her, it lives in her, it is just waiting to emerge in all its horror.

Her husband, her ex-husband as she needs to start calling him now, even though she misspeaks initially and says my husband when she talks about him, sees that she lives alone in the house. No new man moves into the house where she lives. She hasn't had a secret affair which can now be revealed and openly lived. He hasn't been left in that way, for another man. It makes it easier for them to be decent to each other. They maintain good boundaries, that is important. What other way is there? One night they sleep in the same bed, wake up in the same bed. Under separate duvets and with a pillow each, but on the same sheet. Does she dry herself with a towel that stays in his bathroom? She can't remember. The next night she sleeps alone, in another house, and he sleeps alone, she thinks, in the house she has vacated. Can he sleep? Four weeks later he gets a girlfriend. Perhaps she loves him. It sounds like it when she hears about her, the other woman, the new woman. He rings her bell if he has an errand and stays outside the front door. He doesn't ask: What did you do yesterday? Where are you going? Unless it affects his plans. He visits his friend in Copenhagen, meets a young woman and starts dating her. He calls Ida and asks in an exalted voice if she can keep the kids for a few more days. She is no longer the love object. She is no longer the one who gets coffee in bed. She can imagine it, she has dreams about it at night where he wears protective clothing when he goes to bed with her, the new one, a helmet, a gas mask and an enormous jockstrap. Perhaps he sees other women when he is in Norway and the Danish woman is in Denmark. Perhaps he sees their children's teacher, the woman who lives next door. Perhaps he meets her friends in cafés in town when the children are with Ida. All women are possible, available to him, he is attractive and kind and she was the one who let him go, she has made her bed and must lie in it. Perhaps he sleeps with her girlfriends and talks about their divorce. Perhaps they have come straight from his bed when she bumps into them, isn't there something odd about the way they smile? Do they know something she doesn't, which might affect her if she was told. Does he experience something with them that he didn't have with her? Has he discovered, now that he can compare, that she wasn't quite as funny, erotic or interesting as he had told himself. Does he meet others who make him change his view of her and being married to her, so that he realises that their marriage was a mistake and their divorce a blessing? Can other women's naked bodies make him see that she was never the right one, and will he change his mind about her and be pleased about the divorce? So what? Wouldn't that be for the best? Why would she want to be the right woman for him, the man she left? How selfish you are, Ida. She doesn't go out when the Danish woman stays with him, not to meet them hand in hand in the street. Does she in fact love him, is it only now that she is losing him that she feels it?

She never meets the Danish woman, had she met her, shaken her hand, greeted her, it would have helped. She does meet the nurse with the calligraphy hobby whom he dates afterwards. By then it is Christmas. She is going to Trondheim to visit Erik Grøver, she is on the train with the children. The children are getting off at Røros where their father and the nurse who does calligraphy will be meeting them at the station. She feels as if she is suffering from exam nerves. The train slows down, she gulps and she gulps again. Her hands are trembling and she has been to the lavatory several times to study herself in the mirror. Don't look nervous, don't look beaten. Don't look humiliated, lonely, alone, superior, effusive. The train slows down. The children sit silent in their coats on the seats. There's Daddy. Yes, there he is, he waves and runs after the train and is followed by a woman with long dark hair, wearing his coat. The children are ready at the door. The train stops, Ida opens the door. Outside is her ex-husband, the children's father, and behind him, wearing his coat, the dark-haired nurse who does calligraphy.

'Hello,' Ida says.

'Hello,' he says.

Their breaths cloud around them like smoke in the cold.

'I guess I should say hello to you too,' Ida says and extends her hand towards the nurse and the nurse takes it and they say hello and smile cautiously. The nurse is nervous, she realises, even more nervous than Ida, and relieved that Ida isn't hostile, doesn't have the stern, dismissive face she might have had. The children wait in the snow. Ida pats their heads and gets back on the train and the train begins to move and the two adults and two small people walk along the platform in the snow. Ida waves and the children wave and then it is over. She leans back. It is over. She didn't break down, she didn't lose face, she did it.

~

April starts. April ends. May starts. The first. The second. The third. The sky is high and blue. Tulips and daffodils pop up outside her house. The leaves on the birch trees are small and luminous. She has imagined this a thousand times. She has planned every detail, then changed her plans. What she will wear and how she will arrive, rushing in with pink cheeks at the last moment so he will be thinking that she isn't coming and feel disappointed and then, when she appears in the doorway after all, finds himself *love-struck*. Like a revelation, like a proof of the existence of God as it had been for her, as it had radiated through her when he came down the steps to Tostrupkjelleren with his autumn coat flapping behind him. So he would experience the power of love as she has done and find the strength to face another breakup. Be strong enough to say: I want a divorce. And to his child: We're getting divorced, your mother and I. Strong enough to count spoons, divide up wedding presents. To say: Which ones do you want?

How little she knew. How naive she was.

She buys new lingerie. It is May the sixth, the seventh. The tenth. She flies up to Trondheim on the eleventh. On the list of participants she receives on arrival at the hotel, there is no mention of Arnold Bush, nor is there in the programme in a folder in her room.

It is eight o'clock in the evening, she can't call him now, but she has to know. She tries his office anyway, but he is not there. It must be some mistake. It is probably just an error. She is convinced he will be there. Nothing else is possible. He couldn't help himself. She has been waiting for this moment for six long months. She dresses, applies her makeup, gets ready as if he is coming. But at breakfast the following morning she bumps into the organiser of the seminar and asks as casually as she can, though her voice trembles. Arnold Bush has cancelled, that is all they know. She has to go outside and sit down. What now, what does she do now? She must call him, she runs up to her room and rings him at the office, but no answer, he will probably be there later. During every break, as soon as she gets the chance, all that day and all of the next, she calls, he doesn't pick up. She even calls the forbidden number, ready to slam down the phone the moment someone answers, but no one does. He didn't come, he isn't there. He is elsewhere right now while she sits on her hotel bed, defeated. Now, right now, he is elsewhere, it is unreal. Because he practically doesn't exist in their story, he is still just a ghost, a flapping coat.

She has waited for May and May doesn't happen. It rains. She walks in the rain with Erik Grøver and cries. Perhaps it is at this point, in his company, that she asks herself for the first time if her feelings might be rooted in something else. Related to love, a past experience of rejection which this current one has brought back. She stays with Erik Grøver after the seminar has finished. They sleep in his rickety double bed under the crooked ceiling from which a withered plant is hanging, but they don't have sex. He is so burdened, he is fossilised. It rains and rains. She calls Arnold Bush's office and one day he picks up the phone. His voice becomes intimate as she says her name, he has been thinking about her, he has been thinking about the seminar. It was his father's seventieth birthday, he has been away with his family, he says, that was why he didn't attend the seminar, that was why he had to cancel. He offers details, which mean nothing. His father celebrated his seventieth at the Pers Hotel in Geilo, he says. She asks in a calm manner, which is new for her, if they can meet. Her new manner frightens him, he is alarmed and sharpens his tone. Just a straightforward meeting with him during the day at his office. She isn't flirting, she is serious. She needs to find out whether this infatuation, she says, the strongest she has ever experienced, is about him, is about Arnold Bush, or whether she needed to be in love, needed the strength which being in love gave her to do what was necessary, to divorce. She needs to know in order to get on with her life.

Can Arnold help her with that?

He listens, silent on the other end. He doesn't say no, but he makes it clear that he thinks she is asking for something to which she is not entitled.

He says she may visit his office the next day at two o'clock.

She goes there the next day at two o'clock. Makes herself cold, no matter how hard her heart is beating, don't think, don't stop, just do it. Go there and don't let yourself be overcome by the body, that shouts: Stop, it will hurt, it is dangerous. It doesn't rain that day. The sun is shining that day in Trondheim and the air is warm. She hasn't seen him for six months, they had sex then, now she is divorced. He has told her which floor, which door, she knocks and he calls out: Come in. There he sits in real life. She stands in the doorway, he gestures towards the sofa, he has a sofa in his office, but it is too intimate. Did he think they would kiss, fuck on his office couch, that she would pounce on him, it is not until now that she knows him, that the thought crosses her mind. She asks if they can go out.

'Go out?' He sounds surprised. He checks the time. She asks if he can spare just five minutes. He says he can spare an hour. That will suffice. He fiddles with something on his desk, turns off his computer. He is nervous, she isn't nervous anymore. They leave together, they keep their distance, she gravitates towards the wall. They say nothing, he chooses the bench by the shingle entrance so everyone can see them, they sit down at opposite ends of it, she does the talking. She is honest. She tells it like it is. She isn't ashamed, why should she be. It is not difficult. She has been preparing in the long months leading up to May, albeit for something else, she had imagined something else, the seminar, the dinner afterwards, the bar. But her story hangs together. It lacks a source, a catalyst, but it is coherent, it hangs together. Only she can know how strong it feels, how much it hurts. He barely looks at her because when he does, his face reveals that he loves her, he melts.

He listens, he smokes a cigarette, he glances at her from time to time for appearances' sake and loses himself.

What does he say? He says that he has a child. He says that his wife's job is problematic and demanding. He says they are considering another child, but he doesn't think it is such a good idea. He says that his father has a heart condition, which might be hereditary. He checks the time. She gets up immediately, but he says he has another five minutes and she sits down. Now she doesn't say anything. They stay where they are for a little while, then they stand up. They say: Take care, they don't hug one another, she walks away. She doesn't turn and look after him. She is content, he loves her. For an hour or an hour and a half, maybe two, she is happy. She runs back to Erik's and enthuses about the meeting, but the thought forms slowly: And now what? She writes a letter telling him where she is staying, that she will be in town for a few more days and gives him Erik's telephone number. They can meet if he wants to. She hurries to the central post office to post it. He might get it as early as tomorrow. He *has* to go to the office the next day. She is in his town, but he doesn't call. Then he rings, but hangs up. It gets worse. She doesn't go down to the waterfront. It rains again. She is not alone. Erik Grøver is there, with all his problems. He wants to hit all women, pull their hair and bite them. Poor man. She keeps hoping. Right until she leaves Erik's place with her suitcase, she thinks, she hopes, right until she is on the plane going back, she hopes that he will come running after her, across the runway, in through the door of the plane, but it doesn't happen. May comes to an end.

At home the sea is warm. Seagulls perch on the jetties. Roses grow along the wall. Now what? Find another? When everything is about him. When he is the only man in the world. Forget him. Kiss another. She tries to move on. She doesn't say no to anything that might ease her pain, distract her. She drinks. She gets drunk. She kisses other men. She sleeps with other men. Afterwards she feels remorse and shame, she trembles in the grey dawn from fresh, unbearable pain. An earthquake is rumbling. She is caught up in an avalanche. It is happening now: the destruction of the old. She isn't doing anything, it just happens. She is a mute, somnambulant part of it. She is free from her external past, but she has yet to step into her present, she has no idea about the future and every kind of emotion whirls around this space.

Sometimes in the morning, while the children are playing in the garden, it comes over her. Suddenly she has to lie down and she can't get up. The children play in the garden, they come asking for biscuits or juice, but she can't help them. Wait a moment. Mummy is sick. She can't get up, can't speak. It lasts an hour and a half. It consumes her, it eats its way through her body, that is how it feels, it starts from the inside and devours, hollows out her body, without anaesthetic.

~

When the fourth attack happens, she knows that it will pass. That it will last an hour and a half and then slowly it will pass, and that makes it more bearable. It is true, as someone has said, that when you are in pain, you are doing the work. Pay attention to your crisis, the book says. It is telling you that something is wrong. If you regard a crisis as an external disaster that has befallen you, it will simply intensify; she tries to view it as a message.

During her fifth attack she thinks, as she did when she had her second child, that the experience is similar: it's part of the process. It is impossible to imagine, as is giving birth when you are not in the middle of it, just like you can't imagine hunger when you are sated, can't imagine thirst when yours has been quenched, yet still you know that that kind of pain exists, the body remembers. During the fifth attack she asks herself when it is over, what happened just before? She was writing. Writing what? In her diary. She goes to her computer, she checks her calendar and finds the dates of the attacks of pain, she has marked them with a red star. She finds her diary entries from those dates, those five pages, she never writes more than one page per day, she finds them. There it is. The noose. The executioner ready and waiting. The condemned person trying not to faint from terror, desperate to preserve their dignity. Who doesn't scream, who doesn't try to flee because there is no escape, who just stands there and lets it happen, what else can they do? It says so in black and white and it changes her, that is the moment when she becomes herself, one single tremor and there is Ida. It can happen from one moment to the next. But perhaps, she thinks later, years later when she has grown accustomed to her new self, it had emerged slowly and not as subtly as she had hitherto believed. Wasn't it that same realisation that made the houses shake in Copenhagen all that time ago? Slowly until the time was right, until she could bear it, it had smuggled itself into her writing and given itself away.

She rings her sister in despair. She doesn't reflect, she can't reflect, she has been hurled into it, she is fighting her own self. Should someone happen to drop by or call, she is compelled to tell them because it is all-consuming, but she tries to breathe, to be alone, to handle it on her own.

She turns from it, but it doesn't go away. She closes her eyes and still it doesn't go away. Is that what happened to me? Does that explain it? She spins on her own axis until she collapses from dizziness, it is still there. She dreams at night and wakes up in the morning filled with dreams and looks out at the swaying branches; it is coming. She rides her bike downhill, the wind in her hair, it is still there. She swims underwater, it is coming from inside her though it feels as if it is cascading towards her from the outside like a pressure wave, it comes towards her and enters her body through her ears, her eyes, into her mouth and down her throat, through the pores of her skin, into every cell and chews up the old Ida: she is a new person.

~

Whom do you tell that you have changed? I'm not the person I used to be. Whom do you tell that you have turned into someone else? She meets one of her old nursery school teachers who says: It's Ida, isn't it, but she shakes her head because it isn't.

She tries eventually, when it no longer feels so dramatic, to tell her new story to a member of her family. They don't believe her. They think she must be mistaken. Don't you see it, look closely, she wants to shout. Something must be damaged in you too, something broken in you too, because you can't damage just one child. We lived in the same house, we ate at the same table, it can't just be in me, somehow it must also exist in you. Something was wrong all the time, and now I have found the missing piece!

'What are you talking about? You're stirring things up. You're out of your mind.'

'But if I *am* right, just imagine that I'm right. Doesn't that explain it, everything that was wrong, something *was* wrong.'

'You're crazy. You need to get a grip.'

'But what if, think about it, please try.'

'Why, what's the point?'

'The point is to understand.'

'What are you talking about? You regret your divorce, you should never have gone through with it, you're out of your mind.'

'Please, just for a moment! Imagine that I'm right, think about it for just a moment. Don't you all think there's something wrong with you too?'

'No. We don't, as it happens.'

That was pretty much how it went down, although not in so many words. There was never a conversation because they never talked. She had gone mad and sought to infect them with her madness. She had fallen ill and wanted them to be ill too. She had destroyed her own life and wanted to destroy theirs too, wanted to ruin them because she was ruined. She was lashing out at everyone because she had divorced from her safe existence and wanted to hurt herself and those closest to her, and if she couldn't have this strange Arnold Bush in Trondheim, then they would all go down with her.

'She's not herself,' they say when someone asks about her.

'It's the divorce,' they say, 'a disaster, it's the stress,' they say.

'And now she has got it into her head that it all goes back to her childhood.'

'Poor woman,' her family says and they shake their heads when they talk about her. It would almost have been better if she had been sectioned: look, she really is mad. If they meet someone who says: 'I listened to her last play, it was very good,' they are embarrassed, their stomach lurches as if they were hearing bad news. It is not that they don't love her. It is not that they don't think it is sad that they are losing contact, that they see each other less and less, then finally not at all, or that she has lost her mind. It is sad, but she courted that madness herself and has chosen not to let it go. On the contrary, she clings to her madness, whatever the cost, what do they say, that she enjoys her crazy performances, casting herself in the leading role, not only did she always have to be the centre of attention, but now we have to feel sorry for her as well?

It becomes impossible. Impossible for both sides, impossible for everyone. They can't meet, eventually they don't talk or see each other. Silence ensues. Only her mother rings, crying, begging her to come to her senses. Why is she so contrary? Why can't they just be together like a normal family? Why does everything have to be so complicated? It wasn't always so complicated.

How can she explain that it is not her choice, that it isn't a decision, that it just *is*, that it is her body's choice?

Two kinds of pain. The first is paralysing as during her five attacks. It is quiet, it practically turns into death as she nears the answers, holy almost, timeless. The second is the pain of hangover and regret, restless, thumping pressure in her chest, she got drunk, talked too much, met men, lost control. She wakes up alone with a pounding heart and it lasts all day. There is nothing to hope for. No one to talk to. There is no one who feels the way she does with whom she can share it, she will be alone for ever, how will she manage, she can't stand her own company, what is she going to do with herself?

~

When she was a child she would get palpitations from the sheer joy of being alive. How far away that seems now, how insane. On summer mornings in the throes of a happiness so strong that she would run across the fields with her arms outstretched and small sobs in her throat: There's so much! I can't keep it all to myself! I have to share it with someone! Convinced that nothing could go wrong, that she would never be disappointed, dancing across the fields, but was she bursting with the wrong feelings?

Now she is so steeped in pain that she can never be happy again. Once this pain arrives, it can't be suppressed. Nor can it be lived through, it is too great. When you are in pain, you are doing the work, but the work never ends. You're growing now, Ida, she tells herself. Oh, really? All growth, she tells herself, involves pain. Oh, does it now? You are losing parts of yourself and everything linked to those parts; all relationships must be rebuilt and some can't be, that's why.

She prays to God, it makes no difference. She takes the Bible from her bookcase, flicks through it, wanting to open herself to it, it makes no difference. She writes to a psycho-analyst, a cry for help, he calls it later. She is surprised at this because she strives to be as detached as she can be, as matter-of-fact as possible, in order not to seem overwrought, difficult, hysterical and be dismissed. She reads her draft letter several times during the night, the mere act of writing makes her feel better. She writes the final version the following morning with a date and her name and address so it won't seem impulsive, so that she doesn't come across as frenzied and unnerving, a tiresome woman. I need help. Can you help me? Up into the air where she can breathe, be reborn in the air, by the air.

She takes out her photo albums and leafs through them, she looks at the pictures with fresh eyes. She takes out the books she read as a child and rereads them. She finds the books she read as a young woman, as a student, and reads them over and over, and sees her own underlining and comments in the margins. Messages from the person she was to the person she is now. She discovers to her dismay what she didn't read, what she put aside, skipped. The books she didn't finish. The pictures in the photo albums she cut, how she cut herself out because she thought she looked stupid or ugly. She tries to remember the off-cuts, she tries to reconstruct the censored pictures, the fragments that were scrunched up and thrown away. She retrieves her earliest memories, the few clear glimpses and tries to remember the moment before, the moment after. It is like reconstructing an aeroplane. Civilisation ends and the only thing that remains is a three-thousand-year-old plane wreck which the next civilisation is trying to reconstruct. The screws are in one pile and long, coloured cables lie neatly next to each other in a row, the lavatory bowl is at the centre, judging by its round shape it is likely to have been an altar.

~

One bright morning the psychoanalyst calls her, sunshine in the garden, the children are with her, playing in the garden. He has to remind her, she has completely forgotten.

'You wrote me a letter,' he says. A letter? To whom? Once she remembers, she is overcome with the enormity of it; she can hear it in her own voice, as can he. She goes there. She goes to see him. He sends her for a Rorschach test at the Rikshospitalet. They show her images that look like X-ray pictures and ask her what she sees.

'Skeletons,' she says. 'Intestines, lungs and ribs. Skulls,' she says and qualifies for psychoanalysis, five hundred kroner per session, three times a week, but the state will pay. If she fails to turn up, she will be billed in order to ensure compliance and so that she won't skive off when it gets bad, when they approach difficult issues, they, the therapist and her, the two of them together, gathered together to make her feel better.

'I need to warn you,' the Rorschach test man says. 'Psychoanalysis will have major consequences for every aspect of your life.'

'Yes?'

'Major consequences for your relationships with other people.'

'Aha?'

'Your most intimate relationships.'

'They're already ruined.'

~

She lies on the couch and talks. She needs to be as honest as she can be. She can't know if he is listening, she can't see him. Perhaps he isn't listening, perhaps he is daydreaming, perhaps he is bored, perhaps he is yawning. She can't see him. He can see her, that she is lying there, but not her face, there is no point in smiling or smoothing her hair. There are only words, only her voice.

'I was the favourite,' she says, her life story always begins like this, she always opens with this line. It hangs in the air. What did she just say? I was the favourite. What is she saying?

'Oh,' she says.

'Oh, no,' she says.

'It's not true,' she says. She is unable to speak. He must be getting bored by now. You're supposed to talk, so talk! The words lie, they grate in her ears, it is embarrassing, she is ashamed.

'That's not what I mean,' she says.

'Forget it,' she says.

'I mean,' she says, but she doesn't know what she means, she thinks that she needs to start over.

'I wasn't the favourite,' she says, it is better, but it hurts, she is close to tears already.

Three times a week for two and a half years to uncover the losses, early ones and the most recent one, the loss of her beloved Arnold, the latter has brought up the former, she understands that, her fresh experience of loss is exacerbated by the old one, which was dormant. He is just a catalyst and she knows it, but she loves the catalyst. She doesn't try to dress anything up. She is as frank about herself as she is able to be, as merciless towards herself as she can be, in the pursuit of the greater good, for her own benefit, so that she can possibly feel better in the future.

But what should happen, doesn't. What is supposed to happen in order for the treatment to succeed, doesn't. There is no transference. She doesn't let him in. Arnold is there already, he takes up all the room. She wants him there. After two and a half years of psychoanalysis, Ida Heier is still in love with Arnold Bush, and not with her psychoanalyst. She storms in without looking at him, lies down on the couch and when he says her time is up, she runs out again. He is there, he is a witness, he gets her to tell another narrative. Simply because he sits there and listens – presumably – she uses different words, looks at it from different angles and expresses what she sees in new ways and understands more and more. That is what she wants. But it is not enough. For the psychoanalyst, for the psychoanalysis. Her car keys slip out of the pocket of her dress and are left behind on the couch. She rushes back upstairs when she realises it in the car park. They are already on his desk. He has picked them up from the couch already.

'You keep forgetting something here,' he says with a knowing look before he holds out his hand and gives her the keys. What is he implying? Because she left behind a hair slide on the couch the last time. It slipped out of her hair without her noticing, he drew her attention to it when she was in the doorway, pointing meaningfully at the couch. Is that supposed to be something subconscious?

If she has a dream about a man sitting unperturbed in a chair while she herself is in a battle, where she constantly has to cross fields raked with sniper fire and dodge lethal bullets, her first thought is that the paralysed man in the chair is Arnold, while the psychoanalyst thinks that the static man in the chair is him. Who does he think he is, why would Ida dream about him?

He doesn't like her talking about Arnold. He squirms in his chair when she talks about her beloved Arnold in Trondheim, whom she hasn't seen for a long time. It bores him, her trivial love affair which she refuses to give up on. He doesn't believe in her love, he doesn't believe that she loves. He believes, she senses, that Arnold is a random object of her complex emotions. That the only thing which isn't random is that he is unavailable, married, lives far away, in another city, in another part of the country, that he is out of bounds in every possible way, unobtainable. That is why she picked him, to relive her early rejection and loss, to fix something that can't be fixed.

And if the psychoanalyst doesn't believe in that power, the strongest she has ever felt, which points clearly to one person, which is unequivocal, without doubt, which has made her understand poetry and plays. If the natural phenomenon she is experiencing right now, if LOVE in capital letters doesn't exist in his vocabulary, can he still help her?

Three times a week for two and a half years, and she continues to insist that she loves Arnold Bush. Somewhat reconciled to her new narrative about herself and still infatuated, she ends the sessions.

Arnold Bush is made a professor. She reads it in the newspaper. He is taking part in a Brecht seminar in Munich and his title is listed as professor. She tells everyone she knows. He has been made a professor. He is going to Munich to speak at a Brecht seminar. She is always talking about him to everyone, even when she is meant to be talking about other subjects she will talk about him or about her love for him. But not to anyone who might throw spanners in the works of her love. Those who know him well or know his wife, though she talks to them too, but in a different, calculated manner in order to maybe learn something new. But to her own friends, she speaks openly and always about Arnold Bush and she bores them with her talk. She tells them over and over what he has written, what he has said, even though the things he wrote, he wrote a long time ago, the things he said, he said many years ago, she interprets his sentences word by word and in ever new ways. On a good day as declarations of love and promises, on a bad day as betrayals and rejections. One moment as if he chose his words with care, the next as if they were signs from his subconscious that give him away. She goes over them again and again with the same diligence and commitment, possibly with more attention than when she analyses Ibsen's plays in articles for *The Journal*.

Occasionally someone voices a thought that has never crossed her mind, namely that very few people are as interested in the professor from Trondheim as Ida, and she will take offence. She prefers, later this becomes clear to her, the company of people who know him or have met him, people who can contribute with information about him. Friends or acquaintances or random people who studied with him or have heard him lecture or worked with him somehow. She asks those who don't pose a threat, how he looked when they met him, what he wore, what he said, what he ate, what he drank, who he arrived with and, more importantly, who he left with. How he had *seemed*. Depressed? Unhappy? That is what she is hoping for. Depressed and heartbroken. Even when she talks to someone who met him just once several years ago, she hopes for the same thing, that they will say that Arnold seemed depressed and unhappy, so that she can imagine that his only happy hours in life so far have been the hours he spent with her, with Ida.

If she bumps into anyone who has met his wife, she asks them what she looks like, how she *seems*. If it is someone she knows well, she will ask them outright, if she doesn't know them, she will ask them in a crafty yet innocent way, but always the same questions: what does she look like, what is she like, how does she *seem*. Always hoping to hear a negative description such as grey, forgettable, uninteresting, or preferably: charmless, unsympathetic. Ida focuses with such intensity on her conversation partner, she asks with such glowing anticipation that even the most decent person might give in to the temptation to grant Ida her obvious wish and describe Arnold Bush's wife, whom they have barely met, with words such as mousey or dull.

Ida Heier nods adamantly. That was what she thought all along.

She is aware that she is harassing them, but she can't help herself. Also when it comes to his ex-wife; should she happen to bump into someone who has met her, she practically begs to have her described unfavourably. So people start to avoid her. Just like her family, other people too start to view this as an obsession rather than an infatuation. In time she stops speaking so openly about her passion for Arnold Bush, he becomes an 'A' who can only be whispered to a chosen few and mentioned in her diary.

She seeks out new environments where they know A and his work. She mentions, casually, a play he has reviewed, an article he has written, a topic he has recently covered on the radio in the hope that the person she is talking to will mention his name. If she doesn't get a bite in this way, she will herself bring up the article or the review:

'I read an article the other day, about one of Brecht's early plays, written by, oh, what is his name?'

'Who?'

'The Brecht guy.'

And at this point her interlocutor will usually mention his name, the beloved name: 'Arnold Bush?'

'Yes, that's him.'

And if they don't, she will introduce it herself: 'Something beginning with A? Arnold something or other?'

'Bush!' her interlocutor will most likely say, and Ida will respond: 'Yes, I believe that's him.'

And if they don't, she herself might say: 'Bush, I believe. I think his name is Arnold Bush,' she says, sounding critical, as if she disagrees with everything he represents in order not to arouse suspicion, and her breathing will quicken as she forms the words with her mouth, his first name, Arnold, then Bush and says them out loud in a public space, and grows hot and slightly dizzy. At times she plays it safe by being more direct and negative: 'That Arnold Bush who is never off the radio. Isn't he a bit past it?'

And many will nod and agree with Ida. Arnold Bush is past it, finished and Ida Heier doesn't get angry that her secret lover is discussed in negative terms, she is just thrilled that he is the topic of conversation so that she, for as long as it lasts, isn't alone in thinking about him. At times her remark will trigger a long and aggressive tirade against Arnold Bush and his entire style of writing and thinking, and Ida isn't hurt at hearing her beloved and everything he represents characterised pejoratively, on the contrary, it just makes him human, more earthly, it drags him down from the metaphysical sky and makes him approachable, attainable.

If she bumps into someone who disagrees with her negative point of view, who defends Arnold Bush and lists his strengths, she becomes – if it is a woman – instantly suspicious. A lover, a rival, a hidden agenda? If the speaker is a man, she will ingratiate herself with him to learn as much as possible, smile as she argues passionately with him using arguments she has learned from Arnold Bush's opponents and make the conversation last for as long as possible and it feels sweet, like revenge.

People who can't tell her anything about A, who don't somehow stimulate the A in her, don't interest her. Why should she be entertaining or interesting to them? The men she spends a night or two with, know him. Otherwise she wouldn't have bothered sleeping with them, talking to them unless she can – overtly or covertly – introduce the subject of A. She sleeps with his best friend and close collaborator, a dramaturg. He comes over to her at a seminar, in the bar after dinner, and she lets him flirt with her purely because he is A's best friend and collaborator, because he flirts with her on behalf of A, touches her in A's place, at A's request.

A has confided in his friend because he can't help confiding in someone, just like she can't help confiding, he has confided in such a way that it has aroused the desire of his friend, the dramaturg. His overtures can be regarded as messages from A. A's spirit floats over the bed sheets and all she thinks about, hopes for and imagines as she lies underneath A's friend is how he will hint to A about his night with Ida and how A will be intrigued and ask, and how his friend will smile mysteriously, yet say something that can't be misinterpreted, but to the great surprise of A's friend, the dramaturg, who has assumed that the relationship between A and Ida was casual, a fling, A will explode with rage and demand to know the truth, and when he hears it he will be consumed by jealousy and understand, at last and in one fell swoop, how fiercely, how hopelessly he loves her, Ida Heier in Oslo. Understand it in such a way that he can't stay where he is, but has to get up and run to the door, grab his wallet and leave his home, his wife, his child, hurry to the airport and catch the first plane, which can't get to Oslo fast enough, agitated and excited to take her, Ida, in his arms, for ever so that no one else will ever, never ever get close to her, *his* woman.

Meant only for him. The only person in the whole wide world. The void in her body, the hollow of her vagina, made only for him, her beloved. The place where he, his penis, is absent.

She plays a game of Patience, she asks her Patience if he loves her and she doesn't stop playing until it comes out, she can't rest until it comes out, she stays up all night to make it come out, it is not until then that she can sleep, that she can relax, sometimes all of the next day, sometimes for twenty-four hours.

Arnold Bush writes theatre reviews for the radio programme *On Stage*. It airs once a week, on Saturday morning at noon. If not quite every week, then nearly every other week she hears Arnold Bush's voice on the radio. She turns on her radio, Saturday morning at twelve, restless, her heart pounding to hear if the host will announce a review by Arnold Bush. If that happens, her restlessness increases, she becomes more agitated, snappy if one of her children comes to ask her something, *wants* something. On hearing his voice her knees go soft, that is the right expression even when she is sitting down, her ear pressed against the radio and with one of her children on her lap.

'Shhh. Listen,' she whispers into her daughter's hair as she rocks her. 'Do you like that voice?'

The girl tilts back her head and looks up with her thumb in her mouth. Ida kisses her on her forehead and whispers: 'Shhh. Listen. Do you like that voice?'

The child nods cautiously. They listen and breathe quietly. A stylised, strangely unfamiliar voice. Because he is talking on the radio, because he is on air. Because he is sitting in a studio in Tyholt wearing headphones, talking into a microphone. It reaches its intended recipient, Ida in Oslo. An assured, distant, almost superior voice. Different from all others, different from the one that during his orgasm had whispered: I love you. She is frantic with desire. It discusses German literature, translated as well as untranslated, contemporary dramatists, the classics – or that is what most people hear, his colleagues and acquaintances, his wife and son, who sit with him at the kitchen table with coffee and newspapers when the programme is broadcast at twelve noon on a Saturday. But what he is really talking about is his love. His loss. Being unable to live with the one he loves. About hope. Well-hidden to the others, evident only to Ida. Camouflaged behind sophisticated literary analysis, long, convoluted sentences filled with foreign terms, but introduced with a line from a song, 'my love, so far, far away' and concluded simply and with, Ida detects, a hint of tender trembling in his voice:

'In spite of the apparent meaninglessness, the seeming disconnect, this random, yes, bordering on the surreal or absurd action or lack of action, there is a line, a clue for anyone who has the ear or heart for it: the loss of love. Love that can't be released into the world, love that can't be explored. And yet when the curtain falls we don't know what happens next, to use a hackneyed phrase. We don't know if the two people who stand either side of the stage at the end with their arms outstretched to each other, will ever reach each other behind the curtain, precisely because the curtain has come down and blocks what the audience can see, because the meeting of lovers can't be understood from the outside, it can't be seen.'

She is able to write. She is able to do that. She writes a play, *Old Ophelia*, about a woman driven mad by love. But she makes sure it has a happy ending. That she survives him. Her previous play has been produced. It will be broadcast soon. She goes for a walk on the day it happens. She has been to the studio to listen to it, why would she want to listen to it at the same time as everyone else, the very few other people who listen to radio drama, most of them older people. She listens to her answering machine when she comes home. There has been a feature in the newspaper discussing the play with a picture of her that same day. Erik Grøver has called, he listened to the play, he liked it, he says. One of her friends listened to it as well and liked it, she says. Ida is delighted. She doesn't know if her parents or her siblings have listened to it, but it means nothing, it was written a long time ago, *before*. She doesn't know if Arnold Bush listened to it, but she can't believe otherwise. She brought her Arnold sailor with her, just for him.

One of Arnold Bush's colleagues at the Department of German at the University of Trondheim invites her to discuss a German play she has written an article about. She accepts. She wonders if Arnold will be there, if he is behind the invitation. It is autumn again and dark in Trondheim. It rains as usual.

She is meeting his colleague, Leif Asnes, in a café before the event. He smiles, she thinks it is a knowing smile. He asks about the German play and about her own. All she can think about is if Arnold will be there, if she is about to meet him for the first time since May. He is there. The room is filled with students and he is there, he is sitting with the other staff members behind a column, pretending he can't see her. Arnold is in the room, but she is someone he doesn't know now, a survivor. She has been through an ordeal by fire and submitted her new play the day before. They make eye contact, he nods softly. While she speaks, he looks down. He does not dare to look at her because then she will see it, he can't hide it if he looks up. Perhaps he looks up when she looks down, when she flicks through her papers. As long as they are in the same room, she is the braver.

They take a break. He has to come over and say hello, anything else would be odd. Perhaps he has told his colleagues that he knows her. Perhaps he drew their attention to her article. Perhaps he even suggested that they invite her during a meeting about the Department's evening events. He has to come up to her. But perhaps he can see that she has changed and is doubly scared and might end up giving himself away to her, to everyone. He approaches her reluctantly with a colleague.

'Hello,' he says.

'Hello,' she says.

'How are you?' he asks.

'I'm all right,' she says.

'I'm on a sabbatical,' he says, looks down and then to the side. 'I'm writing a paper on Faust,' he says, odd little details like that.

His colleague wants to step outside for a cigarette. Arnold tries to hold him back, reaches out his arm and grabs his coat sleeve to keep him there, an intuitive movement so as not to be left alone with her, he doesn't dare. His colleague frowns, snatches back his coat and disappears, now Arnold is on his own and helpless. In this brief moment it is inconceivable that she can be afraid of him, that she feels like a supplicant towards him every day and every night. He and only he can bring salvation. Yet now he is too scared to meet her eyes. She helps him, she chats to him. He looks up, surprised at how direct she is, how effortlessly she manages it, she who has written him desperate letters, doesn't she love him anymore?

Oh yes, her eyes reply. Oh yes, I still love you, I'm just in a different place now, I've changed, my darling.

He needs the loo, he says, and turns and leaves, and as she watches his back disappear, she feels the first indication of the familiar pain. He could have stayed, but he leaves, he disappears.

After the break, after she has finished speaking, after the discussion in which she doesn't participate, the German Department invites its guest for a beer in town. Arnold's colleague stands next to her and waits while she gathers up her things. The others have made their way out into the rain and down to the bar they tend to go to after such events. She is ready, she has put on her coat and slung her bag over her shoulder, but her host, Leif Asnes, doesn't move. They are waiting for Arnold Bush, he says, who has gone upstairs to get his coat. They wander outside and wait under the entrance canopy. He takes his time. Because he is scared, because he has to steel himself. Perhaps he takes a swig from a bottle, it is long afterwards, now that she knows him, that she thinks this thought. He keeps a bottle in his office for Dutch courage. There he is. It is the same coat. It flaps after him in the wind in the same way as the last time, which she will never forget. Out into the darkness, into the twilight rain, it is cold, they stuff their hands into their pockets and hunch their shoulders.

'So you're going to Rome?' Arnold asks.

'Yes.' Ida is going to Rome. She has just submitted a new play and a friend, who is currently renting a flat in Rome, has invited her to stay and she has said yes. Yes, she is on her way to Rome, she is leaving tomorrow, the timing is fortuitous. She wanted to go to Arnold Bush's city where she might meet Arnold Bush and there might be pain afterwards as there usually is and then it might help to get on a plane and fly away, to the sun, and visit a man in Rome. They end up sitting next to each other. She doesn't know how it happens. Almost as if they tacitly and imperceptibly are treated as a couple. They sit next to each other, but he talks to the person on his other side. It doesn't matter. His body, his attention, is aimed at her, at Ida, his ear is tuned to her. A young man leans across the table to her, he compliments her on something she has said and is keen to discuss it, she makes room for him on her other side and Arnold Bush gets up abruptly, knocking over his glass as he does so, he swears, sweeping beer from his trousers, and reddens. He goes to a neighbouring table, bends down to an attractive, young woman who looks up, surprised that the professor has decided that now is the perfect time to comment on her last essay. Five minutes later he is back, he drains his glass and says he has to leave, he is driving, he says. Not to Ida, he isn't addressing anyone in particular, he just speaks into the air. He's going *home*, he says, snatches his light-coloured coat and leaves. The pain starts. His back, his bald head against the door and then he is gone.

She empties her glass. She orders another beer. She tries to concentrate, to focus on what the others are saying, on something else. She drinks quickly, she drinks another beer, she stays there until they break up so as not to be alone. Leif Asnes walks her to her hotel. It is as if he, too, is sad, as if he senses that he is walking next to someone who is going to pieces. Outside the hotel, he quickly strokes her cheek and says that he wishes her all the best, then he leaves. She is unable to thank him, her throat is dry. Outside it is dark and cold. She goes up to her room, she doesn't turn on the light, she doesn't close the curtains, she doesn't undress, she gets into bed, under the duvet, this feels like the worst attack, it hasn't been this bad for a long time. She is in freefall again, she doesn't have the energy to fall, but she can't fight it, control it, she collapses in pain. And it is unbearable. If this is the way it is going to be, then she can't meet him, can't see him. If these are the consequences of a meeting, she must avoid him. She had thought she would be fine, she had been looking forward to going to Rome, having finished her play, now it is ruined, she will never be happy again.

She has experienced this before. Her mind tells her that it will pass, that it must be endured and then it will be over – for now. She keeps reminding herself, but doesn't believe her own words. She will never smile again.

It lasts a day and a half. She writes to him on the plane while she drinks miniature bottles of white wine. To explain to him what happens, what their meetings do to her because he might be behind the invitation, because he turned up; to share with him something she has learned about herself, to explain to him how fragile she is so that he doesn't do it again, in some ways it is a goodbye letter.

Her friend meets her at the airport. It is hot in Rome. She takes off her heavy coat. It is bright, it is sunny in Rome. She can smell herbs, there are cobblestones. There is cooking with gas, red wine and white bread. There is a double bed. There are mornings and evenings and museums with pictures of fruit that must be eaten right away or it will rot.

Back home his reply is in her mailbox.

Dear Ida. I wanted to see you the last time I was in Oslo, but started to shake when I was about to call. I don't know if it was because I was afraid that you would say: Fuck off, you bastard. Because I don't want you to say that and that's not who I want to be. Or was there another reason? But perhaps we could discuss modern drama or life or the weather over a glass of mineral water at some point?

And as regards Trondheim, I didn't find it relaxing either. And while we are on the subject of big questions, I have not, still not, whispered the poem to more than three people. Apart from that I am lost for words and thinking of other things.

All the best,

Arnold

He is thinking of other things. Of small questions. When it comes to the big questions such as love, he hasn't whispered the poem to more than three people. Which poem? Did you whisper a poem? What poem did you whisper? And you haven't whispered it to more than three people. And I am one of the lucky three. Lucky, lucky me!

They met for the first time at a seminar in late March. They spent a night together and wrote to each other for a couple of months, then met again in early June where they spent a night and an afternoon together. They still write, but more rarely now, it is the summer holidays and besides, it has become too serious, potentially uncontrollable, but they can't help themselves. They meet a few times that autumn, but it only becomes more dangerous, more difficult, they have to end it, they end it and don't see each other until May, at her insistence, the following year. By then she is divorced and living on her own.

They see each other in the autumn, she has been invited to the University of Trondheim, and he is there, she still loves him, but he goes home without saying anything, he just disappears, and she realises that she has to put it behind her. She writes to him telling him that and tries to forget, to be free so as not to live half a life, so as to meet someone else, love someone else. When she writes to him it is no longer to move him, she has given up on that, but to pour out her heart because it helps, it makes her feel better, it is purely for her own sake, her letters become increasingly rare.

She takes a quick look around and when she drinks, she wastes no time. She brings them home or goes home with them, and some of them ring her afterwards, there are phone calls to wait for other than the silent ones. They invite her to dinner and she dresses up and feels excited and one evening she meets a decent, intelligent and funny man. She spends the night with him and when she drives home the next morning she is cheerful, she drives too quickly, it is the first time for a long time that she is happy. This man calls her. He sends her a book. She thanks him. They go for a beer and she sleeps with him again, they go for a walk and he stays over at her place, in the morning they make breakfast together. She doesn't tell him about Arnold. She is not sure that he needs to know. With him it is like a game. In his old apartment in the city where the trams rattle past. Without her children it is as if she has become young again like him, carefree like him. Stacks of books and piles of records on the floor. Red wine and fried prawns in garlic cooked at night on the old stove in the large, derelict kitchen, she sits on a second-hand chair while he tells her about his time in India. She dances naked through the big, almost empty rooms. They make love on the wobbly waterbed and she does all the things she has never dared before, each night might be their last one. Neither of them ever says: What are you doing tomorrow? Or this summer. One of them will call the other and they meet, every time for the first time, every time a new visit and no one knows about them. He invites her to dinner, she rings the doorbell and they pretend that it is the first time, as if she has never been there before, as if they have never slept together, have never kissed each other, how does he do it? Oh, no, I'm not in the mood. But he charms her. He gets her into bed as carefully as if it was the first time, as passionately as if it was the last time, and no one knows about them. They walk across the ice to the nature reserve in the winter darkness. He is freezing and borrows her big scarf and ties it around his head like a woman. She has coffee and alcohol in her bag, he didn't know that, then they go home and he chops up her old bookcase in her garage while she makes the bed so they have firewood for the night, then they go to bed with the fire blazing.

'My name is Trond Hagfors!' he says when he comes.

While she has her children, he has his friends and projects and his job at the publishers. He lives not far from her psychoanalyst, at times he waits outside when he sees her car parked there, she still goes to therapy. She doesn't see her parents or her siblings, her old friends think she has changed, but Trond is leaning against her car, smoking while he waits.

'Soooo?' he asks.

It is December. It is windy. The smoke disappears into the air before she can smell it, but she smells it in his beard which tickles her throat, it tickles between her legs, he puts his arm in its bottle green coat sleeve around her and takes her home if she needs him to and makes coffee.

'Are we a couple?'

She doesn't want to say no, but she can't say yes either. She loves Arnold. She still hopes, when she picks up her post, that there will be something from Arnold, there never is. She still hopes that there will be a message from him on her answering machine, there never is, but she hopes and every time, every single time, she is disappointed, she feels the disappointment when there is nothing, in the post, on her answering machine, from him, the man she loves, a disappointment that lasts for a while, it doesn't pass immediately. She can relax with Trond and forget about it with Trond, for a while, for as long as it lasts, but it never passes completely. If she makes a wish, if she finds a four-leaf clover or a coin, if she throws a coin in a fountain, she wishes for *him*, Arnold. At the library she looks for his name in newspapers and journals, and if she finds anything, she sits down to read where he has been and what he has been doing, every time it hurts her just as much because it doesn't seem to impact on his writing that she exists in his world, in his reports on seminars, his responses to arguments, his articles on a new Goethe translation, but she can't help herself. She can't be Trond's girlfriend.

She can't walk hand in hand through town with Trond. She can't introduce Trond to friends and acquaintances, to anyone and say: this is Trond, my new boyfriend. It's impossible. Yet she doesn't want to lose him either, she wants to be with him, sleep with him, hold him. And more importantly she wants to be held by him.

'You're like a little girl,' he says, 'an adult child.'

She has strange dreams and he buys her a book about dreams and at night before she falls asleep, she asks her dreams for guidance: What will happen to me? What am I going to do? My subconscious, please tell me!

'Are we a couple?' he asks. It is February. The sun shines over the city. Smoke twirls slowly in the clear air. She walks with him through the grey park to his office, he is pale. 'Do you really want to be with me?'

She snuggles up to him, he is tall, she buries her face in the armpit of his jacket, she nibbles his neck up to his ear.

'Is that your answer?'

They turn and head back. He calls in and says he isn't coming to work. The whole day is spent in the soft, swaying bed until the evening. But Arnold is always present, will it never end? Nothing is ever completely good, completely true, completely funny, completely whole, something is always missing. Will it never end? They go out for something to eat, it helps to drink, but in the morning something is still missing, something is still lost, she is on the verge of tears through the grey park to his office, she whispers to herself.

'It feels as if the whole world can see I got drunk yesterday.'

'It feels as if the whole world can see that I'm in love.'

'But that's nothing to be ashamed of.'

'But what if someone sees us together.'

He borrows a cabin in the mountains and invites her to come with him. Her children are with their father, she doesn't have to tell anyone, there is no one to tell, if she goes missing, no one will wonder where she is, no one will miss her except Trond. Trond is on his own as is she. They pack the car, outdoor clothes, indoor clothes, bedlinens, towels. They stop on the way to buy groceries for breakfast, lunch, dinner, wine. He jingles the keys: We're going to a cabin.

She drives, he drinks beer and reads Thomas Bernhard aloud to her as it grows dark. Years later it feels unreal and it remains unreal, her former closeness to someone she no longer sees, whose smell she has forgotten. The drive seems unreal, their arrival unreal, that they struggled through the snow together. How they made the bed, how they walked across the snowed-over roads and talked, unreal. She tells him about Arnold. He knows Arnold. He works for Arnold Bush's publishers and is in regular contact with him. What does he make of it all? He smokes. He has a nice smell, a-smoke-in-winter smell on his clothes, in his beard. He smokes in an unfamiliar, manly way. He raises his hand to his mouth and she is drawn closer to him. What does he make of it all? He doesn't say anything. He looks straight ahead. She frowns, his expression is stern and he stares straight ahead, not at her. Then he looks out of the window on the passenger side and she must keep her eyes on the road. He shakes his head and stares straight ahead again and is quiet with this stern expression. Is he or is he not taking this seriously? Arnold Bush is married, he has a child, Arnold Bush lives in Trondheim. Trond sits next to her, he walks next to her on the deserted road across the wide expanse, lies next to her at night, lies on top of her at night, in the newly made bed, they will get there soon, they make the bed, they drink red wine in front of the fireplace, they talk and go to bed and talk some more. She takes his arm. She holds his arm.

Is this happy? Is this sad? Looking back, the times when nothing was certain have a unique quality. When everything was up for grabs, when she couldn't even make a guess at how it would pan out, how the ending would unfold, that is how she remembers it. Is it when you don't know what to feel, when you don't know what will happen, when your questions are truly open-ended and sincere, that time stops?

She chairs the Dramatists' Association's annual general meeting. The secretary slides a note across the table, it says: Arnold is ready now.

Has he called? She freezes. Is he in Oslo? Is he free right now? Is he in a café, bored, did he miss his plane and is he expecting her to drop everything and come running to him? She is chairing a meeting, she is actually busy, who does he think he is? She looks at the secretary who smiles in response. 'Did he call?' she whispers, 'how do you know?' 'He made it,' she replies, nodding toward the audience. 'He's here.'

And there is the poet who was supposed to read a poem at the start, who didn't show, who was delayed, Arnold André Olsen. She invited him herself, she called and asked him and sent him a written confirmation of their arrangement, she wrote his name on the envelope and not for a second did she think of him as Arnold, there is only one.

At times she thinks: There, I didn't think of him! And she is happy. Perhaps it is fading. Then she relapses. In the wake of some incident or other.

Trond asks: 'What do you want from me?'

Sometimes he works from home and they spend the whole day in bed together. As long as he makes sure he has read whatever he needs to read for the Monday meetings and has edited the texts for which he is responsible, then it is fine; he doesn't talk to Arnold Bush as often as he used to.

She starts to doubt that it will ever happen. It feels as if she is wasting time, days, her life. She longs to put it behind her, to get through it, to start over, she needs a clear 'no'.

They haven't seen each other since the autumn in Trondheim. And before that it was on the bench in May. Twice in one year, altogether two hours and forty-five minutes in one year. No touching, no phone calls, that adds up to a NO, yet still she needs it. Then again it might make no difference at all, perhaps nothing will, but she has to try.

She writes, for the first time in a long time, matter-of-factly and briefly, without a hint of seduction. A single question, a single wish, my life is at stake. Say no. Tell me that it won't happen. Turn me away.

She gets a postcard back. *Le monde perdu* by Magritte on the cover. *Paysage, personnage perdant la mémoire, corps de femme, cheval.* Postmarked Trondheim, but bought in Stockholm the day before. Is this to tell her that he has been abroad, out in the big wide world?

Dear Ida. Thank you for your letter. I bought this postcard in Stockholm yesterday. You deserve a better answer. Sleet, melting snow from Arnold.

Is that supposed to make her feel lyrical? Sleet, melting snow from Arnold. Because it is spring and the snow is melting? Or is his intention that she will seek to interpret it, take it to mean that it is Arnold who is melting.
Idiot. Coward.
It is better than a no. It is more helpful than a no.
A real man would have written no.
His period of grace is over.

A *Minor Passion* has been entered into a competition for radio drama in Amsterdam and she is invited to attend.

April follows winter. The snow has melted, there is no sleet. I'm so happy, she writes in her diary. And a little scared. After all, the two often go together.

Trond will join her there. He has been to Amsterdam before. She sits in the April light, on the plane, high above it all. Her shoes clip-clop on Amsterdam's cobblestones. She attends the big event alone. Has she never been truly free until now? Nothing goes wrong. She returns to her hotel with a new feeling of this being a proper spring, as if it is her first. Her room is on the tenth floor, she sits down by the large window and gazes across the city. High up, behind glass. It glitters below, underneath her, everything is quiet, the world is at peace. The children are safe, at home with their father. Her house waits patiently. She was called to the stage and presented with a framed certificate. Her words from the darkness, from her foggy brain read aloud in daylight, broadcast and translated and spoken by earnest, foreign voices as if it was about them. She exists, the unmentionable is sung out loud.

Morning. Empty streets, sunshine. She is meeting him in the lobby of the Grand Hotel Krasnapolsky. His suggestion, he knows the city. She has bought a map and new sunglasses and sits down in a café to have a cup of coffee. She is meeting Trond soon, she is looking forward to it, she misses him. He is walking through the city now, thinking about her. She can feel it and she thinks about him, and about Arnold. He wears his leather jacket, which smells of leather and smoke. When she arrives, his face lights up, he can't help himself. She wears shoes suitable for walking, shoes that clip-clop against the cobblestones, it sounds almost like birdsong. She is pretty because she is happy, she looks forward to him seeing how happy she is. There it is on the map. Half a kilometre, fifteen minutes left and she will see him, she will have his arms around her. If only Arnold could see her now. How pretty, how happy she sits in the café. How lovely a time she can have without him. How pleased she is to be meeting someone other than him. If only a passer-by would spot her, someone who knows him, who could tell him so that he will be sorry.

He sits behind the windows in the hotel's winter garden, she is in the right place. Wearing his leather jacket, smoking and looking serious. Her arrival makes him happy. He can't help himself. He tries not to give himself away, but he does. She kisses him, she sits down on his lap, she tickles him, they order beer, they are on holiday now. He tries not to be a young man, but he is a young man. She buys a leather jacket that looks like his, that smells like his, she smokes like him. She buys champagne and antique champagne glasses with broad cups, they sit by the bridge in the evening and toast A Minor Passion, and he asks:

'So, are we a couple?'

'Yes,' she says, and he looks at her in surprise.

'Are you serious?'

'Yes.' She is serious.

'Do you mind if I get wasted tonight?'

May comes. She is at Fornebu airport. She is visiting Erik Grøver in Trondheim. She has just signed off *The Journal* for printing and she is happy. She wears a summer dress and a denim jacket, it smells of smoke because she has borrowed it from her boyfriend. He smokes, it smells of him. She has just made love with him. She's come straight from his flat. She stopped by to see him on her way to the airport, he was sitting on his balcony, reading, then she turned up in her summer dress. Warm, the first day of summer, he lifted up her dress and they made love on the balcony, quickly because she had a plane to catch, so she smells of him. 'I'm taking this,' she said, snatching the jacket from the coat rack when she left, and he didn't object.

That morning she had sprayed herself with the perfume she wore the first time *they* were together. For some reason she had found that very perfume in her cupboard. Underneath her boyfriend's denim jacket she perceives the scent though she hasn't worn it since the last time she saw Arnold, almost one year ago. So that the scent wouldn't become associated with any memories or experiences other than those which relate to *him* and *that time*. So that when she inhales the scent she can embrace *him* and *that time*. She hasn't worn it in order not to use it up and so as not to mix those memories with other memories. And because it might hurt, because the scent might send her back into the pain. But now she feels safe. And the pain didn't come, the pain has been replaced by a kind of melancholy that gives way to excitement, optimism, as it has today.

Because she has made love. And because the man she made love with is in love with her, and because when someone is in love with you, as Trond is with her, as she is with *him*, with Arnold, they are smitten by infatuation and will consequently fall in love, even if their feelings are not as strong. Just like Ida is in love with Trond and just like Arnold has to be in love with Ida, and one day the two of them will be together. Because she has the infatuated man's jacket over her shoulders and it smells of him. She is at the airport. Down by one of the domestic gates furthest away from the departure hall, she stands by a payphone, talking to Erik Grøver, telling him which plane she will be arriving on. The last plane, it is late, it is evening, there is a faint grey spring light outside the windows and it is warm. It smells of spring. It smells of evening. She stands by the payphone outside the lavatories and talks to Erik Grøver, and she can see that they have started boarding passengers for Trondheim at gate 22, and then she sees Arnold Bush getting up from a seat with a briefcase in one hand, his airline ticket in the other.

'Guess who I'm looking at right now?' she stutters into the handset.

'Arnold?'

~

He goes through the gate, crosses the tarmac and boards the plane while she waits by the payphone. She hasn't seen him since the event at the Department of German last November. She walks towards the gate, she is the last passenger to board. She shows her boarding pass and steps outside, into the evening, into the spring light, the smell of spring. She isn't as nervous as she thought she would be, if anyone had told her that she would bump into him accidentally like this. Perhaps he is seated at the back and she won't see him. She can take a seat at the front and avoid meeting him, she smiles because she isn't nervous, because she isn't trembling. If she really is over it, then she is free. She is not the same person. When one thing changes, everything changes. He sits near the front, she realises that he has seen her. He has sat down near the front to make sure that they see each other, he has put newspapers on the seat next to him as if to reserve it, when she boards he will clear them away as if it is natural that she would sit there, as if it is nothing, as if they are old friends.

'I can't talk to you right now,' she says and walks past him, it is true. It is too sudden, she wouldn't be able to handle it, she takes a seat at the back and smiles, pleased to be on the same plane as him. The most important person in her life – except for her children, but there is no comparison – sits at the front of the half-empty plane to Trondheim. For months, for years she has thought about him incessantly. She has also thought about other things, other people, her work, but she has thought about him all the time. There he sits, she counts, fifteen rows ahead of her, she can't see his head or his newspaper. The last few times she met him, in May, in November, she had been prepared. She can't just sit down next to him and make small talk until they get to Trondheim. With him it is only the big questions. Do you love me? Will you come to me? Will we be together? When? Nothing else matters. Why would she discuss current affairs with him? Love is a serious business. There is nothing more serious, only death. He waits at the luggage belt for her. He has no luggage, he is waiting for her. He asks her where she is going. He has a car and says that he can give her a lift. She accepts, what else should she do? She has drunk beer on the plane and is calmer now. They step outside, it is colder in Trondheim than it is at home. Darkness has fallen since Oslo. How dark Trondheim is in May. The streetlights are on. They light up the twilight, making it almost pink. He has given a talk on Brecht, he says, at the Goethe Institute. His car is white, he puts his briefcase on the boot and opens it, searches for his keys. There is an engraved cigarette case in the briefcase, a disposable lighter. Three black pens and a red pen. A typed manuscript, a stripy notebook. An open letter with his name and address on the envelope written in a female hand. A newspaper cutting folded so she can't see the headline. His wristwatch is metal and small, on one hand he wears a ring she hasn't seen before. Three stamps, a corkscrew, then he closes the briefcase. They get into the car. He gets in first and reaches across to open the passenger door for her. The car is clean. There is a packet of chewing gum on the dashboard, that is all, a child seat in the back. Nothing on the floor, no ice cream wrappers or apple cores. What do they say to each other, she doesn't remember. She is agitated, smiling, slightly manic, she remembers that, yes, she talks about "jump into the deep end, after all, you're wearing a life jacket" under Capricorn, her phone call to *Adresseavisen* and her phone call to the author of the horoscope, the astrologer Wendy Manters in London, and laughs at herself, how crazy I was! The implication being, and he doesn't like it, that she is not that person anymore.

He asks where she wants to be dropped off, she gives him the address. He says he used to live not far away from there. His son went to nursery two streets away, odd little details, they don't interest her at all. Only one thing matters between them, yes or no. He wants her to tell him who she is visiting, but she doesn't. He knows about Trond. It was in the papers. Trond praised her play in a newspaper column and criticised a novel in the same article, and the novelist wrote a furious letter in response stating that Trond Hagfors should not be allowed to review Ida Heier because they lived together. Trond had bought yet another second-hand chair at a flea market and Ida had helped him carry it through the streets of Majorstua to his flat, and since then rumours have abounded. Trond responded by writing that he didn't live with Ida Heier, and the offended novelist wrote that even if they didn't live together, they were certainly very close, intimate, and Trond consequently ineligible, and Trond didn't respond to that. Yes, Arnold knows about Trond. He wonders who her Trondheim host is, if it is a man, Ida says nothing. They turn into the street where she is getting out. Almost casually he mentions his plans for the foreseeable future. He will be going to Oslo, among other things, in a fortnight, on his way to a stay in Germany where he will be translating some previously unknown texts by Brecht, only recently released. She doesn't seize the opportunity. She doesn't say: Then we can meet. Or: Please call me. That is what he wants, but she doesn't take the bait; if he doesn't have the courage to ask her outright, there is ultimately no point.

'Aha,' she says. Nothing more. He won't dream of touching her, she is unapproachable. He won't dream of leaning towards her, hugging her, caressing her cheek because he doesn't know where she is now. He doesn't dare, that is fine, that is how it should be. She is new to him. He has to fumble his way forwards, get to know her all over again. Yet even so it is there between them in the car. He looks at her cleavage and says he recognises her perfume. He says that.

She doesn't leave the house on the day he arrives in Oslo so as not to risk missing his call. Nor does she leave it the next day, in case he calls while she is out. A friend from university calls to say that she saw Arnold at Herregårdskroen last night, he was at a table on his own so she invited him to join them. He had some beers with them and they had a nice time.

'Did you sleep with him?'

'Of course not.'

'Was he with anyone else?'

'No. At least I don't think so. I don't know anything about that.'

And she is back to square one. He is in town, but he doesn't call. He would rather sit alone at Herregårdskroen than call her. He is punishing her for Trond. Then he calls. He has never asked her for her number, he knows it by heart. It is the first time he doesn't hang up when she answers. He wants to meet her at eight o'clock, that evening, in two hours. If she hadn't been in, if she hadn't answered the phone, with whom would he have had dinner? He knows she is at home, that is the point, he knows she is waiting, that she can't help herself. They haven't touched each other since November eighteen months ago. Now it happens. He calls, she says yes, they meet at Herregårdskroen. They drink beer. They go on to another café, she doesn't think about Trond, that he might turn up, that he might be passing, it doesn't matter. He has found the courage now, he has been drinking and she came when he snapped his fingers, she didn't say no, they end up on a bench, she doesn't remember how, and he strokes her cheek. She can't say that it comes as a total surprise. Because she knows what he wants when he calls. Even so she is taken aback, almost shocked when it happens and looks at him so astonished that he starts to smile. Is she like an innocent girl to him because she loves him? He smiles and kisses her, she surrenders, they walk to his hotel, they make love. Is he coming to her now, is it for real now? She leaves early the next morning, she has a meeting at *The Journal*. She doesn't ask if they are going to meet later even though he will be in Oslo today. No, she doesn't ask. He will have to call her. She is happy because he is going to call her. If he has a choice between eating, drinking wine and sleeping alone or with her, he will choose the latter, and he has a choice. She goes straight home after a meeting at the radio station in order to be there when he calls. Three o'clock, then five o'clock. Six o'clock and he still hasn't called. Seven o'clock, he still hasn't called. She starts to get angry, she is back to square one again and she hates herself. He wants her to call, but she's not going to. At least that's something, she thinks: I'm not going to call! Eight o'clock and he hasn't called. Women going on dates are already waiting at bus stops. The sun is still shining, cafés fill with happy people. Her children are with their father, she can do whatever she likes, she waits by the telephone. It rings. It is Trond.

'I'll call you back,' she says and slams down the phone to keep the line clear. She drinks beer, she can't help herself. She stares at the telephone. It mocks her. She picks up the handset to make sure that it is working, that there is a buzzing tone. There is. She glares at the phone in order to make it ring. It doesn't ring. She hates it. It is evil, it looks innocent but it is evil, it laughs at her. If it wasn't because it wouldn't be able to ring anymore, she would have hurled it against the floor, smashed it. If only it had had skin, she would have stabbed it. Nine o'clock and he hasn't called. She will give herself ten minutes and then she will leave. She will give herself fifteen minutes and then she will leave. After twenty minutes she calls a taxi and hopes the telephone will ring before it arrives so she can use it to go to Arnold, to Arnold's hotel, but it doesn't ring. Then she calls Trond and tells him that she is on her way over. Right until the moment she locks her front door, she is listening, yearning for the sound of the telephone, as she walks to the taxi she listens through the closed door and into the living room to the sound of the telephone, she has her keys ready in her hand so she can run back, unlock the door and answer it before it stops ringing, she keeps hoping right until she closes the taxi door and it drives off, she hopes.

It hurts to look back on it, she will definitely get drunk tonight.

She turns up at Trond's and clings to him in bed and drinks quickly to steady her nerves. When he goes to the kitchen, when he goes to the loo, when he goes out into the passage to fetch something, she calls her own number and listens to her answering machine. You have no new messages. At ten minutes past ten she has one new message, it is from him, he wants to meet her, he says, but you're not at home, he says, it sounds like a reproach, it is a reproach. She should be at home waiting for him. She jumps out of bed, calls out into the bathroom that she needs to go, that

113

she is going to sleep at her own place after all and runs out, down the stairs, out into the street where she hails a taxi. She doesn't think she can call him from a payphone or go straight to his hotel, her respect for him is too great, she takes a taxi home and it can't drive fast enough. Dear God, please let him be there when I call! Dear God, please make sure he hasn't left or called someone else! She jumps out of the taxi, runs up the steps, lets herself in and flings herself at the telephone: I'm here! I want to meet you!

Except now he doesn't know what he wants. He chuckles. Now she has been put in her place, now she is where she should be. His voice is calm as it was on her answering machine, laid-back as if he can barely be bothered to talk, as if there is nothing at stake for him, as if he doesn't mind either way. She is gasping for air. Say yes! Say yes!

'So do you want to see me?'

'Yes!'

'Do you know where I am staying?'

'Aren't you staying in the same place as last night?'

He laughs. It was a joke. He was joking!

'I think it's too late,' he then says.

'I don't mind. I'll take a taxi.'

He hesitates. 'I think it's too late,' he says again.

If she had been at home, he says, when he called, but she wasn't. That is her punishment. She begs, she pleads, he says no, he has made up his mind. Hurt me, hurt me so I can feel who I am.

~

She calls Trond, sobbing, he has to come over. He comes over, she can't be alone, she tells him everything, he mustn't leave. She is utterly destroyed, how did she end up here? He holds her and listens to her, he makes love to her, he bites her breast. She has to call him, she can't stop herself.

'Don't do it,' Trond says.

'I can't help it,' she says.

'Don't do it,' Trond says.

'I can't help it,' she says, 'please don't go!'

She walks upstairs to call him.

'I have to meet you before you leave,' she says. 'I have to! I have to tell you that I love you.'

'You're telling me now.'

'This doesn't count. I have to tell you properly.'

His plane leaves at ten in the morning. She can meet him at nine, by the escalator, he will allow her to do that. She feels better now. She walks downstairs to tell Trond. He is lying on his back with one arm under his head, he is smoking, he blows out smoke.

'Ida,' he says.

'Yes?'

'Ida, Ida,' he says.

Her alarm clock goes off, but she has been awake for a long time. She tiptoes out and gets ready, she doesn't know if Trond is awake or watching. It is light, it is almost summer, she puts on a white dress, she remembers everything. She drives to the airport, she arrives early. He is queueing at the post office and doesn't know that she is watching him. How pale he is, how bald, in a pale-yellow T-shirt, so thin. Who is he sending letters to? She meets him by the escalator as agreed.

'I love you,' she says.

'You told me that yesterday,' he says.

That is all she wants to say. She has nothing else to add. He can leave now.

He gives her an envelope, a letter, then he takes the escalator to Germany.

What does the letter say? I'm going to be away for such and such a time, I'll be in touch when I get back and then we can discuss what we do about our love, about our lives, does it say that?

No.

It says, as far as I remember because this letter doesn't exist anymore, she tore it into pieces and threw the pieces into the sea that night while she sobbed, something along the lines of:

Dear Ida, woman in the wind.

I don't often write poetry, but now I have.

A poem follows, four lines about waves and shadows, noncommittal, opaque. Who does he think she is? That that is enough? That she will be grateful for his 'poem', for having been his muse? Send it to one of your students! He is through passport control. She sits on the bench by the escalator with his letter in her hand. She can't scream at

116

him. This time the pain returns more violently, the scab cracks, the wound is reopened, every time it hurts more. Saturday in June, sunshine in Oslo. She may as well die. Please let Trond be there when she gets back, please let Trond be there when she gets back. He is there when she gets back. Sobbing, she throws herself at him and she can't stop crying.

'Does it hurt that much?'

He strokes her hair, brushes hair from her eyes, wipes away her smeared makeup, her sobs send her into spasms. He kisses her cheeks, pats her, undresses her and tucks her up in bed and cuddles up behind her and holds her tight, firmly, squeezing her as if to help the tears come out.

'Does it hurt that much?' he asks again in a thick voice and brushes hair away from her neck and kisses the back of her neck and strokes her head.

'Darling girl,' he whispers. 'Poor Ida,' he whispers. Why can't she love him?

She has the feeling of being faced with an immutability. The departure of trains, the departure of planes, as if their separation is permanent. A physical limitation. Or being faced with a crying mother. The coldness of constellations, their indifference to our pain. Who can bear it without pain relief, without drinking?

He calls from Germany and leaves a message on her answering machine.

'It's Arnold. I'm in Bonn.'

And adds his telephone number.

She is such an idiot that when he says Bonn, she thinks he is talking about bonds that bind. Because he misses her, he loves her and it is only now that he has gone abroad that she understands. But she soon works out that he means Bonn, the city of Bonn in Germany, and then she gets angry. She calls the number in a rage. Because yet again he has done exactly what she told him not to: visited her only to leave her again. She has told him she can't handle it. He has given her a vague, enigmatic letter when she has explained to him that vagueness, enigma make her sick, she is destroyed by enigma when she has asked for clarity, for even the most brutal honesty.

He is very quiet.

'This isn't a game,' she says.

'Thank you for calling,' he says before she hangs up.

Five postcards.

He had already posted the first, she gets it the following day: Dear gracious lady. I send you greetings from the back of the cathedral in Bonn, where we, that is, I, am drinking a profane pilsner. It is, however, unrequited. Metaphorically from A.

And that means what? She puts it away. It is not doing her any good.

~

Four days later a brown envelope: You forgot this (a post-card she bought from a pedlar at Herregårdskroen). Sorry about the silly postcard. I realised it was completely wrong when I spoke to you on the phone. Elegant or elephant from Arnold.

Elegant or elephant, that is fine. But she has tried everything. Trond is still around. She hurts him. She is honest, nevertheless she hurts him or maybe that is why. When she cries, when she is beside herself, all alone in the world, he is there. She is all alone in the world, she doesn't see her parents or her siblings. When she gets drunk and does stupid things, he is there, supportive during the after-math. That summer they travel far away. She thinks she is pregnant, what if she is pregnant. No, it doesn't bear think-ing about. He is so young, one day he will leave her because he can love and wants to be in loved in return.

A postcard in October, from Hanover, Germany: Highborn lady. After forty-four lectures on aesthetics, I ask: Where is beauty. *Wissen Sie es?*

Yes, she could reply. It is here. With me! But she doesn't reply, there is no point.

In December a postcard, from Munich: To Ida. The woman in the wind (what is that wind obsession all about?) who blows in the mist (what does he mean, does he want her to feel lyrical?). No, I just wanted to say hi! I'm enjoying the sun and the wine, and I'm hoping, without being enigmatic, that you're fine where you are. The coffee is OK. Espresso is better. Or perhaps cappuccino? Coffee greetings from Arnold.

She is pleased and puts it away. She doesn't wonder about what cappuccino might mean when compared to regular coffee or espresso, she can't see the point.

Just before Christmas another coffee postcard from Germany: Sunny outside, raining inside. Everything happens in coffee shops. All dates – including Kjersti's. South German coffee culture is fundamentally different from Norwegian: everybody drinks coffee all the time and with everyone else. Coffee greetings number two from Arnold in a café. And diagonally along the side: No one here believes Father Christmas can find love, is it possible?

And his Munich address.

Poor, helpless man.

Between Christmas and the New Year she visits Erik Grøver. Erik Grøver in Trondheim, who is still travelling back in pain, lost, he has no family like her, there are so few of them in the world that they stick together when they bump into one another, at Christmas, during the holidays. He meets her at the railway station in the evening and they go out. Candles are lit in every window, big piles of snow, they walk through the streets to a café to drink beer. Arnold turns up with a university colleague:

'What are you doing here?'

'I thought you were in Munich. I just got a postcard from you, from Munich?'

The café is crowded. So they join them at their table. Arnold Bush and Leif Asnes at Ida and Erik's table, Arnold next to Ida, it just works out like that. Erik goes to the lavatory and Leif Asnes goes to the bar to order beer. Arnold turns to Ida and says that he has told his wife about her: 'I have told Kjersti about you.'

He is not feeling well. She can tell from looking at him that he is not feeling well. He is trying to pay her a compliment. He thinks he is paying her a compliment. He isn't well. His wife is having an affair. Ida has said that she loves him, can it be true, can a woman love him, can this woman? What should he say to her? He thinks he is telling her that she was important, that what they had mattered, that it was so important that Kjersti had to know. But it is not true and she knows it because she got the coffee postcard from Munich. He said it to hurt his wife. He sacrificed a story about Ida on the bonfire of their marriage, for revenge, so that Kjersti would burn. He sees that she realises it and regrets telling her.

'Now she hates me and we can never be together,' Ida says.

'That's what I've been thinking,' he says.

He loves her, they love each other. Why can't they get up and leave together? Erik returns. Leif Asnes returns. When the café shuts, they walk to a bar which stays open late. Arnold and Ida on a sofa. He kisses her. Her body says: This always leads to hurt. To unbearable pain. She frees herself and runs through the streets to Erik's front door. When Erik comes home a little later, he tells her that they went outside to look for her, and Arnold said:

'Perhaps I should have said something.'

Is it as tiresome to read as it is to write? Won't something happen soon? She walks through the streets of Trondheim strangely pleased because she knows that he feels worse. She is through it, he is still in the middle of it. He will come. All she has to do is wait.

This is what she says to the few people she discusses him with: He's coming!

They don't believe her. Her obsession with the professor in Trondheim is unhealthy, a sign of how damaged she is.

'He's coming!'

'Ida!'

'He is!'

'When did you first meet him?'

'Three years ago.'

'How many times have you seen him during those three years?'

'Seven.'

'How many of those times did he make the first move?'

'Two.'

'How many times has he called you?'

'Many times.'

'How many times has he called you and actually *said* something?'

'Three.'

'Do you think that's a lot?'

'It's enough.'

'Ida!'

'Yes?'

'Was he at a seminar in Oslo three weeks ago?'

'What about it?'

'Did you write to him suggesting you meet?'

'Yes.'

'Did you offer to climb through his hotel window at night so that no one would see you, if that was what he was afraid of?'

'Yes.'

'Did he respond to your approach?'

'No, but that was because of Trond, Trond was at the same seminar. That's why. He rang and hung up!'

'He was with another woman at the seminar, wasn't he? You've heard that he was with someone else, haven't you?'

'It doesn't matter. He loves me. He's coming.'

Why would she ever think so? But she did. I thought I was over AB yesterday, she writes in her diary. I cried and let it go, then my phone rang twice without the caller saying anything and I was back to square one. I heard nothing on the other end, it made me so happy.

She calls him in January, she has already won, she is sure of it. He has had a breakdown, he says. And no wonder given that Ida freed herself and ran away when he tried to kiss her. He calls her back that evening. The fourth time he calls he doesn't hang up.

Easter is coming, it is some months before the new era begins. Arnold is attending a seminar in Copenhagen. He calls to ask if he can stay at her place on his journey there. See, that is what she has been saying all along, he is coming. With baby steps, but he is coming.

'Shall we meet at Håndverkeren at six o'clock on Friday?'

'Yes!' It is the annual general meeting of the Dramatists' Association that same weekend, there is a board meeting the day before, on the Friday, but it doesn't matter, she sends her apologies. He is there when she arrives, they have dinner, they drink, he puts on a leather cap and a leather jacket, he looks like a gay man and they take a taxi back to her place.

'I want to see how you live,' he says as if she is taking part in a contest, perhaps she is. Perhaps she wins because he likes her home. She wins because she has proved steadfast, because he is starting to believe that she loves him. He isn't someone who loves, who chooses, he is chosen, to be loved is more important to him than to love. She lights a fire in the fireplace as he wanders around to see how she lives, they drink some more, then they make love, the usual, perhaps they make love again before they fall asleep, she doesn't remember any of it, you never remember such things when a relationship is over. They drink and make love and make love again, it must have been like that. Perhaps they lie tangled up in each other while they sleep as they will do in the future or perhaps they don't. She has to leave early next morning, before him, for the annual general meeting she is chairing. Perhaps he is half awake, aware that she is leaving, perhaps he isn't. Perhaps he is looking forward to her going so he will be on his own, so he can wander round undisturbed and study her home. They make no plans, they never do. She goes to the annual general meeting and she is happy, happier than last year, it is exactly a year since she got the note saying: Arnold is ready now. Now he is lying in her bed. No, he will have gone by now. Put the key under the mat like she asked him to. He has sneaked around, pulled out drawers and looked through them by now. He has left something behind for her, a greeting, or perhaps he hasn't.

Or perhaps he hasn't. There is nothing. No note. The bed is messy, the glasses still where they left them when they went to sleep. It makes her sad that he didn't clear them away, put them in the sink. Didn't make the bed, that he cares so little for what she might think that he leaves behind an unmade bed, half-empty wine glasses on the bedside table, that he doesn't bother to make a good impression, to sell himself – then again there is no need. But there is a pen by her phone that isn't hers. One of those he writes with, from the University of Trondheim, she is thrilled, she kisses it.

~

She doesn't know how long his seminar lasts. They made no plans, she didn't ask, she doesn't ask. She isn't pushy and he tells her nothing, she can only speculate. Will he stop over in Oslo on his way back? Will he call? Is she facing months of silence as usual? He doesn't call. No postcards arrive from Denmark. It is Tuesday, he left Saturday morning. He does it every time. With every passing hour she becomes more desperately unhappy. She prays to God, she tries to conjure up his spirit. The children are playing in the garden, it is sunny as it often is in March, there is a smell of wet soil, of flowers about to bloom, luminous green colours, pushing up and out. The children ask for squash, she hasn't got the energy to get up. It has to end. He isn't worth it. He is incorrigible. This pain is new and viscous like fluid. She loses faith.

Then her phone rings. She knew it. Hello? From a payphone, then it cuts out. He calls back. He has to find another phone box, then he calls. She sits by the phone, it rings, it is him.

'Hello?' He is at Copenhagen airport. His plane leaves in ten minutes, he will be landing at eleven-thirty, will she pick him up? Yes. She organises a babysitter who can stay the night, she showers and gets dressed up, singing, excited, she drives to the airport, picks him up, drives them to an airport hotel. He goes to the bathroom to shower, she waits on the bed, he comes out and gets dressed, stands before the mirror in a clean shirt, asks her if it goes with his jacket, he behaves as if this is uncomplicated, ordinary. It doesn't go, but she doesn't tell him, she doesn't dare. They move down to the bar and drink. He tells her about the seminar, then they go back to the room and make love, one time or perhaps more, then they fall asleep, then they wake up and then it ends as it always does with him leaving. He is dreading Easter, he says, spending the holiday with his in-laws. What can she say? He doesn't say that he is unhappily married. He doesn't say that he is thinking about getting a divorce. He doesn't say that he loves Ida and appreciates that the situation is complicated. He doesn't say: What's going to happen to the two of us. And she doesn't ask. It is bad enough as it is without her asking him that question. But perhaps he wants her to ask, perhaps he is creating an opening for that. For her to ask: But what about us, Arnold? What will happen to the two of us? His plane departs at eleven, but he calls and rebooks to a later flight, he doesn't want to leave the bed. They need to vacate the room at noon, but he doesn't want to go to the airport, they stay in the hotel restaurant, he drinks beer, she is driving, she drives him, when he gets out of the car, he takes a bottle of perfume from one of his tax-free bags and gives it to her.

'For me?' she says, genuinely surprised. He looks away, he looks down, he feels guilty towards all of them, airport perfume reeks of a guilty conscience, he probably bought it for his wife. She feels his absence before he has gone. She is used to it and fed up with it, perhaps it is the first time for him, one of the first.

~

127

She doesn't hear from him. It doesn't matter. Now he is the one who is trembling, in limbo. Easter comes and Easter goes. She spends a day or two with Trond, then goes to stay with a girlfriend in the mountains. She skis in the sharp, white light, across the wide expanse until the evening. There is no wind, the sun goes down and the light grows eerie. It is happening, but there is no urgency, she is completely calm.

One of the contributors to *The Journal* has something to tell her. They sit on a bench in town, he looks serious. He was at the same seminar as Arnold in Copenhagen recently. Arnold was with another woman at the seminar. He knows this because he has spoken to her, her name is Agnete Tveit, she is connected to the Goethe Institute. Arnold left her in the middle of the night so she was rather upset. Ida calls him the next day and asks if he has no respect for her. He doesn't respond. He doesn't say anything. She isn't angry, she has deduced something which he will later confirm, which is that it was being in another woman's bed that made him call her from Copenhagen airport, that made him understand that she, Ida, is the one. She knows it.

Some months before they get together, some months before the new era, he says that even if he gets a divorce, he can't be sure that he will be with her, be with Ida.

'There are so many women,' he says. At least six:

Tone, who joined him on trips to Bergen and Stavanger, she already knew about.

The woman he was with at the seminar, which Trond also attended, where Ida had offered to climb through his hotel window at night, a teacher at the teacher training college, married and skinny, she already knew about.

Agnete Tveit from the Copenhagen seminar, connected to the Goethe Institute, she already knew about.

The woman whose husband has cancer, she didn't know about her, she learned about her the night when everything was confessed.

A female friend from his student days, the same age as him, married, but with an unfaithful husband. Erotic on the dancefloor, but not in bed, she learned on the night of confessions.

The student from the Berlin trip which he organised for his students, a redhead top and bottom.

'Have you got yourself a new wife, Arnold?' the Institute secretary, who was also on the Berlin trip, had asked him.

'I'm getting a divorce,' he had replied, that was in May, she learned that on the night they told each other everything.

'She's a grown woman,' he said, he didn't want to get a reputation for pursuing his young students.

When he started his confessions, he was guarded at first until he realised that she wouldn't get angry or use them against him, then he became confident, eager, almost excited: redheads, brunettes, blondes, students, a Swedish poet. And now this great lover, this proper Don Juan has finally decided, at long last, in conclusion, to surrender, of all these willing women, to none other than Ida!

Thank you.

She rings him every now and then, sometimes he is present, other times he is remote. He makes no promises. He intimates that the marriage is failing, but these are only hints. It is just before it happens. It is just before he comes.

In her diary:

Friday 7. Enough, enough. It has to end. I'm miserable, consumed with sadness, I'm at a precipice, I have to turn away from this, I can't stay here any longer, it will destroy me.

Thursday 13. 11:35. He said he'd call, he hasn't called. Same old same old. I'm waiting for something that will never happen. The disappointment is exhausting. If it doesn't happen now, then I will put it behind me. I've had some red wine, but not much, I'm exhausted, he has drained me of my energy, my vitality, what I need for life to be OK.

Monday 24. I'm so angry, I can't help myself because here I am again waiting, waiting, waiting, less than a week has passed, but I know he isn't going to call, he isn't going to write, I will never be able to trust him, how could I, I'm about to explode with rage, I want to get it out of my system, start the process of getting over him, I haven't got the patience to wait a week, I want to tell him right now, I'm desperate for a resolution, I'm desperate, desperate for a resolution. I have to have one! When I feel the way I do now, I'm mortified by all the validation I have given him, that I have written so much about him here, it is embarrassing, he isn't worth it, it is just embarrassing. I feel better now. Writing helps. Happier now.

Tuesday 1. I'm so angry, so angry and desperate to be over him, to have put it all behind me. I must ring and tell him not to come. Not to get a divorce. It won't ever work out, I'm furious.

Thursday 16. I'm in a holding position yet again. One and a half weeks ago he told me to give him a week. He hasn't called. There is nothing in the post. This is how he succeeds in deflecting my focus, the question no longer being if I can live with him, have him in my house, now all my hopes are directed at the telephone, at the mailbox.

~

Sunday 19. He called. I can't be bothered to relate what he said. He has nothing new to report. It is pointless.

Now, just before it happens, she doesn't chase him. Her feelings have been mastered, if not conquered. She doesn't think, she doesn't hope. Yet she calls all the same to ask how he is. He says that he has moved out. She doesn't know what she feels. He calls back that evening and says:

'I want to tell you three things. Number one: I don't know how this is going to pan out. Number two: if we divorce there's no guarantee that you and I will end up together. There are other women. Number three: I would like to see you.'

It's a breakthrough. It is the first time he puts his cards on the table, open and honest. She cleans the house. She changes the bedlinen. She buys wine. She jumps whenever the phone rings in case it is him calling it off. He calls her on the day to ask her to buy wine. Sure, sure, everything is ready. Four bottles? Sure, sure. They will go for a walk along the coast. She has decided that. The following morning she is going to Slovakia with the Dramatists' Association, he is travelling on to Germany. She picks him up from the airport. He has brought her a present, a CD. He has dressed up, has she noticed, he says. A white shirt and tie.

They go for a walk along the coast. She has brought a picnic basket with wine and glasses. They sit down on a jetty, she uncorks the wine. He is nervous, he drinks quickly.

At this point he tells her, as she knew he would eventually, that it was in Copenhagen, at the seminar, after going to bed with someone else, that he realised that Ida was the one. In fact, it all started with Ida, he says. He is lying, but it doesn't matter. He is wearing black jeans, a white shirt, black shoes and black sunglasses although the sun isn't shining. He fears her open gaze. Her gaze is open. They go home, they go to bed, they make love, he cries as he comes. It makes an impression on all women. When he goes from one to the other, he cries about the last one with the new one, and the new one thinks she is the one triggering the tears, that their encounter is too intense for him. She pats his head and his wet back, the sweat is dripping from him, dripping from his head onto her face. He comes and he screams out loud, and then he cries. They sleep wrapped around each other, when she wakes up and realises it, she is happy and presses herself against him. She has set her alarm clock, she leaves first. She gets up, gets ready and calls a taxi. She kisses him goodbye, but when the taxi arrives, she goes back and kisses him again, kisses him passionately.

'I won't forget that kiss,' he says, much later.

She is shining. She is full of joy. Everything is changing, the new era is starting. There is a note on her dresser back home. *Wonderful, wasn't it?* And even though there is a question mark, at least there is a note this time. The glasses have been put in the sink and he has tried to make the bed. He is not going to walk away now. She is winning. He calls her in the evening on the day she returns home and asks if she flirted with anyone.

'No,' she says although that is not strictly true.

He asks her if she would like to come with him to Denmark.

'Yes,' she says.

He will be translating Brecht and she can write a radio play there.

'Yes,' she says.

She doesn't believe it until it happens. In two weeks. He lives in Trondheim. In a house she has never seen. How little she knows about how he lives, how he is reorganising his life. He says something about it on the phone, but how interested is she really. Why should she help him through it? She had to go through it alone. Come to me is what it is all about. Not the logistics of how. She is going to Denmark in a week, that is all that matters. She is teaching a writing course up in Røros. He looks after his son in Trondheim, not very far away from there, it is so unreal. He exists, he is breathing, he is coming. She wears something light and white, fortunately she isn't as skinny as she used to be. Her hair is lush, glossy, the air is clear. It is happening now. Right now, this summer. What she has prayed to God for. She will ring him in an hour. The forbidden number. Yes, it is happening. She is nervous. Perhaps there is too much to be repaired. Perhaps too much has happened, perhaps she knows too much. Though it is beyond her control. She has no choice. But she has faith. Has she tried to get over him for too long? The final step has yet to be taken, she can still turn around. He mustn't get a divorce for her sake! Has she promised to be there for him? His marriage isn't ending because of her, it would have ended anyway. She has a choice of ways to retreat should she want to, she walks among the old buildings which smell of tar and tries to feel free, as if that were possible. She rings, as they have agreed, between two classes. Her students are outside smoking, she runs to the phone box with her heart pounding. There he is, light and gentle as if he doesn't have a care in the world, with the booking reference for her plane ticket and a joke.

Her diary reads: Thursday 17. Don't forget, all the damage must be repaired.

She has put on her prettiest clothes. She is coming from Oslo, he is coming from Trondheim on the last plane, they meet at Copenhagen airport. They hug, they have been drinking. They take a taxi to a hotel where he has booked a room, the apartment where they will be staying won't be ready until the following day. They drink, she doesn't remember if they have sex. They wake up with empty miniatures scattered across the carpet in a small dark room.

It is bright outside. It is sunny outside. They stand together in the lobby and split the bill. Then out on the pavement, each with a suitcase. They will be together for a week. Broad Copenhagen avenues spread out. There is a café in the park.

'How about a cup of coffee?'

Yes, that's a good idea. They sit down, order coffee, and while the waitress is still at their table with her notepad in her hand, he asks with a sideways glance, tentatively: 'And a beer?'

'Yes, one beer, please.'

'Two beers.'

It will do them good. Advertising slogans on posters around the city proclaim that there is something human about a beer. Sunshine in the park. Beer. It is twelve-thirty, beer is acceptable, one o'clock, two o'clock, three o'clock, more beer, it is good, it helps, it is necessary.

A bedroom with a single bed, a bathroom with a shower, a living room with a desk, he can have that, she can work on the sofa. A communal kitchen in the corridor, but no one else is staying on their floor. He showers. She looks at the desk where he has laid out his things. His laptop, a pile of books, three pens lined up, his watch, his engraved cigarette case with eight brown cigarillos she sees when she opens it, the shower is still running in the bathroom, a present from his wife's sister when he received his doctorate. His wife gave him a ring on the same occasion, he still wears it, he will wear it for another year until he gets a new ring from her, from Ida. Freshly showered and in clean clothes they hit the town. No work today, no, no work today. He takes her hand and they walk through the city. Later they will always walk like this. He looks at her and smiles. And she smiles at him and later they will always walk like this, hand in hand or with their arms around each other. She tickles his palm, it means: Want to make love? He nods, he wants to all the time. They make love in parks, behind bushes, behind bus stops.

'Isn't it fine,' he says and looks down proudly at his penis.

They make love, they have done that before. They drink, they have done that before. They work, they haven't done that before. In the same room. He is translating Brecht's erotic poems which have recently been released. If he needs a word that rhymes with whore, she suggests claw, war, folklore. He squints at her through the smoke. She is editing her one-act play about a clairvoyant woman, whose love is destroyed because she can foresee the end. He sits at the desk in beige chinos. He spends more time looking out of the window and thinking than writing. Occasionally he bends over his laptop and writes, still gazing into the air, out of the window, he must have learned how to touch type. Every now and then he will open his cigarette case, take out a cigarillo and lick it pensively before he sticks it in his mouth and lights it, is this performance for her benefit? He leaves it hanging from his lips while he writes, puffing out small clouds of smoke through the corners of his mouth, he squints to avoid getting smoke in his eyes, narrow eyes, as he leans forwards. He takes it out with his right hand and taps off the ash with his forefinger over the ashtray, smiles, pleased with his solution. Would she like a bitters, he asks. No, thanks. He goes to the bookshelf where he has put the half bottle of Gammel Dansk he bought at the airport and sets the bottle down on the desk. Fetches a small shot glass from the same shelf, places it next to the bottle and fills it. Screws the cap back on and returns the bottle to the bookshelf before he sits down, lights a new cigarillo and drinks the Gammel Dansk so slowly that it looks healthy. There, in the same room, she can't believe it. In the afternoon they head out, she doesn't remember what they talk about, only that life is easy, that they laugh, that it is like it is in novels about happy lovers: exuberant, simple, euphoric, fits of laughter, no danger. Anyone who sees them will think: There's a couple in love.

They make love on the sofa in the living room, in the bed, on the desk, kissing, lying close, pushing against each other, swaying, rubbing. Afterwards one of them will walk naked into the kitchen and fetch bottles of beer that they have put in the freezer and which have frozen almost solid. Whoever doesn't get the beer will fetch a pillow, a duvet, the engraved cigarette case. He lies on his back blowing clouds of smoke towards the ceiling. She lies on her side, watching him. He quotes Brecht in German, a passage he is struggling to translate. To his surprise she comes up with the right word, doesn't he know yet who she is, that she is like him? Perhaps he is afraid. She is afraid to ask him, she doesn't know how to express it. They head out in the afternoon, arm in arm in the afternoon light. Anyone who talks to them, talks to them as if they are an item, as if they have been together for a long time, as if they know each other's preferences at the bar.

'What's the lady having?' Bogdo the bartender asks.

'What do you want?' Arnold asks.

'What are you having?' Ida asks.

'White wine, I think.'

'White wine, I think.'

'You have a lovely wife,' Bogdo says to Arnold and they laugh.

'You're a nice couple,' Bogdo says and they laugh again.

'Aren't we just?' Arnold says, pulling her close, no one can be as happy as she. But give it time.

Bogdo invites them home for dinner and they accept. The next day at five o'clock through unfamiliar, empty Sunday streets in neighbourhoods they haven't been to before, hand in hand, the table is set for three, he is lonely, an outsider, as are they. They help themselves to food awkwardly, they have never visited someone as a couple before. She misses Arnold. He is so far away on the other side of the table. Is that what he looks like? She can't look him in the eye over the melon, how do they do this?

'When were you born?' Bogdo wants to know. 'Well, that makes you a pig.'

'That's it, a pig!' Arnold says, 'I knew it.'

When she gets home, there is a letter from him in her mailbox. He must have written it furtively in Copenhagen, on their third day and posted it in secret, without her noticing:

And on the third day of the new era, he learned to his surprise that he loved a pig! Bogdo the swineherd, a man from the unknown, made him aware of this, something which until then had been unknown, also to her: that she was loved by a zebra. Your hands are like rain, he said to her in a poem: rain in rainfall!

Five things. Five tiny things:

The first time in a café. He has stubbed out his cigarillo and is pushing the stub around the ashtray.

'Now Kjersti would have said,' he says pensively and with a wry smile, 'now Kjersti would have said: Look, Arnold is tidying up the ashtray.' Ida looks at the ashtray, the stubs are in one pile, the ashes in another.

'Kjersti has an *eye* for these things,' Arnold says.

There is nothing strange about it, it is just the way it is, it is natural. Except that Ida is the one who has an eye for such things. If anyone has an eye, it is Ida; he still doesn't know who she is.

Kjersti thinks he has gone to Copenhagen on his own. It doesn't matter, it is fine.

The second time in a café in the evening. He points to a woman and says: 'She looks like Kjersti.'

A beautiful, blonde woman. It might have been relevant information if she had asked: What does she look like, your wife? But not like this, out of the blue, showing her how present Kjersti is in his mind, even though she, Ida, is sitting next to him on the sofa. There is nothing strange about it, it is just the way it is, it is natural, but does he understand, when he sees her face, that it hurts that he doesn't push aside images of Kjersti but lingers on them almost proudly as he scrutinises Ida. Nor does she believe him. She has asked about Kjersti, she looks nothing like the beautiful, blonde woman.

The third time. He phones home. There is nothing strange about it, it is just the way it is, it is natural. She, too, calls her children's father to tell him where she is and check that everything is all right. She stands in the window and watches him cross the square, then the street to the phone box on the corner seven floors below her, his characteristic gait that makes her tremble, which she lusts after, just like when he came down the steps to Tostrupkjelleren with his light-coloured coat flapping out behind him, she wants his gait inside her, to eat and swallow if it were possible. She studies him as he walks away from her, like she does when he goes to the gents in cafés or crosses the street to buy a newspaper, and experiences a desire she doesn't feel when they walk together, close to one another and she can *feel* his gait, his hip against hers, this is different, seeing it with her own eyes is different. Across the street to the corner and into the phone box, he picks up the handset and presses it against his ear. Raises his other arm and inserts coins into the slot, enters the number and waits. He is talking now, he is moving his head now, what is he saying, can she trust him? Does he miss her, is that what he is saying? The reassurance she feels when he is in the room, when she is holding him, is gone. Then he walks back across the street, the square, to the front door, through the door, it takes time before she hears the lift. I only managed to speak to my son, he says. Kjersti had an appointment. What kind of appointment, he wonders. I wonder what kind of appointment it could be, he frets. Eventually he decides it must be her therapist and calms down, relieved that it wasn't another kind of appointment, a date.

There is nothing strange about it, it is just the way it is, it is natural. It is Ida who doesn't pay attention to Kjersti's story, she understands that now, much later, but that is not strange either, that is just the way it is, it is natural.

The fourth time. She offers to call them a taxi. She offers, yes, she does all the running. She goes out to buy breakfast, she offers, yes, she nips out to get it. She makes coffee, yes, she offers, and carries it and milk and cups on the tray and washes up afterwards.

'I'll do it,' she says and does it, and he lets her do it, and thanks her for doing it and says he is not used to women doing things for him, a nice surprise, he says, and she is delighted. If he forgets his jacket, she will run up seven flights of stairs to fetch it from the wardrobe for him and seize the opportunity to look at his clothes, they are so different from other men's clothes. She thinks once or twice or several times: I can't do this for ever.

142

It won't be like this for ever. It is because he is torn, but she can't know that when he doesn't show it. Never drink spirits on an empty stomach, it says on posters in the bars, have a few beers first. The state of emergency in which he exists, the breakup he can't face, the chaos he feels. Perhaps he is still hoping that it won't happen, that all will be well again. Poor Arnold.

Does he fall in love with her in Copenhagen? Was he so successful at getting her out of his system originally that he didn't know what he felt, as he told her, until now in Copenhagen. It feels like being in love, it is effortless, and yet it is not a fairy tale, not an affair, the big question still hangs in the air: Are we a couple?

'Why do you need me?' he says.

'I don't need you. I love you.'

The fifth time, their last day, after they have been together day and night for seven days, after they have carried out their experiment and the seriousness dawns on them. That is when it happens, not all that surprisingly, on their very last night. They have been out, they have danced. He flings out his arms to the rhythm, but suddenly and without a plan, he looks like a jumping jack. His controlled gait, the way he smokes, speaks, so softly that you have to concentrate to hear him, the slow turn of his head, his lingering gaze are all gone, everything she thought was the essence of his character, the languid quality, completely gone, it was a façade, it turns out, and now the real him appears as he dances, as he flings out his arms and legs. As it does during sex, towards the end of intercourse, in the moment of orgasm when he cries out or howls weirdly and collapses in sobs, the kind of sobbing that turns into laughter.

He starts to cry in the taxi back. They are drunk, she doesn't remember how it begins, who says what, but at some point he starts to cry in the taxi as they are going home. It is late at night, they have been out dancing, their last night, he is drunk and starts to sob: 'I've been so bad. You'll hate me, you won't be able to forgive me.'

The crucial question, that last drunken evening. The absolutely crucial question, which she can't yet answer if she is to be entirely honest, something she wants to be, but has had no opportunity to be because this must be experienced in real life, there are no guarantees, but then again, neither can they pretend he didn't bring it up, although she says: 'Of course I can, of course I can, my darling.'

If they are to be together for real, commit themselves to each another, it is on condition that she forgive him, can she do that? Not a little bit, not superficially, but deeply, properly and then trust him from now on. She doesn't know if she can do that. She hopes so.

'Of course I can, of course I can, my darling,' she says as she helps him out of the taxi, he slumps onto the pavement. She manages to pull him to his feet and slips her arm under his, through the front door, into the lift and up.

'Of course I can, of course I can, my darling. Don't worry. It'll be fine.'

Pulls off his shoes, jacket, shirt. There. There we are. I love you. No, I won't leave you. No, never, have no fear. Trust me, she lies and thinks that while she is glad that he has asked the crucial question, that he understands what the crucial question is, she still wonders: When is it my turn to be held and comforted?

He lies naked, almost unconscious on the bed, and she can study him without being studied in return. She keeps looking at him. Does she love him? This strange body. So unlike other bodies she has known. Is it really him, suddenly accessible, right in front of her on the bed, before all her senses, for so long the forbidden fruit, defenceless on the bed, warts and all. This week, especially late at night when they have been drinking, she has wanted to tell him, not in an accusatory manner, oh no, not in a reproachful manner, oh no, just calmly, matter-of-factly, perhaps even humorously how she felt during the years she waited for him. Tell him what it was like, how he was in her thoughts, in totally crazy ways. But she has refrained in order for him not to misunderstand, to interpret it as an accusation or reproach for which at some point he will be held accountable, as a threat of future punishment.

But he appears to have expected that story, that reproach, she realises now, so that he could ask the crucial question:

'Can you forgive me?'

And when she didn't tell him her story, he asked the question anyway, on that last night when he was drunk, but he paraphrased it: You won't be able to forgive me! So that she would say that together they could start a new story. She must put the old Arnold behind her. Here he lies, the new Arnold. Hello, darling, this is you. So naked and vulnerable and tearful. Yes, everything begins here, at this moment. That is how it must be. She undresses and lies down next to him, rolls him onto his side and snuggles up to him, sniffs his neck, his smell, is it familiar now? Does she smell Arnold and not Trond? Does she remember his smell, can she trust it, does it change? From year to year, week to week, from woman to woman, does it change like his hair, what little he has left, it was fair when she first met him, like that of his wife's, Kjersti, it grew darker in the time he was with her, with Ida, darker still, like Ida's, it might be ginger now. It doesn't smell the same. It has changed its smell, it is unrecognisable.

She pulls the duvet over both of them and tucks it under them, under him and herself, little Arnold, my darling, my beloved. But at the same time a little voice at the back of her mind is saying: Is this how it's going to be? Will he always be the child?

They drink the whole week. In the morning, at noon in order to cool their overheating brains, to calm their agitated senses, in order to survive, in order not to take off, disappear, in order not to remember the impossible. They find themselves a regular bar, a local, a corner shop where they buy milk, coffee, orange juice and beer, a regular route from the flat to their regular places, a holy map of their world. Set phrases emerge in one week. They develop their own language, their own holy places. The shop in whose changing room they make love. The shop where he buys her a skirt with a zip from the waistband to the hem, which can be unzipped in one movement. The shop where she buys him a box of cigars, later they will always walk past it: Do you remember?

Mind you don't drink it, the first sentence. Then as if nothing has happened and the ringing bells of nothingness. And Arnold my sailor and Bogdo's year of the pig. You can whittle a coat stand if you find a coat-stand-shaped piece of wood in the forest, the top of a small tree with branches in several directions, cut them off seventeen to twenty centimetres from the trunk and polish them, some thick, others thin. Before you hang it on the wall to hold your hats and scarves, you can try it out, can't you, will you be my coat stand?

It makes no sense to anyone but the lovers. It can only be expressed in their new language for two, shared only by them.

'I get electric,' she says when she has come so many times that he has to stay away from her.

'I'm electronic,' he replies.

~

Dear relatively stylish pig! I was going to surprise you with a personal ad in *Dagbladet* on Saturday, but then again, I know about newspapers: coat stands, hats and pigs can be strong stuff.

He has sent in a personal ad to a lonely hearts club in *Dagbladet*; it is refused *due to its wording* as the red stamp across his proposed text makes clear: Coat stand with hat seeks relatively stylish pig. Interests: Getting drunk. Ref. number: As if nothing has happened.

Beer-for-breakfast days. The first beer-for-breakfast day happens in Røros. He has booked himself into a hotel near the railway station for a week in order to work. Late autumn, everything is red and bright yellow. He comes by train from Trondheim, she comes by train from Oslo, they meet in the hotel lobby and hug. There are hardly any other guests, it is off-season, but there will be a wedding on the Saturday. That morning people in city clothes and ankle boots get off the train and struggle through the snow with their suitcases. They stand at the window, watching them. Every time a train has arrived, six or seven during the day, they have gone to the window and looked down at the platform to see if anyone gets off, it is rare but it happens. That Saturday morning, however, their second-last day in the mountains, many people get off the morning and midday trains wearing city clothes and city shoes. Darkness falls quickly. As early as four o'clock. They stand at the window and look down on the platform where the snow has been cleared. Snow lies in bright white piles to all sides. The lights are on in the fifteen houses on the far side of the railway tracks, yellow lamps in the windows, yellow lamps outside the doors, above the steps, they colour the fluttering snowflakes yellow, they don't settle, they whirl, dance, snow, snow. From time to time someone will make their way through the snow, stumbling in padded coats and survival suits, a husky barks, while the twilight seems to grow from the ground up. At four o'clock people appear outside, in national costumes and on skis, carrying torches, the couple is to be married next to one of the snow-covered slag piles. They wear tunics and jackets with furs draped over their shoulders as they cross the platform where the snow has been cleared, with a blazing torch in one hand, ski poles in the other. They can't see the wedding ceremony from their window, but they stand at the window while it happens, leaning forwards, their noses pressed against the pane. Until the procession returns, at a swifter pace than when they headed up, happier, a little unsteady as if they have already drunk champagne.

The newlyweds are the last to return, in a dogsled that makes a tour through the snow-white town. Some time to themselves before the festivities begin. They have pledged their troth to each other in the presence of witnesses, now they want to be alone, pulled by dogs through the town, just the two of them, snugly enveloped in furs in the darkness with champagne flutes cold against their lips, reflecting on it, underneath the stars which shine brightly this evening in Røros, closer to them than to most other places on earth.

Ida and Arnold get dressed and go downstairs, attracted by the occasion, the abundance of emotion, it is off-season, there are hardly any other guests, just Ida and Arnold and the wedding guests in the lobby with champagne flutes. They are waiting for the happy couple and their dogsled, they can see them through the large windows that overlook the railway tracks. They sit deep in the sled on its runners, drawn by eight panting huskies. Are they happy? In the presence of witnesses and with their eyes locked on each other, they have just said: I do! For better or for worse, till death us do part. It will always be you and only you. Is that happiness? Is that salvation? They sit down to watch from a distance, each with a beer. There is the best man with a carnation in his buttonhole, he flicks through his notes. There is a mother, flushed with excitement, she receives presents and orders a younger woman, a daughter or sister to open them, and don't get the cards mixed up! We mustn't lose track of who gave what, that's important. There are friends who know each other well, who drink quickly and laugh a lot. An old uncle, a grandmother, some children run around and grab hold of random trouser legs when they lose their balance. Ida and Arnold sit further away, behind a pillar.

The bride and groom arrive. Flushed, smiling from champagne, from all of it, so is it salvation and happiness after all? Their friends raise their glasses to toast them. Moments like this are worth celebrating. The love between two people who pledge their troth to each other, it is rare, enviable, there is nothing more provocative than a truly besotted couple. Over at the beautifully laid table a brother or brother-in-law is placing red and green song sheets under the plates. In a corner a middle-aged man with a crumpled piece of paper in his hand is mumbling to himself, a father, a father-in-law or a favourite uncle. Ida and Arnold follow the guests and sit down as near to the open dining-room door as they can without drawing attention to themselves.

The father of the bride makes a speech, he welcomes everyone, no one will ever get to hear what Arnold's father would have said. Then the bridegroom speaks, what Arnold would have said, no one, not even Ida, will ever hear. I would have made a great speech, Arnold says. No one will ever hear it. Outside the snow glistens, darkness seeps from the ground, but the snowdrifts light up the night, the clouds clear and the stars shine more brightly. No one will ever get to hear Ida's speech to Arnold and his scar. The well-rehearsed one she composed when she wandered the streets during her long, lonely evening walks that first wretched, hopeful winter. Nor will anyone else, ever.

'Will you marry me?'

'Yes,' she says every time, but they never marry.

'We love each other,' he says, 'don't we?'

'Yes, we do.'

'Cheers.'

~

In order to avoid the potential heartbreak before it is too late, she looks for signs: He doesn't love me anymore. One day he won't love me. There! And there! They never get married. Would it have made a difference? They thought at one point that they ought to get married if they were to be together until death do us part. That their parents, while they were still alive, his and hers, while they were still alive, ought to meet on one occasion, their siblings with their spouses, their nieces and nephews, just once. She didn't see much of her family and neither did he, but shouldn't they, if they were going to be together until death do us part, meet one another, Arnold's father meet Ida's mother, Arnold's old mother, Ida's mother, Arnold's brothers meet Ida's brother and sisters, see each other's faces, meet each other's eyes, hold out their hands to one another and say hello, just once.

They listen to the wedding songs where family members have composed new lyrics to well-known tunes and think about what they themselves would have written, to each other, what their best man would have written and to which tunes, something unique, something extraordinary because their relationship isn't ordinary, it is rare. They join in the chorus to give it a bit of oomph. They raise toasts to the happy couple and all the golden nuggets of wisdom being served up. Never let the sun go down on an argument. Always kiss and make up before you go to sleep. Carry each other's burdens. They clap and sing along to the chorus and the mood in the dining room is so convivial that the guests laugh towards Ida and Arnold and raise their glasses to them, and as the atmosphere grows more exuberant, Ida taps her glass and tells a joke. A couple is preparing their silver wedding. The wife is bursting with ideas about the venue, the guest list and the menu, salmon as the starter, rack of lamb as the main course, ice cream parfait for dessert and she is deciding on the wines and cakes, floral decorations etc., when the man pipes up that they could always celebrate the occasion with a two-minute silence. Ha-ha! If he really had loved me, he would have married someone else! Ha-ha! They laugh and she sits down. Don't go over the top. Everything in moderation. But if it had been their wedding, they would have given their all, gone all out, they will do it one day, show the world. Pledge their troth while everyone is listening. When it is time to dance, they dance. When the happy couple dance their first dance, they dance as well.

'We have to do it. If anyone should get married, it's us. People who love like we do should get married.'

They wake up around eleven, it is Sunday. He always sleeps in the recovery position in order not to die in his sleep, she lies behind him, curled around him, her arms around him, they are spooning. The next day, Monday, they are going home, to their respective destinations, he to Trondheim, she to Oslo. She wakes up first, she is thirsty, she opens the curtains cautiously to check the weather. The sky above the town is dark, but it isn't snowing. Arnold is asleep, curled up like a ball under the duvet, only the top of his head shows. She goes to get something to drink. There is nothing in the minibar, no juice, no mineral water. Only beer, many bottles of beer and white wine. She takes two beers, opens them, pours them into glasses and goes to him, opens the curtains fully and gives him a glass, he doesn't open his eyes until he is drinking.

'Beer?' he says afterwards.

'It was all there was.'

They drink out of sheer thirst and sit with the empty glasses in their hands. They need a day off, it is acceptable, it is necessary. To do nothing all day, just stay in bed. Abandon all plans, all resolutions, no one knows where they are. They have made no promises to anyone. She fetches more beer. They can sit in bed all day and look out of the window. At the shifting weather, at the sky changing colour. At the drifting clouds. And talk about anything they want, about getting married, pledging their troth. How to do it, about people who do, what makes them do it, what is it they do, those who make a marriage work, what is the most impor-tant factor? Honesty. Not to humiliate the other. To listen to each other. To take an interest in each other's work, to understand the other's work, the other's passion. Sex. More beer, it relaxes them, it helps them let go. Let go of all their worries, brush them aside, forget about them. Shoulder to shoulder, but still alone in the world. No one knows what it is like until now. It hasn't existed until now. Thigh against thigh, arm against arm and face against face. They are only apart when one of them goes to the loo or fetches more beer and wine, and they miss each other.

'Where are you going?'

'I'm just going to the loo.'

'Don't be long!'

And when she comes back: 'I missed you.'

'Me too.'

The week in Copenhagen is over. The city, the scene of the crime, the real beginning of their love, lies behind them in the sunshine. They have packed their bags and are going to the airport. His plane leaves before hers, but they go to the airport together. They have lunch there and drink beer, always the same, in that restaurant, which at the time was on the first floor from where you can look down at the crowds of people in the departure hall. He walks down there to call Kjersti and he is gone a long time. She can still see him from the restaurant where she sits on her own, calmly above all the people. The handset against his ear, he is talking now. Uttering sounds, words to her, his wife, who knows him better than Ida does, who washes her clothes with his after they have lain in the same laundry basket, mingling together. He has been in a furniture store and chosen furniture with her, he has a child with her. What does he say to her, to whom he pledged his troth in Trondheim registry office not all that long ago, to whom he gave the groom's speech? It undoubtedly went down well.

What is he saying now? He walks back slowly. He tells her that she is sad. Kjersti is depressed and desperate and it makes him, Arnold, sad too. It is natural, it is the way it is. Kjersti wonders if she might still love him, he says. And that makes him feel really bad, he says.

'Because we've had such a good time. Do you see?'

'I'm not married. I'm not deceiving anyone.'

No. It is true. They have to leave now. Arnold has to leave. He stops by the duty-free to buy body lotion for Kjersti, can Ida recommend a brand. No. That is a mistake. He understands that.

'That was a mistake,' he says.

They walk as close to his gate as he dares. People from Trondheim catch the Trondheim plane, his colleagues, students or members of Kjersti's family. He stops and turns to her. This far. No further.

'Take care,' he says, kisses her quickly on the lips and looks at her, and she accepts the kiss and looks at him and replies: Take care, then he leaves.

She watches him until he has turned a corner and can no longer be seen, then she goes back to the departure hall, finds a payphone and calls someone. She is full to bursting, they are still in the same building. She has never been as beautiful as she is now, she is sure she gives off a scent, people turn to look after her.

His gate is closing. Now he is on the plane, wearing his seatbelt. Reading his newspaper. Is he thinking of her? He has to be! Is he thinking of Kjersti? So what? Now he is in the air, the illuminated letters of his flight number on the sign disappear.

Perhaps she goes to see Trond. To be calmed down. For one last orgasm. To let go, to scream out loud. Touch me here, it echoes through her body. Trond welcomes her. He has a hunch, but he doesn't ask, he can just see that she is on edge. He sees her better, he knows her better than Arnold. She doesn't know how honest she is, what honesty is. That, too, is unbearable. It is like coming home from a party that went on for too long, to an empty house to be alone, a party you should have left earlier, before something happened that shouldn't have happened, something that no one can endure. Shame and fear follow in its wake, but only until her children come home and normality and daylight come back. And with the daylight, she calls him and says: I love you!

She has to! As an affirmation, as a prayer. Then she can breathe again. He plans a trip for them, to London.

'Yes!'

She can breathe again.

Every day brings it closer. Two weeks, one week. Five days, four days, three, two, a single day. And then the day itself.

The children are back at school, it is early autumn. She is going to London with her beloved. It is like an unopened present. Her son has a football match. She walks with her children across meadows into the forest where the match will be held, they pick flowers, find stones, sticks. Mummy is so happy. Mummy is singing. Mummy hugs them and strokes their hair. Mummy runs down the path with her arms outstretched, thinking the sunshine is almost too bright.

'Isn't it pretty. Isn't it amazing!'

Mummy tickles them under their armpits and behind their knees and rolls around the grass with them. How giddy she is. The raspberries are ripe. There are still wild strawberries where it has been cold, behind the boulders, where the tall trees cast their shadows. Everything is clear. Everything is vivid. There is nothing more to wish for. If only she could tell them. Salvation, the greatest feeling in the whole world. Once I have driven you to Daddy's house, do you know what I'm going to do? Meet my beloved at the airport and fly to London! Is there anyone happier than me?

'Go, Trym! Come on, Trym! Go for it, Trym! Score a goal!'

Home again through the darkening forest. Early evening, early autumn, twilight. One child on her shoulders. She can smell the forest, the children. She is trembling. What if. She can't stand still or breathe normally, she can't stop smiling. When she has taken them and their stuff to their father's, when they are out of the house, she showers, gets ready, drinks a glass of wine. No one can be happier than Ida is right now. A taxi to the airport. Thank you, God! Soon he will be there, in front of her, and she won't be nervous like the last time, in Copenhagen, because now she knows that they will be together. There he is.

Sparkling wine while they wait. To celebrate. That they have met each other and have made it this far, that they are on their way to London. A whole week, just the two of them, alone. Everyone thinks they have just met, that they are newlyweds. More bubbly! The English flight attendant thinks they drink because they are scared of flying. Yes, really scared of flying, look how they tremble, how they cling to each other. They get through many miniatures.

'On honeymoon?'

'Yes, honeymoon!' Lots more little bottles and an invitation to the cockpit during the flight. Ida accepts. They come for her after take-off.

'Would you like to come with us, madam?'

Just like that. High up. Floating. Completely free, utterly light and bright blue.

They kiss and kiss. They still don't know the other's clothes, the other's underwear, the other's things in bags and suitcases, adventures await, black areas on the map, an explorer's trip.

If there is anything they haven't told each other yet, they can tell it now. Stories they have already told can be retold the same way or in new ways. Siblings born to the same woman a few years apart, with the same father, who grew up together, in the same house, shared rooms, childhood, teenage years. How is it possible, twenty years on, that they know nothing about each other's lives? Children who would snuggle up in each other's beds at night and sit together in the back of cars on long driving holidays summer and winter. Who once slept with their arms and legs tangled up, they show pictures, and now they are no longer in touch. They played together, they knew each other's smell and belongings, they shared friends, activities and meals until they left home and for a while afterwards, but at some point, a moment in time that is impossible to pinpoint, it happened, they started to drift apart and now they are strangers. When was it, how, and does it make any sense? They don't know what their families are thinking and they don't want to know either, there is no point in trying to explain themselves, they wouldn't be understood anyway. She asks herself questions and he tries to answer them. To come up with a fresh perspective, to work out the answer. He asks: Why did my brother become an addict, what was it he couldn't cope with? When did it start? And why? Could it have been any different? Could he have done something? It is so far away, it is almost impossible to explain, but if you insist. The link to the past has weakened, faded, eroded, shrunk to insignificant anecdotes, but I will try. How did it start, the movement that brought them here, made them so that they fit together now, like a special key for a special lock, like a miracle.

On the last day he suddenly stops her in the middle of a street:

'But what's going to happen to us?'

'What do you mean?'

'I work in Trondheim. You live in Oslo. I have a child. You have children.'

'We'll be fine,' she says, she is not worried. 'We'll be fine,' she says. 'I'm flexible. Don't worry about it,' she says. 'Time is on our side.'

She has waited so long and now he is here. This is salvation. He mustn't leave her again! She will do anything, anything!

The winter she met her husband, when she was nineteen, he asked her shortly afterwards if she skiied slalom. Someone had suggested a weekend trip to the mountains to ski slalom.

'Yes,' she said. But she lied, she didn't ski slalom, she never had. So she couldn't come to the mountains with him. She would have to invent an excuse. Something about her knee. Or her stomach, a sudden stomach bug. And then she would have to break up with him. Because her lie would be discovered sooner or later, he would see what she was really like and then it would be over. For several years afterwards she was terrified of her lie. She would toss and turn at night because of her lie. She worried herself sick over that stupid slalom lie. How weird to think about it now, so many years later. How we lie and thus end up living a lie, how we get used to living in fear of being revealed, to impending doom.

They are in a pub in London, Ida and Arnold. He got a first with distinction, he says. You can get no higher grade than that. Arnold Bush has never heard of anyone else who got a first with distinction, he may well be the only one.

'I got a first with distinction,' Ida Heier says, but it is not true, she just blurts it out. They raise a glass to toast that they are probably the only two people in Norway to get a first with distinction who have found one another. Arnold Bush returns to this fascinating fact several times during the evening, that not only he but also Ida, the woman he is now sitting with in London, got a first-class degree with distinction. He doesn't think she is lying and perhaps that is a compliment of sorts. And yet he is not quite as happy about it as he pretends, she can see it. He is a little disappointed that he is no longer the only person with a perfect score and wrong-footed that he can't impress in the way he normally does and is accustomed to and had expected to. But cheers, he says, and Ida raises her glass and is now forced to mention during the evening this remarkable coincidence so that it doesn't seem suspicious that she isn't quite as excited about it as he is.

Ida got an upper second so she is lying, but it doesn't feel as if she is lying. It is not really a lie, only a minor fib, that is how it feels because she studied independently while she was doing a language course in Spain, she didn't attend a single lecture, she studied on her own in the evenings, she had no tutorials, she didn't submit any essays, and yet she did well, she got an upper second. That is not bad, all things considered, so imagine how well she would have done if she had studied like Arnold Bush, she visualises him bent over his books. Countless exclamation marks in the margins, constantly underlining, eager and excited, sentence by sentence, page by page. In theory she could have got a first with distinction like Arnold because she is just as clever as he is, that is the point she wanted to make!

But softly, softly! Baby steps, don't hurt him, don't threaten him.

Later, sober, the next morning, she regrets it. Not her reasoning from last night, not the conclusion, the crucial point she wanted to make, which is that he is not superior to her. But the fact that her lie can be uncovered and if it is, she will look ridiculous, pitiful, and that will make him superior to her after all. She imagines how Arnold Bush will introduce her to his friends and colleagues: This is Ida Heier. She, too, got a first with distinction, just like me!

And a friend or colleague decides to investigate and finds out that Ida Heier boasted about her degree result in order to impress Arnold Bush, and you can't do anything stupider than that. That is fatal.

She thinks about it all the next day. Has she ruined everything before it has even begun? She destroys, she self-sabotages, she doesn't want to be happy. Live in truth this time, that had been her resolve, that was what it was all about. Truth, love, honesty, no pretence, that was her ambition and where is she now after just six days in London?

She has to tell him before he mentions it to anyone, before it comes out and it is too late. Prostrate herself, laugh at herself in order to prevent further damage.

'I need to tell you something,' she says the next day, he realises it is serious and he blanches.

'What is it?' he says anxiously.

'I've written it down,' she says, she has written it on a piece of paper and put it in an envelope, she has it in her pocket. She pulls it out and gives it to him, he grows even paler. She gets up and leaves the room in order not to be there when he reads it. Now he is reading it. She is ashamed, she cringes. How can she look at him now? What is he thinking? She is scared. So strange to think about it now, so long afterwards, how scared she was. Of what, what can he do? Reject her, that is her fear. And then her life will go back to the way it was, the unbearable waiting. She never foresaw just how relieved he would be. Now he is the only one again, the rarity. He is laughing heartily when she returns, she is so happy, so relieved. He kisses her passionately.

'My little Ida,' he says.

His wife doesn't know about them. His wife doesn't know about Ida. Every other week, one of them lives in the house with their child, every other week in a flat they borrow for yet another month. So he is not unfaithful, he is not doing anything illegal. He doesn't have to tell his wife anything, it would only add insult to injury and serve no purpose. His wife doesn't know that he is in London with Ida. He says he needs to call her and Ida leaves the room. It is not strange that he wants to be on his own when he calls, it is entirely natural, but what does he say. The air is clear, there are still green leaves on the trees.

'She's upset,' he says when Ida comes back. 'She says that maybe she still loves me.'

That is how you feel when you are on the verge, when you are about to experience loss.

'What are you thinking?' Ida wants to know.

He runs his hand over the back of his head, the heat has left small beads of sweat on his scalp.

'I like her better when she's like that,' he says.

Life is strange. People, who have never met each other, have the greatest possible impact on each other's lives, they determine what may or may not be possible for us.

'Do you want to be with her?'

'No,' he says and ponders it. 'I want to be with you.'

Where are her children? Does she go on holiday with them? Yes, she goes on holiday with them, to Trondheim. They fly, what fun, to Trondheim, and stay in a hotel with a swimming pool, that is fun too, what more could you want. Arnold's wife has gone away with their child, and Ida's children are in a hotel room with big bags of sweets and Donald Duck comics in front of the television with multiple channels. Arnold picks her up in his car. The white one in which she has sat once before. Now she will see his house. It turns out to be ordinary, how can it be that this unique man, this extraordinary, quite remarkable man has an ordinary house, pine dining chairs with pink upholstery, an IKEA sofa, pictures on the walls, candlesticks in the windows, everything is so ordinary.

He points to a poster on the living-room wall.

'Kjersti likes this,' he says, then goes to the curtains and holds them up:

'And these,' he says, referring to the curtains made of a golden material, 'Kjersti's taste again.'

'Right.' Why does she need to know that?

He shows her the bedroom, the marital bed is nicely made, a copy of Van Gogh's *Sunflowers* on the wall, some old books, a wooden sculpture he was given by a surrealist artist, the view from his study, then he says:

'That's all I have to show you.'

How restrained he is. He has cooked, he tells her what he has made, it involves sage and cooking with wine for an hour, he goes into detail. Big questions sit on the tip of her tongue. He learned to cook in Italy, he says. They drink wine. Admittedly, there is a very nice view of the fjord. If it wasn't for the fjord, she wouldn't know where she was, far outside the city in a valley. The house smells of a different family as does the bathroom, the towels, she sniffs the clean ones in the linen cupboard. Afterwards they head back to town and make love in a flat he has borrowed from a friend who is away because she doesn't want to make love in the marital bed where his *wife* will lie when she gets home, *home*. When they have done it, made love on his friend's leather sofa, in his friend's flat, in town, when they have got dressed and drunk some more and are heading to her hotel, he walks her there before he takes a taxi home, she says something to him, which she feels that she has to say. Which she hasn't dared to say yet, which she has dreaded saying and which she hardly dares to say now. That he never asks her a single question which doesn't involve him. About the trauma she struggles with.

He has never asked: 'Do you sometimes feel all alone in the world?'

He has never asked: 'How come you see so little of your family?'

He has never asked: 'Please will you tell me what happened, your childhood trauma.'

Nor has he ever asked: 'What are you going to do about it?' Or: 'How was your therapy and can you share it with me, talk to me about it?'

He has enough on his plate. He has so much more on his mind than she knows, than he tells her. She brings it up that evening in Trondheim, her feeling that they never talk about her problems. Only ever about his, about his divorce. If she cries and is upset, she says, if she feels alone and helpless, she never rings Arnold, not to burden him with more troubles and add to his despair. Instead she will ring Trond, she says.

She shouldn't have said it, he can't bear it, he starts to cry, he howls and sobs, distraught, and collapses in her arms outside the hotel. She has to get back to her children, she called them from the flat and they weren't asleep. Only Arnold won't stop crying.

'I didn't mean it like that, Arnold. Please don't cry, Arnold. I love only you, Arnold. I've never loved anyone else, Arnold. Only you, Arnold. I'll never leave you. There, there.'

He calls her from home once he gets back, he is still crying. She lies under the duvet with the telephone so the children won't hear her.

'Please don't cry, Arnold. I didn't mean it. Forget it. You misunderstood.'

'I'm a heartless bastard.'

'No, no, Arnold. Please don't say that. I love you.'

It is all so long ago now. Since then she has learned the brutal truth. Their tragedy wasn't that they didn't get to be together, it was that they did.

Then she goes home, one of them always has to go home, it is agony and relief at the same time. Finally free, but she feels as if she is bleeding from her groin and her heart.

She goes to parties and drinks too much to fill the absence, the void. The flat which Arnold and his wife had borrowed from a friend, which they took turns to stay in, is no longer available. They have to live together in the terraced house where Ida ate Arnold's Italian food. They have separate bedrooms, Arnold says, and Ida trusts him because she loves him. She doesn't call the forbidden number because his wife might answer the phone and his wife must be shielded from Ida. So that she won't be hurt, feel betrayed, become difficult and cause trouble. Ida goes to parties with people who know Arnold and drinks too much. Because it is a secret, because she can't bear the secrecy, she wants to shout it from the rooftops, but she has to hold it in. That is the odd thing about great love, it wants to be on show and seen, as if everything that two such happy people do must surely demand the full attention of the whole world. We have been to London! We have been to Copenhagen! She is agitated, hypersensitive, nervous, she drinks too much, talks too much, goes home with a man after a party and has a fit of remorse in the morning in case Arnold finds out and changes his mind. What if he doesn't come? He has to come. Or she will die. Or kill him. How could she be stupid enough to risk everything now that she is so close, it is madness.

On the phone, however, he is the same. Thank you, God! He knows nothing!

'I love you. I miss you. I can't live without you. When are you coming, when can I see you, I need to see you.'

He likes to hear that, he melts.

'I love you too,' he says. 'I miss you,' he says. 'I miss your body,' he says.

'I miss your body too,' she sobs, 'you have to come, I have to see you.'

~

He is teaching in Stavanger the following week and she can travel there and stay at the hotel with him. Yes! It is a date, they have a date, they are going to meet, now she can breathe again. She arrives at Stavanger. He is waiting with white wine, they make love, they morph, it is all that matters now, here, with him inside her, the only time she feels whole. Filled by him, by what was lacking. She looks at him as he talks, he lies on his back and looks up at the ceiling afterwards, she lies in his arms, sniffing his armpit. Does he feel the same way she does? Does he understand how rare this is? Has he had so many women in the hotel where he stays when he is in Stavanger that the encounters blur into one for him? Is the white wine the same, the room the same, he has a routine, but at some point he will come to realise that this is completely different, unique, but has he understood it yet? She knows that it is, she has known it all along.

'Aren't you glad I didn't give up? Now that you can see how perfect we are for each other. That I pursued it, wasn't that prescient of me, aren't you happy?'

Sometimes passion goes wrong. You fall in love, but when push comes to shove, it doesn't work out. She has read about it.

'Yes, I'm happy,' he says, but does he understand it yet? He says strange things. She marvels at it herself, that her passion wasn't mistaken.

Arnold and his wife share a house, but not a bedroom, he says. Ida calls his office from the office of *The Journal* or the

Dramatists' Association, from home, from payphones all over the city to say: I love you. Come, take me, soothe me, ease my unrest, come!

How unreal it seems now. That time had a smell, she realises it now that she thinks about it, a distinct smell. She can smell it inside and out: Arnold is coming soon, he is almost here.

There is a seminar in Oslo and he comes. Officially he is staying at a hotel, for his wife's sake so she won't cause trouble, but he stays with Ida, she doesn't have the children, they are with their father. Life is wonderfully ordinary, as if they were married, as if they were a couple. During the day he goes to the seminar, borrows her car, kisses her goodbye in the morning, leaves and comes home at five o'clock and she has organised dinner, wine, bought flowers, planned their lovemaking, made the bed, showered, covered her body in lotions, dressed up, a geisha is waiting at the door. They drink, they eat, they make love and they drink, they discuss the seminar, who said what, she knows all the participants. They don't talk about Ida's day or things she cares about. Friday night he attends the final seminar dinner, but they will see each other when it is over, around ten. It is late autumn now and cold. The leaves fall from the trees, yellow and brown through the air onto the street and people's hair. She doesn't mind that their relationship is a secret so long as she knows: I will see him tonight. She doesn't mind that they are apart so long as she knows: We will see each other tonight at ten. She is beautiful, passion makes her beautiful, anticipation makes her beautiful, just one more hour to go. She waits with a beer at the place where they have arranged to meet. Will she ever experience that feeling again? Beloved! Here he comes along the pavement, that's him. They get drunk, take a taxi home, fall asleep in each other's arms and wake up in the same bed the next morning and another morning after that.

Is it this time her children turn up. On their bicycles, their helmets askew on their heads. It is Saturday, they don't have school. She sees them from the window, they have spotted her car and know that she is there, they stay outside wondering, as if they sense it. That the man their mother has mentioned to them when they ask is there, the scary one. She asks Arnold if he minds, he nods anxiously, then she opens the window and calls them in.

'Come and say hi to Arnold,' she says.

Do they want to? They exchange glances. Then they get off their bicycles, they lay them down gently on the ground and walk reluctantly towards the front door, poor kids. Arnold rubs the palms of his hands on his trousers. Dear God, please let it be all right.

They stop in the doorway and look at her, they glance at him, but they look at her. They give her the come-here-look, she walks to them and puts her arms around them.

'This is Trym and this is Helga,' she says.

'Hello,' Arnold says and glances up before he looks down again in that soft, sweet way of his which she loves.

'Aren't you going to say hello?'

Do they have to? Arnold gets up unsteadily and walks over with an outstretched hand and they shake it in turns while looking at her all the time.

'Arnold,' Arnold says.

Trym doesn't say Trym, and Helga doesn't say Helga, but then again, he already knows their names. Now they have greeted him politely. Please can they go now? She asks if they want a snack, they do, but she doesn't have anything, she opens every cupboard, but can't find even a single raisin. Afterwards, once they have left, the mood is weird, as if she has done something wrong. She didn't want to mix the two, but neither does she want to keep them apart. If it were possible she would keep them separate in two distinct worlds because they don't fit, they don't go together, but it isn't possible. What she has prayed for and wanted is in the process of happening. And yet it shouts at her from all sides. How complicated it is. It is uncomplicated only under the duvet, mouth to mouth, except on the day he leaves. One of them always has to leave. When he has left, she breathes a sigh of relief.

When they are apart, at night, when they call to say good night, they have phone sex, she sticks her fingers deep inside herself, closes her eyes as she grips the handset. He comes with the same howl as always.

'Why don't we go away together?' he suggests.

173

'Yes!' He plans a trip abroad, just the two of them, away from it all. Three weeks in Athens. Free accommodation at the Norwegian Institute. He can translate Brecht and she can write a radio play. Three weeks. It turns out to be a test.

Something happens for the first time there, later it will happen frequently and eventually she gets so used to it that she forgets that two people can have more than one nice week together. The dramas, the scenes, the quarrels and the sweet reconciliations. Howling, screaming, breaking things, fighting, hiccupping sobs and passionate lovemaking. Drunkenness and arguments, then confession and someone's childhood wounds. All dregs whisked to the surface, shame meets shame and makes love more passionate. Still in a state the next morning and out into the too-bright light of the world, late, wearing sunglasses in all kinds of weather to the dingiest of bars, dives, the darkest corners, drinking beer until their hands stop shaking. Until they laugh at themselves as if what happened was funny: We're crazy! There's no one like us, no one understands. Their love is impossible to explain.

They unpack in the same room. In an old house where Norwegian researchers and students are put up. A window overlooking a courtyard, laundry flapping in the wind, cats on the flagstones. His suitcase in one corner, hers in another. His toiletries on one end of the bathroom shelf, hers on the other. His travel alarm clock on one bedside table, her diary on the other. She doesn't make any entries while she is there, she is never alone. The sun at its zenith. They have plenty of time. Out into the city to cafés or into the pine forest. Crooked trees form canopies over them in the twilight. Lanterns and the voices of children who stay up late, who race around. She wants to finish her play about the clairvoyant woman's difficult love, he intends to translate poetry. Two beers. This is how it should be, how it used to be. They walk on the dusty road, arm in arm and with a bottle of white wine to the Institute in the evening, to type into a computer when the others have gone, when it is dim and empty and quiet. They manage it. Working in the same room. In the same room, at separate computers in the empty reading room, opposite one another. They work on their individual projects and from time to time they look up and catch the other's eye and smile, vaguely distracted, lost in their work, but at the same time complicit: we're in the same place, literally and metaphorically. If one of them goes to the loo or to the kitchen to fetch more wine or anything else, and passes the other, a hand goes out to caress a head or hair. Things are good between them.

On the balcony in the darkness afterwards, once the computers have been turned off. The Acropolis illuminated on the mountain right in front of them. The traffic below a faint, soothing hum. They talk about what they have done. There is understanding and commenting. One word inspires another, one thought prompts another and they go inside for their notebooks. Each of them in their own thoughts and in the other's at the same time, it is rare. The room expands, they understand each other more and more. When one of them laughs, the other has to laugh too. When one of them laughs, the other feels light-hearted. They help each other grow, they give birth to each other. When one of them falls, the other catches. When one is angry, the other absorbs it. If she cries, he is the father, if he cries, she is the mother. It happens on their way home, late one evening, the last drink, the last bar. She says something, a name is mentioned.

'Have you slept with him?'

She smiles. Serves him right. Did he think she did nothing but wait for him? For almost three years. That she was faithful to him, in absentia, that there was only Trond. Oh, no, honey. Did he imagine she was faithful to the faithless Arnold, not only in thought but also in deed? Oh no, she smiles. This time he can't slam down the phone, hit back with weeks of silence. Now he sits here, dressed in black, his eyes black across the table.

'You told me Trond was the only one. You swore to me Trond was the only one. That berk. You told me you were just friends, acquaintances, that it was purely platonic with Haakon, with Toralf, with Espen. Now you're telling a different story. Anyone else I should know about? Any more berks? What else have you lied about?'

They are drunk, they don't stop. Is she bad? She lets it happen. Because she has lied, there are more, she thinks, in her alcohol-sozzled brain. Then he gets up:

'I'm off! That's it!'

And he staggers towards the city, back to the old part, in the opposite direction to where they are staying, but she doesn't run after him, she doesn't call out to him, she walks the other way, home, towards the house where they are staying, there is a party there that evening, a Friday, Icelanders, Danes, Swedes and some Norwegians are sitting on the benches and on the flagstones in the courtyard, drinking wine, singing. Serves him right, he will be back with his tail between his legs. She joins in the singing, she drinks, she is sitting on the lap of some Norwegian man when he returns, he sees and turns around in the doorway, in the archway, but this time she does run after him.

'I didn't mean to hurt you. Arnold!'

She calls out to him. Reclaims him.

'Arnold! I love you.'

He pushes her away. She throws herself at him.

'Arnold! Arnold! Darling Arnold!'

He cries, he howls, she takes his arm, puts her other arm around his shoulder, she walks him back and helps him undress, they go to bed, she lies close to him, holding him. 'Arnold, Arnold!'

He cries, he howls. She has never seen anyone surrender to crying, relish crying the way he does.

'Only you, Arnold. I've never loved anyone else. Never. And I never will. I promise!'

~

He also cries in the morning, before they make love. It is his breakup, she realises that now, long afterwards. He is in the process of breaking up. It tears him apart, but not her, she lies close to him, singing her songs. Perhaps he is thinking about his wife, perhaps he misses his wife, she thinks now, long afterwards. She can think only of him, there is no one else, and she can't imagine how it could be any different for him. Does he feel guilty, she wonders now, years later. Is he missing his child, does he struggle to see how it is going to work out with the house, with the finances, with everything? For her part everything is in order, everything has been dealt with, and she can't imagine any obstacles now that they are finally together and will be together for another two weeks in Athens. Arnold, my friend. Arnold, my sailor.

She keeps stroking him. She sings her songs to him, into the back of his neck while he shakes. She continues to caress him, she has plenty of time, there is no rush. She whispers poems to him. Go to the beach with your sorrows, pick up a stone and throw it in the water, then throw another stone. They make love and scream when they come so everyone in the building must be able to hear them, and if anyone saw them argue and fight last night, they will realise now that they have made up.

They get up in the early evening. They shower and dress and go outside, they walk closer to each other, even more closely, it really is possible. It's because we love each other, they say. It's because we're so passionate. We're enthralled by the power of love.

'I've never felt like this about anyone.'

'Me neither.'

'Kiss me!'

'Never leave me!'

'If you leave me, I'll kill you!'

There is savagery and passion as in great world literature. This is the unchained passion they have read about, the dream of total union, the obsession about which so much has been written, they know, but which brings with it fear and horror too, a kind of death.

They eat with just one hand because they always hold hands. They swap places so they can take turns eating, drinking, writing with their right hand. They want to show their love, it demands to be shown, they can't in Norway, but it is possible abroad, so they travel constantly. They want to be alone, but love must be manifested in the world, paraded, love grows when it is on display, when they walk wrapped in one another down the streets, when they kiss on benches, stand close together in shops, in front of paintings in museums, when they sit in cafés kissing. Look at us, how we love, more and more united, more and more a couple. Copenhagen, London, Athens, that's just the start. The scene in Athens is just the start, the first of an incomprehensibly vast number of scenes. His storming off in anger is only the first of thousands of future times he will storm off in anger. And she will storm off as well, in big cities and at home in Oslo, in Trondheim, from the terraced house to a hotel in the city centre, thinking:

'It can't go on, it has to end, I can't take any more!'

From one hotel to another in big cities abroad before the next day's reconciliation. Perhaps it was necessary at the start, to cleanse, have it all out, get even. Confess in order to mend, repair. Drink to find the courage to tackle the knots, fight their way through them to forgiveness and reconciliation. Trembling, sobbing, utterly exhausted. They fling their arms around the other's neck and promise fidelity until death. They know, they have realised yet again that neither can live without the other. It was necessary, inevitable at the start, but then it doesn't stop. It continues, it grows, it becomes their hallmark. Because they are not like other people. Their love, their story isn't like that of other people. It isn't ordinary like the others. They may look like any other couple in love, but it is an optical illusion. For them it is a matter of life or death and it can be no other way. It is impossible to explain to those who haven't experienced it for themselves.

After two weeks in Athens he has to write a letter to his wife. A letter telling her about Ida. So that she will hear it from him rather than anyone else. They are working at the Norwegian Institute, they share a building with other Norwegians, Athens is full of tourists, who knows who might have seen them?

He has to do it. They are going to divorce. They no longer live together. Technically they have already separated. But he needs to do it properly, tidily. So that his wife won't be the last to know. In order to control the narrative, he must phrase it so it sounds as little like betrayal as possible, so that she will be as little angry as possible, so she won't cause any trouble. He keeps putting it off.

They are sitting in a restaurant under the trees, each with a beer, at separate tables. Ida furthest away, nearer to the forest with its sounds of birds and crickets, she can look down on him. It is morning and warm, even in the shade. She tries to work, to think of something, he writes his letter. She looks down at him to see what he looks like, if he changes while he writes to Kjersti, to her, the addressee in his thoughts, the woman who will read it. Who will open the letter, unfold it and read it. Words about Ida. Ida Heier, whom she learned about almost a year ago in Munich when he wanted to get his own back because she, Kjersti, was having an affair with a German man, Ida has imagined it. Now it is the two of them, Arnold and Ida, he writes the letter down there below her, the sky is high above this scene, it is solemn and painful. It is like saying it out loud to everyone. As if it doesn't become real until now, hasn't been manifested in the world until this moment, now it is official. She watches him, he stares into space, thinking. Perhaps he can't do it. He is thinking, he mostly thinks for almost two hours. Stares into space, pondering the words. He doesn't read everything to her, only the paragraph that mentions her. It says that Ida is there, in Athens, with him. That is all, nothing more, nothing less. Of course not. Did she think he was going to write how much he loves her? She loves him. She takes his arm. They must post it immediately. He doesn't have a stamp, he says. Ida gets a stamp. They find a post office and the envelope with his wife's address on it, probably the right one, is slipped into the post box.

Then home to children, to duties, to Kjersti who may already have received the letter and read it, to their daily lives in their separate cities, they drag it out, they linger in the bar at Fornebu airport after they have landed to prolong it and numb themselves. Has Kjersti got the letter yet? He catches the last plane to Trondheim. It doesn't leave for another hour, fortunately, but how quickly the time flies. Now there is only half an hour left and he might have to board soon. Time keeps passing, they can't stop it, his plane is boarding now. Don't go! Not yet! Soon the other passengers have been boarding for ten minutes and the gate could close at any minute, he has to go, he goes. He disappears through the gate. Now she is alone. It feels so strange. So odd. She takes a taxi.

'I'm coming, I'm on my way!'

Her children come back. They have waited, they have called and waited for her to arrive. She has bought them presents, she is giddy. The children are there before she has switched on the lights, unpacked. They tumble into the hallway with backpacks and suitcases and questions. As if she is the same as always. As if nothing has happened, as if she has not been gone for three weeks. They cling to her, they jump up at her, they touch her as if she doesn't belong to Arnold. But surely Arnold and her are the same now, symbiosis must have taken place. They need her, unashamedly, they demand without embarrassment her attention as unquestioningly as always, as if she is genuinely interested in ice hockey matches and RE grades, as if she isn't completely filled up. She can't call to ask him if Kjersti has received the letter because he lives with Kjersti in their house, perhaps she picked him up from the airport, for all Ida knows Kjersti picked him up from the airport and still hasn't got the letter. This evening just has to be got through. These hours just have to be got through. Until it is time for work and the office, until university professors are back behind their desks where they have their own telephone, which no one else answers but them.

She calls him at his office the next day when the children are at school and the house is quiet and she can focus. No, Kjersti hasn't got the letter. However, she had been in a good mood when Arnold arrived and said she was moving in with her parents, so they don't have to share the house anymore. It turns out she has met another man; while Arnold was with Ida in Athens Kjersti met another man, so there. It won't be long now until Ida can ring the forbidden number.

~

She gets a postcard a few days later, written in Athens while she was out somewhere: Dear Ida. I'm drinking in Athens with my new girlfriend. I have shown her Parnassus! I love her very much! Even though life is damp during the rainy season! Otherwise I'm spicing up life with loving arguments. Call me whenever you like. You know the number. Hugs from the Oracle in Delphi.

Arnold Bush has been invited to give a talk at a Dramatists' Association seminar about the state of modern European drama. He turns up in a new suit, nervous, this is Ida's world, not his. She, too, is tense, not as tense as he is, but still tense. How will it play out, how can Ida Heier, who usually attends on her own, whom no one has seen holding hands with a man, who smiles, who dances with everyone, suddenly appear all wrapped up in Arnold? They can't do it. His way of being a man doesn't fit with her way of being a woman and vice versa, they look odd, they become awkward, they don't suit each other, no one gets why the two of them are together. They are good at being two, just the two of them. Their love is asocial, antisocial, it doesn't work among others, it is hell. Back home, home at last, just the two of them in front of the fireplace, she gives him a ring. He has taken off the one Kjersti gave him, his finger is free. She runs to the small, dark cabinet on the wall in her bedroom where she keeps her jewellery and fetches it, an antique signet ring her grandfather gave her when she wrote her first play many years ago, to wear on a chain around her neck, a man's ring from Phoenicia. He puts it on his finger, it is a little too big, but it suits him. He goes to Bergen to work as an external examiner and she arrives in her winter coat in the December darkness at the Hotel Norge where he waits in the bar with champagne. Underneath the winter coat she wears a backless cocktail dress with deep cleavage, she caught a plane to spend this one night with him, a night of love. She flings her winter coat with the fur collar over the broad leather armchair like they do in the movies, her lipstick is dark red. He slips his hand into his inside pocket, his right hand under his left lapel to his inside pocket, like a man, like they do in the movies, produces a small box and offers it to her with a knowing look, like a man to a woman. A ring. A little too small, but it suits her. She pities anyone without a lover.

In the morning he goes to the university, she stays in the hotel room writing, when he comes back they make love, share a bottle of wine and go out into the city, they eat, they go to bed, they make love, they will never tire of it, they carry on, carry on, carry on.

'What can I get you,' the flight attendant asks them on the way to Trondheim.

'Four beers,' Arnold says, 'each.'

To Trondheim, to the terraced house. His son is with Kjersti, Ida hasn't met his son. They are alone, it is better this way. Just the two of them. In the terraced house, she can still remember its smell, the unfamiliar smell. How the bedlinen smelled, how the cupboard smelled, the bathroom, the smell of another family. Kjersti's things are there, she has only packed the essentials, things she needs every day at her parents' house where she is staying. Her toiletries are gone, most of them, her clothes are gone, most of them, but her wedding dress still hangs in the wardrobe. So much still hangs there, stands there and lies there that it smells of family in the house rather than just Arnold. When he is at the university, she goes through their things, Kjersti's things. She tries to be restrained, but she is ashamed. She just opens drawers and looks at them, she doesn't touch anything, she doesn't move anything. She opens a drawer and she looks at it. Well, she takes out an old school certificate and studies the photograph. Notes on pieces of paper, magazines, unopened bottles of perfume, jewellery, some letters, letters from Arnold. Dead things, Arnold says. Kjersti's coats in the hall, old jumpers in the wardrobe, her books on the bookshelves with her signature on the title page, photo albums. She lives among these things with a cleared-out bedside table on her side of the bed, the double bed where she sleeps, on the same side where Kjersti slept, Ida now sleeps there every other week.

She reads the few letters from Arnold that she finds, how very like him they are. She sees how he covered himself, after all, she knows something about how he lived while he wrote them. She flicks through the photo albums to study the woman who has lived with him these last few years, her body, which he must have loved, been close to. And she studies how they look together, how Arnold looks with his wife and child at Christmas, on a skiing trip, at the top of a mountain.

When her children aren't with her, she flies to Trondheim. She wants to be with him because she loves him, but something undefinable intrudes, an oppressive feeling she experiences every time the taxi pulls up in front of the terraced house, a tightness in her throat. One time she bumps into an acquaintance at the airport, he is flying to Trondheim as is she. Their plane is delayed and they drink a beer while they wait. Almost like life used to be, before she had children, when she could do whatever she wanted. They sit next to each other on the plane, they drink more beer and their conversation flows effortlessly, they laugh, they catch the airport bus together and when it arrives at his hotel she wants to stay with him, go to the hotel bar, head out into the city to have fun, have a good time rather than go to Arnold's terraced house outside the city where Arnold is sitting on the sofa, waiting, morose. He is in the middle of his breakup, it is grim. In the morning he goes to the university and Ida tries to write. She sits at the pine dining table where she has a view of the forest, rather than in the kitchen from where she can see stay-at-home mothers on the bench by the playground, drinking coffee from Thermos flasks while their children play in the sandpit. The house is in the middle of nowhere. It is, however, near Arnold's separated wife's childhood home, that explains it. In a valley outside Trondheim. She is a terrible human being. But that is the price she pays for love. She arrives in the evening with her suitcases, he sits, almost catatonic, on the sofa in a blue jumper his mother-in-law knitted for him. He is ruined, she realises that now, long afterwards, she has arrived at a ruin, that is the truth. He is trapped and she is trapped by him, unless they are travelling they are trapped by too many things, too many people. They make love in the double bed next to the bedside table and in the morning Arnold goes to work and Ida makes coffee, and yet again she looks through the photo albums, pictures of the terraced house before the family moved in, the first summer, building a brick fence, how they seeded the lawn. Kjersti plants a rose bush on a patch of ground in front of the house, wearing gardening gloves, her hair in a ponytail. In the garden at the back they plant a tree. Kjersti sits in a garden chair on the lawn, reading. Arnold has taken the picture. He sees her sitting there and fancies taking her picture, he goes inside to fetch his camera, zooms in and takes the picture, it is clear that she doesn't know she is being photographed. There is so much Ida doesn't know.

When Arnold comes back from the university she greets him, freshly showered, in a chocolate-coloured silk negligee and they make love immediately.

'All men should live like this,' Arnold says. Then they drink the wine he bought on his way home.

One day in town, they bump into Arnold's old friend, Stein. The man who helped them build the brick fence. It is a chance encounter, they would rather be on their own, but they have a beer with him. He acts as if seeing Arnold with Ida is normal. He acts as if it is unexceptional, normal, while he studies them in order to try to understand it. The day before Arnold's son is due to stay with him, she flies home. To her own things, her own children. To basketball games, ice hockey matches, parents' evenings, dinners, shopping baskets. They call each other every day, they have phone sex in the evening and they plan a holiday. The day arrives. The house has been tidied and cleaned, children dropped off, freshly ironed clothes in the suitcase, it is noon, winter light pours through the windows, midday at Fornebu airport. Everything begins now. Life. She hasn't seen him for a week. She is wearing her best clothes. There he is. At last. She becomes whole again after being a half. Close to the one truly important person. Just him, no one else can disturb them now, they are going to Berlin to celebrate the New Year and to work.

'Champagne!'

From now and for ever, darling! Cheers! My love! The bubbles rise from the bottle and tickle their nostrils, the glass overflows, thousands of tiny beads bursting in their mouths, making their heads light and the sky high: Here we come!

He has been here before and shows her around. They sit in a café in the morning, writing. Side by side at the same table, somewhere with wall sockets. Together all the time. What are you writing? How far have you got? They get on fine. He likes German women, he says. He looks at the waitresses and likes them. She doesn't get jealous, she loves him.

One day they order a champagne lunch. Why not? Think of how other people live. I feel sorry for them. I'll drink to that. Outside, big, slow flakes fall like inside a snow globe. There is a fine white layer everywhere, on the cars, on the pavement, on the streets, on the lamps outside the shops. It is warm inside. Brown wooden walls and burning candles. Pretty, unhurried waitresses with long white aprons around their hips, their hair up and little curls at the back of their neck. It gets dark quickly, it is dark already. No one stops them doing anything. Provided they have money, they can do whatever they like. They don't talk about money. Have whatever takes your fancy. They need no one but each other, they want nothing more. Home to make love and then out again, find a table, plug in their laptops and start writing. Writing equals money. Home again, make love again, recharge their laptops and go out again for dinner, drink wine, go to a bar or a tavern and get drunk. Every night they go to bed drunk.

New Year's Eve in Berlin. Thank God they are not in Norway. I'll drink to that. They have been out for dinner, it is long past midnight, they have toasted the New Year in with each other, with the neighbouring tables at the restaurant. Something is said, something revealing, something that has to be said, which can't be left unchallenged, afterwards there is only fog. She runs away from him on their way home. She has had enough. This time it is definitely over. She doesn't know where she is, she doesn't know where they are staying, he booked their accommodation. A man passes her and says that she should not be out on her own in this part of the city at night, she calms down and finds her way back to the restaurant and from there to the place where they are staying. Arnold has thrown up on the floor, he lies in the bed, sobbing.

New Year's Day and white winter light in the room. They tidy up, they clean up, open the window to air the room, shower and dress. Arnold, the professor, sits freshly showered, nicely dressed in an armchair in front of the television. The traditional New Year ski jumping competition is showing. Blue sky and bright sunshine from the screen. On the small table the telephone is ready, as is a small bottle of beer. He is going to have a nice time and call his son and ask if his son is also watching the New Year ski jumping competition as they usually do together, have done every year until now, until this year, this is the first New Year's Day they are not together.

'Hello, it's Dad.'

She sits on the bed watching him. There he is, over there, back to his old self. As if he can't be truly shaken. Not fundamentally. He recovers quickly, goes back to his usual self. Because he is healthier than she is – or more damaged. Or damaged in another way, they are two damaged people who have met each other, who have become enmeshed in each other and don't know what they are doing, but are compelled. If anyone had told her what was going to happen, how they would be together, she would not have believed them. Their last restaurant bill says fourteen beers and sixteen shots of schnapps.

She must be naked only for him. She must be pretty only for him. She must show cleavage only for him, only for him. If she is with a female friend, he will ring. If she is with her sister, he will ring. If she isn't at home, he will ring and keep on ringing.

'Where have you been? Why were you gone so long? Why, who were you with? I love you. Doesn't that mean anything?'

'Yes, everything.'

'I miss you, I love you. If you leave me, I'll kill you.'

'Arnold!'

'I mean it.'

If she is going to a conference organised by the Dramatists' Association, he insists on coming with her. If he can't because he is in Trondheim with his son, he will call and insist on talking to her for a long time in the evening so she has to stay in her hotel room. If she says she has to go downstairs to join the others, he asks if they are more important than him. She has spent the whole day with them, does she absolutely have to spend the evening with them as well, can't she find time for her boyfriend, who is all alone in Trondheim with no one to talk to? Doesn't she miss him, like he misses her? It doesn't sound as if she misses him like he misses her.

'I miss you, I've been thinking about you all day, but it doesn't sound as if you have been thinking about me. You just want to get back downstairs to the others the moment I call. You've spent all day with them and now you want to spend the evening with them as well.'

If she isn't in her room, he will call the bar at the hotel and the bartender will come over to her and tell her she has a phone call. Then she will talk to him in the bar, but she doesn't want the others to hear what she says, how they talk to each other and for how long, so she says she will go up to her room and call him back from there. And she goes up to her room and she calls him back from there.

As long as they can just keep falling into each other's arms and into bed. They know each other's bodies, but there is so much new to discover, to try. Shall we try doing it like this? Whatever you want! Or like that? Whatever you want! Have you thought about doing it like this? Whatever you want! Exhausted after the last time, still giddy, this wonderful, troublesome desire. Why don't we have a child? That's probably not a good idea. Why don't we get married? If you like.

'Is that a yes?'

'Yes, it is.'

They go out and celebrate with champagne.

'We got married today!' And they get special service. They get married in Istanbul, in Casablanca, in Paris, in Munich. The champagne arrives in an ice bucket. In Istanbul they eat lobster with the champagne, by the harbour on the Galata side, with a view of Asia. In Paris they eat salmon with their champagne. The bar of the Casablanca Hyatt, where Bogart and Bergman were in love, is so expensive that they only have nuts with their champagne.

'We got married today, champagne!'

It arrives in an ice bucket and the waiter takes a picture of them.

'Play it again, Sam!'

And the music plays and they kiss each other yet again and make each other promises yet again and they couldn't ever feel like this about anyone else. Other people will fall out of love eventually, they won't, not ever. More! More! They live the high life. They get married in Paris, by the Seine in the autumn, in Stockholm in the summer and they make love on a slope in Djurgården Park and waltz on the big dance floor with other, older married couples and they quarrel that night because Arnold thinks Ida flirted with someone, perhaps she did, it has been known to happen. He makes his way to the airport, but returns to the hotel when she begs him, and they cry and are distraught and don't know how to cope until they have made up. Champagne!

~

Home to children, to their separate cities. In one week they will meet again in Trondheim, they visit several bars and argue at night, she walks out and books herself into a hotel, empties the minibar, takes a bubble bath and dances naked and clean around the room, finally free. But the morning brings a pounding fear, an unbearable pain and she calls him, begging him to forgive her, and he is silent on the other end and she cries, she pleads.

'I'm sorry, I'm sorry, I can't live without you,' and then she is allowed back and she looks forward to seeing him, as long as she gets to see him, snuggle up to him, the pain will pass, everything will be all right again.

Sometimes before she walks out, he will say: Please don't go! And sometimes she stays, but he rarely begs her to stay because he knows that she will come back and when she comes back she will be so sweet, so nice to him. They make love and laugh at themselves, at their remarkable love driving them insane, no one else is granted love like this.

'Where have you been?'
'With Mari.'
'Why?'
'She's my friend.'
'What did you talk about? What can you possibly need a whole evening to discuss? Here I sit, all alone, waiting for my girlfriend to call. What was so important to talk to Mari about?'
'Nothing special, just this and that.'

'What then?'

'Gossip, about family and friends.'

'I loathe gossip, I can't be bothered with gossip, it's beyond me why you would waste an entire evening gossiping.'

'I've known her for a long time.'

'You said you were just popping out to see her, but you have been gone five hours. You said you were just stopping by to see her, a quick visit you said, I've been waiting, you could have called, I've been worried, worried about my girlfriend, I thought that something had happened to you, you could have called me. When you're not here, it's as if I don't exist for you.'

'But I'm here now, we're talking now.'

'When you're not here, it's as if I don't exist for you.'

'But you do. I think about you all the time.'

'So why didn't you call?'

'I'm calling you now.'

'I called you a dozen times. I've been going out of my mind. I had no idea where you were.'

'I told you I was going to see Mari.'

'A quick visit, you said, just popping out, you said, you've been out for five hours.'

'You could have called me at her house.'

'But I don't have Mari's number.'

'But I've given it to you, you've called it before.'

'Well, I must have lost it.'

'Arnold!'

'Yes?'

'Darling!'

'Yes?'

'Don't be cross, please.'

'I think you could be more considerate of me. I've been sitting here alone on the sofa. With no one to talk to. I had no one to talk to. I've been waiting for you, I had been looking forward to talking because I had something important to tell you.'

'What?'

'It doesn't matter now. I've lost interest.'

'Arnold!'

'I've lost interest, I said. I had actually been looking forward to telling you because it's something that affects you too, but now it doesn't matter.'

'Arnold.'

He hangs up. She calls him back. He picks up.

'Arnold!' she says, then he hangs up. She calls again. He picks up. 'Arnold!' she says, then he hangs up. Five times before he holds onto the receiver:

'Yes, what do you want?'

'Please don't be cross. I was thinking about you the whole time. I told Mari. We talked about relationships. I told her how much I miss you. I talked about how great we are together, how much we love each other. She envies us, how lucky we are to be together, Arnold, to have found each other. Please don't be angry, Arnold darling, I miss you so much, I wish you were here.'

'Me too.'

'What was it you wanted to tell me, something that also concerns me?'

She loves him even though he is small and insecure. She sees him, he is small and insecure. But she can't tell him that she sees him, how small, how insecure he is and that she loves him regardless, because he doesn't want her to see it. She hides her knowledge in order to protect him. And so she can't say what she would like to have said to make things entirely clear and possibly easier:

'I love you even though you are small and insecure, even though for some reason you feel offended.'

He can say it himself or he can write it: I am a fragile human being.

Yes, at times he will do so, he will write: *I know I can be impossible, but* . . . it says on the paper and it looks supreme, like an insight, as if it is something he has mastered.

She makes coffee and brings him a cup.

'It might be too strong,' she says.

'Strong coffee,' he says and she expects him to add: 'for a strong man.'

'Strong coffee,' Arnold says with a smile, 'for a weak man.'

It is so easy to focus on the pain, the problems, the nights turning into days, to create a narrative out of their difficulties as she looks back, in order to endure it, provide an explanation.

The first time he sleeps with someone else.

~

Ida is due to cover a theatre festival in Trondheim for *Adresseavisen* that summer. She has her children half the time, but she can take them with her. Arnold is attending a seminar in Denmark so they can stay at his house. Her children have met Arnold. They once stopped by when the windows were open and heard him play the accordion and came inside to look at the strange instrument.

She travels to Trondheim with her children while Arnold is in Denmark. She borrows Arnold's car and Arnold's house and takes the children with her to plays in the evening and writes at night and submits the next morning, and on the Sunday she puts the children on a plane and she is alone. She checks into the festival hotel where she was meant to stay all along, where the other participants are staying, where the newspaper has booked her a room. In the city centre, closer to the editorial office, to the theatres, to everything that is happening. Arnold calls as she is packing up her things. He has done well, he says, his lecture was a big success. People complimented him. He is having a beer and is so happy, he says. She can hear voices in the background, the other seminar participants, far away in Denmark. He asks how she is.

Ida says everything is fine. That the children are on the plane back and that she is going to stay at a hotel, the Britannia.

'Why?'

'Because it's closer to everything. I won't have to drive, especially in the evening, which means I can have a drink. Everyone else is staying there.'

'So you'll be partying with them all night.'

'No, that's not what I'm saying.'

'But that's what's going to happen. You'll party with them all night, I know it. Why can't you stay at my place, why do you insist on partying and drinking all night with your crazy writer friends? Why do you want to stay there, what are you really up to, tell me! Partying all night! Why are you so flighty, why can't you settle down?'

She goes to the hotel. She knows it, she could hear it on the phone, something is about to go down. He is about to do something. She knows it before it has even happened. Perhaps he had entertained the possibility and now he's made up his mind because she wouldn't listen to him and stay where she was. Because she does what she wants rather than what he wants. If she does something he doesn't like, there will be consequences. She spots it the moment he comes back to Trondheim, that mix of self-assurance in his gait and evasiveness in his eyes, he no longer inhabits his own face. Nor is he angry anymore, that is the most suspicious thing, he is no longer angry that she left his terraced house and went to the hotel. He smiles because he has had a great time, he says. He has had a good time, he says, what exactly does he mean? No, he isn't angry anymore. She is sure. But she doesn't ask yet. She waits for the moment when he might be honest. When they have been drinking, when they have had sex, she does everything he asks her to. When they have drunk some more, she asks him. He denies it, but that only makes it more obvious. Twenty-four hours pass, he denies it, he lies, then she asks in the right way, at the right time when they have drunk the right amount, and he admits it, yes, she is right, he was with another woman:

'Because I knew that you knew. But it was just one night,' he says. 'It's not like I'm in a relationship with her,' he says.

Does he usually form new attachments when he is unfaithful at seminars? Is he with the same woman for several nights, does he eat breakfast with her in the morning? Does he have lunch with her and go for walks in the park with her during breaks? Does he sit next to her in seminar rooms and later at dinner and go to the bar with her afterwards? Should Ida be grateful that it was only the one night, the last night? She knows the answer before he says it, but once it is out in the open, it gets worse. It hurts, it is unbearable, but she doesn't know what to do with the pain, what to say, so she falls mute. She can't bear to sleep in the same bed as him, so she moves to the sofa in the living room, what is she going to do? She can't leave him now that they are together at long last, she has been waiting for him for years, she has finally got him and she can't leave him now, it is impossible, she isn't capable of it, she can't even summon up anger. She is speechless. She falls mute. They eat breakfast in silence. She asks if he wants more coffee, she tries to ask if he wants more coffee, then she falls mute again. By the small kitchen table in the small kitchen with a view of the small playground where mothers sit on the bench with coffee in Thermos flasks as they watch their children playing in the sandpit. What a life. Later she can always retrieve the memory. He lied. How she did whatever he asked her right up until that point.

His separated wife calls and he breaks down. She wants sole custody of their son, she is just letting him know, she says, they have mediation the next day. Poor Arnold, it is too much for him. He goes to take a shower and stands under the running water, sobbing. Poor Arnold, what is going to become of him? She reaches out her arms to touch and comfort him, but he pushes her away. He can't be consoled by a woman he has just hurt so badly, that is how he explains it to her later, and she understands, but at the time she understands nothing at all, she has so surrendered herself, she is so alone, it is so long ago.

When he is not there she goes through his briefcase, she can't help herself. Finds pieces of paper with names and addresses. She calls the numbers and hears the voices of Danish women, exotic, foreign, far away, she imagines them in the rooms where they are standing, the beds where they are lying, imagines their orgasms underneath him. She goes through the pockets of his suit jackets, his notebooks, his papers for compromising receipts for double hotel rooms, dinners for two, and she feels ashamed, but once she starts she can't stop. She knows only too well what he is capable of.

I'm crying on the inside, she writes in her diary, but I don't think he has noticed. I'm crying because I am becoming weak.

Don't feel so sorry for yourself! Don't be so self-righteous. Who were you with that evening, that night at the seminar hotel and in the morning, before and after breakfast, breakfast for two in bed, which you made sure no one would find out about by burning the hotel invoice?

That's different! Because I knew he was going to do it! Because he can't help himself! For him it's a compulsion. But not for me! He needs it, for him it's good, for me it is the other way round, it hurts! He hurts me and I add to that hurt by hurting myself further! It's necessary for him, it is how he grows. But it can also be his ruin.

She mentions it to a fellow writer on the board of the Dramatists' Association. The meeting has finished, they have dinner in a restaurant and drink beer and she has to ask someone about it, a grown man. He writes her a letter afterwards. He can't live with uncertainty, he writes. Personally, he always seeks clarity. Doubting, wondering are not for him. He can handle someone upsetting him, he writes, but not the state of being upset.

At times he destroys his own belongings in his rage over Ida. When he is alone in Trondheim and distraught because he has been to mediation with his wife and they can't agree on custody and their finances are in a mess, and Ida fails to be at home. Ida doesn't have her children and yet she is in Oslo. She has a Dramatists' Association board meeting and in the evening she goes out to dinner with the other board members because why wouldn't she, a pleasant summer's evening in Oslo, a Friday, when she doesn't need to be at home with her children. Should she go home and sit by the phone just to be available to Arnold? She is out with the other board members and having fun at Herregårdskroen. Why should she hurry home when nobody needs her there for once? Merely in case Arnold might ring?

All hell breaks loose when she comes home that night, late at night, fair enough, perhaps it is early the next morning. Thirty-two hysterical and furious answerphone messages from Arnold Bush. He calls again just as she steps through the door, she picks up and he is incandescent and when she tries to say something, he slams down the phone and then he calls her back and she picks up and he screams and slams down the phone and calls her again and she picks up, how long will they carry on like this, she is tired, she wants to go to bed. But she is terrified of losing him and he knows it. She tries to explain, but he is so angry, so drunk, he has stayed up drinking while he waited. He has smashed china, he shouts. Because Ida has been out all night. He has broken one telephone, he howls, because Ida has been out all night. He has smashed pictures, he screams. He smashes a glass while he talks to her, she hears it smash, and he is impossible to reason with because Ida has been out all night.

Later that morning he is no longer angry, he is in despair, he cries and sobs, it is only because he loves her. He has never done anything like that before. Ida sets him off, why does she have to be out at night? Why can't she be at home, having a quiet night in like Arnold? Arnold is at home, having a quiet evening, why can't Ida do the same? He wails, he hiccups and gasps for air. He has never been like this before, he has never done anything like this before, it is only now that he is with Ida. He doesn't have the energy to get up. He is all alone in the world. He can't take it anymore. He wants to die.

Ida jumps on a plane. She flies to Trondheim and sweeps up the broken glass. Arnold is in bed, sobbing. Books are scattered across the floor. Vases and cups and glasses have been snatched from cupboards and hurled against the wall, they have hit pictures and mirrors and ceramic candlesticks, lamps lie broken on the floor. While he was smashing things up, he tells her, still sobbing, he kept repeating his parents' old telephone number to himself. 32 18 14, 32 18 14, 32 18 14.

'That's interesting,' Ida says and pats him on the head.

'It points to your childhood,' Ida says and pats him on the head and fusses over him and when they have made love – he is never so distraught that he doesn't want to make love – when she has cleared up, swept up and thrown things away, returned the books to the shelves, bought wine and poured him a glass, they can analyse Arnold Bush's childhood to find out why he repeats his parents' old telephone number, 32 18 14, whenever he breaks things.

Arnold and Kjersti can't agree on custody. They can't agree on money. They argue. They scream at each other on the phone. Arnold is desperate. He hasn't got any money, he is in debt, it is utter chaos. Ida is going to China with the Dramatists' Association. An exciting trip. Arnold doesn't want her to go, when she tells him she can sense his opposition. She dreads telling him that she is going because she knows he will hate it and he does. Whenever she mentions the trip, whenever the subject of the trip comes up, she senses his aversion and so she avoids bringing it up, she makes sure never to tell him that she is looking forward to the trip. She is leaving *him*, that is how he sees it. Leaving him behind with his problems, that is how he sees it. He calls her hotel in China, it is not easy to get through, but he manages it in the middle of the night, he stays up drinking. It is morning in China and she is in the chairman's room preparing for the day's meetings. Arnold has called Ida's room, but she wasn't there, he calls the chairman's room and Ida picks up. He slams down the phone and calls back. He rages on the phone, slamming down the handset when she tries to say:

'But Arnold!'

He calls back and slams down the phone and calls back and says he has smashed up the television.

'I've smashed up the television!'

Now it sounds funny, like a joke. But it wasn't funny at the time, it was bloody awful at the time, it shook her, she nearly went out of her mind. If he leaves her now, she will die. He thinks she has spent the night in the chairman's room and she doesn't get a chance to explain. She calls, but she doesn't get through, she runs from one western hotel to another to find a working telephone, but she can't get through. She writes letter after letter, she writes that she loves him, begs him to calm down and think about it, and not leave her now, in anger. Through the streets of Beijing, she thinks only of Arnold, her stomach hurts only for Arnold. On Tiananmen Square she paces in anxious circles, fearing for Arnold. Dear God! Please explain the situation to him! When she manages to talk to him at last, two unbearable days later, he is off work sick.

His friend Stein, says Arnold, when he heard about Arnold being off work sick and about Ida being in China, said that Ida shouldn't travel so much.

One time he is with her in Oslo, they attend an evening event in her world where they drink, then argue because he thinks she is too close to another man, a fellow writer, and he goes home in anger before her. She stays behind so as not to give in to him. When she comes back an hour later, he has broken things in her home. Thrown her beautiful red wine glass against a picture, breaking both the glass and the picture, hurled a carafe onto the floor. No more, that's enough. She doesn't say anything when she comes home, he is very drunk and impossible to talk to, but she will say something later. She has meetings at the radio station the next day and is out all morning. But when she comes home, she is going to say something. He is still in bed when she comes back and he is miserable. She snuggles up to him and says: 'Arnold.'

He doesn't answer. He is depressed. He has a migraine.

'When you break my things, it hurts me, it's almost as if you've hit me. It feels as if you don't respect me. You're hurting me.'

He nods silently.

'Do you understand?'

He nods.

They make love. He rarely smashes her things after that.

He has a seminar in Denmark and she is worried. She goes through his papers when he isn't around, looking for a name. He has a secret, that is the attraction, one she has to reveal, has to know about, women are drawn to Arnold Bush's secret, she is mad with infatuation, with passion and jealousy. She makes a note of suspicious names, anyone he happens to mention and the ones she comes across in his papers, then calls directory enquiries to get their number and calls and asks about them while he is in Denmark and sometimes the reply is:

'No, she's not here, she's in Denmark.'

So now what? What can she do with that information? She can't control him. If an opportunity presents itself, he will take it, he is one of those who can't say no. So now what?

He is in Denmark. She sits by her telephone in Oslo.

'No, she's in Denmark,' a child answers.

So now what? What use is that information ultimately to her, she is no further advanced, except now she also feels ashamed. Outside the sun is shining, why doesn't she do something constructive, something healthy, go for a walk, read a book, work. Just because he makes stupid choices, it doesn't follow that she has to. If he is deceiving her, then let him deceive her, it will come out eventually and then she will catch him. Just because he is being an idiot, it doesn't follow that she has to be one. Even if she found the information she was looking for, she still couldn't stop him, but she can stop herself from making poor choices, from demeaning herself. Ida! Take a look at yourself! Outside the sun is shining, the sky is blue while you are inside, sitting by the phone, trapped by thoughts of Arnold with another. If you were on your deathbed, Ida, watching your life flash past, what would you think about the time you sat by the telephone, calling total strangers, asking pointless questions, which got you nowhere except deeper into futility. Trapped, impotent, surrendered, paralysed. It's wasted time, Ida, shame on you! Go out into the world and do something, live, don't shame yourself to death.

~

Can he change?

It is early autumn. They are at Herregårdskroen. His fling in Denmark at the start of the summer has almost been forgotten. Arnold is going to a party with his publisher who will be publishing Brecht's erotic poems in Norwegian. He is looking forward to it, he drinks beer in the sunshine. Ida drinks mineral water. She has to drive her children to basketball practice, cook dinner, put them to bed. He is unencumbered and visiting the capital, she can tell from the look on his face.

'Please don't cheat tonight,' she says.

He smiles.

It means: Wouldn't you like to know. She doesn't read him the riot act. It doesn't cross her mind. She isn't capable of it. She just feels insecure and sad. She just goes home with a sense of dread. She just does everything half-heartedly and anxiously for the rest of the evening and she can't sleep. He turns up at five-thirty in the morning, crying, so something must have happened.

'What is it, Arnold?'

He says nothing in a way that makes her realise that something did.

'What is it, Arnold?'

He says nothing in a way that makes it obvious that something happened.

'What is it? Did you sleep with someone?'

~

The numb feeling of fatigue, paralysis, she doesn't know what to say. He says that it just happened. He is drunk, he wants to sleep and falls asleep. She gets up one and a half hours later to get the children ready for school. She is teaching a course at the radio station and leaves soon after them. She has taught all week and come to know the eight participants the way you do when you discuss and exchange ideas about writing. She can't keep it to herself, they will spot it anyway, she is exposed just as obviously as if she had turned up naked.

'Doesn't it make you angry?' they want to know.

No, that's the thing. She shakes her head. It is as if the blood has been drained from her veins, she just feels weak. Nor would he tolerate it if she were to get angry, he would leave and she can't risk that because then she will die.

'But perhaps he'll change?' she asks them.

They smile and exchange knowing glances.

'How old is he?'

'Forty-two.'

'Do you think he can change?'

The honest answer – that he will never change – hangs in the air. But she can't say it. It is impossible. She believes in love, she has to believe in it, there is nothing else to believe in.

They go for a walk along the rocky shore. Arnold and Ida. No partying tonight. They will spend the evening at home.

She has no teaching tomorrow. They can have a lie-in the next day while her children are at school. They move to a different rhythm, there is no rush. They have bought delicious food, the wine is chilling. It is early autumn. It is too cold to go swimming in the sea, but warm enough to sit outside without a jacket against the sun-soaked wall of an old shed, which smells of sundried wood.

Does he know what she is thinking? Does he suspect that the words 'he's never going to change' are ringing in her head? Does he know that she is debating with herself, that a voice inside her is calling out: Ida! He's never going to change! A voice that demands to be heard.

Does he notice that she is calm? Not like the last time, mute, not like the last time, paralysed. Not like the last time, but infinitely more exhausted. Because he says as they sit there against the sun-soaked shed wall, which smells of wood and late roses: 'Ida!'

'Yes?'

He waits. He waits so that she too will start to wait, anticipate.

Then he says something slowly, he speaks slowly when he thinks he is saying something important, and salvation arrives:

'If we're going to be together. If we're going to be together properly, then I have to stop doing that.'

Is she meant to respond to that?

She nods.

He nods as well, then he smiles: There you are!

Is she supposed to thank him?

They have been together for almost two years at this point.

The Dramatists' Association invites her on a trip to Japan. She is in two minds about going. She wants to, but she doesn't know if she has the energy. There will be arguments, sulking. But she wants to go. She doesn't tell him. But she accepts the invitation.

'I'd love to go,' she tells them, but that isn't what she tells Arnold, she puts off telling Arnold. The children mustn't be there when she tells Arnold. He mustn't have been drinking when she tells him. She will tell him just after they have made love, when they have the whole day to themselves.

'Arnold?'

'Yes?'

'Guess where the Dramatists' Association has invited me this time?'

'Another trip? Seems to me they do nothing but travel. Does it ever lead to anything? What's the point of it? I can't stand the chairman. Bloody control freak. Do you know what he said once, do you know what he did? But you're always so nice to him, you smile, you flatter him.'

She keeps putting it off, her plane ticket arrives, it has been booked and paid for, she is going to Japan, she has to tell him. On the phone, to avoid the worst, she struggles to pluck up the courage.

'It turns out that we, the Dramatists' Association, have been invited to Japan.'

'Aha?'

'The chairman and I and some of the other members in order to set up an international dramatists' association.'

'When?'

'It's quite soon, in three weeks.'

'Are you going to go?'

That's a good question. Is she? Is she going? Her ticket is in the secret drawer, she has to say yes.

'I've been thinking about it. I would like to.'

Silence, silence down the other end.

'Are you there?'

'Arnold? Are you there?'

Silence, it is so silent that she merely whispers.

'Arnold?'

Nothing. Nothing.

'Arnold?'

And then, after a pause: 'Yes.'

The yes says it all.

'Arnold!'

'So you're thinking of going?'

Now it is her turn to pause.

'I wouldn't mind.'

'What does that mean?'

'That it's important. A global organisation. It's interesting, I want to do it, to help make it happen, it's important. Think about it.'

Silence.

'So you're going?'

'It's not confirmed yet.'

'I don't believe that.'

'What do you mean?'

'You've made up your mind. You're going. You made up your mind a long time ago. But you're only just telling me now.'

He is right about that. She has made up her mind, she is going. He is right, he is absolutely right.

'Arnold!'

'So is it just you and the chairman, then? Just the two of you, is it?'

'Oh no, probably more, I'm not sure, it hasn't been decided yet.'

'Oh yes it has. I know it has.'

'Arnold!'

When they speak the next day, he calls her from his office at the university and says that he wants to come with her. He wants to come with her to Japan because he has never been there before. Ida has accompanied him on trips when he has been the external examiner, to Bergen, to Stavanger, she has come with him when he has given talks, in Germany, in Sweden. Arnold wants Ida to come with him everywhere all the time, so surely Arnold can come with Ida to Japan.

'It might be tricky,' she says. She doesn't want him to come with her to Japan. Because then she can't be the

215

person she usually is with the Dramatists' Association, she can't talk to people like she usually does. She can't share with them as she usually does. Arnold will criticise the way she talks to them, how she looks at them, how close to them she is, how confiding, how open, because she tells them things which ought to be restricted to him, to Arnold alone. And in the evening when they return to their hotel room they will argue about it, he will shout at her because of it every night, and the next day she won't be able to relax, she will walk on eggshells because of Arnold. Arnold wants to be close, Arnold wants to hold her hand, Arnold wants to talk to only Ida, he wants only Ida and no one else. Ida will be caught in the middle, trapped in the middle, it won't work, she will never manage being Ida for the Dramatists' Association and Ida for Arnold at the same time, it is impossible.

'It might be tricky,' she says.

'Why?' he demands to know.

'The logistics,' she says. 'Plane tickets, the hotel, everything that has been organised,' she says.

'I thought you said it hadn't been confirmed? Surely they can't have booked the tickets yet if you don't know if you're going. If you're being honest with me, that is.'

'It's not a holiday, Arnold. There will meetings all day long,' she says. 'It's silly for you to spend so much money on a trip when you'll be on your own for most of the time.'

'You don't want me to come!'

'That's not what I'm saying, Arnold. It's just not that kind of trip.'

'How so? Haven't you come with me many times?'

'Yes, I have.'

'So what's the problem?'

'Meetings all day and dinners as an extension of the meetings, we're going talk shop all the time.'

'You just don't want me to come!'

He is right. She will be pressured from all sides. Overt pressure from Arnold, tacit but tangible pressure from the delegation. People will be exchanging glances behind her back:

'Would you look at Ida. The hold he has over her.'

No winding down over a drink in the bar after meetings as is usual for these trips. The events, the analysis over dinner in the evening, the planning of the next day. Arnold nudging her side, touching her leg and when they are alone in the hotel room, he will accuse her of flirting, of being too friendly, of leading people on and accuse the others of coming too close to her, of not respecting their relationship, of not respecting him, Arnold. No, she doesn't want him there, she wants this for herself, but she is afraid to tell him so.

Is he serious? Is that what it looks like to him? That she is flirting, leading people on? Or does he just want to keep her for himself, to control her, because not being able to control her is unbearable for him? If his own emotions have gone haywire, why doesn't he try to analyse them the way he analyses everything else – after all, he is an expert in textual analysis and theories – rather than give in to them? Or does it genuinely look like that to him. As if she is flaunting herself, as if anyone could have her? They will argue about this for years.

'You didn't want me to come with you to Japan!' She will hear it repeated when he is angry, for years to come. And for the umpteenth time she will say that it was a business trip, a promotional trip.

But one time she will reply: 'Yes! You're right! I didn't want you to come! Yes, it's true, you're right, I wanted to travel on my own! Without you! Yes!'

They argue about it every day in the three weeks leading up to her departure. He doesn't come with her to Japan. He goes to Denmark for a seminar. He has an affair while she is in Japan, that is her punishment. She knows it is going to happen before it happens, that is her punishment. She is meant to find out about it, that is her punishment, she finds out as soon as she comes home. She travels straight from Japan to Trondheim. He meets her at the airport and she knows straightaway. And when she asks him that night, after they have made love, he confirms it. He slept with the same woman as the last time. She gets dressed and runs out into the rain, the pain comes back, the anguish, but it is not as bad as the last time, no, it doesn't hurt as much as the last time, it is bad but not that bad, with every single betrayal the pain lessens, she learns eventually and that helps. She comes back and says she is flying to Oslo, it is morning now. His son goes to school, she continues to insist that she wants to go home.

He hadn't expected this. She packs her things. She packs her things and says that she is leaving. She is going to call a taxi. Is she serious? Yes, she picks up the phone to call a taxi. He takes the telephone from her. She can't be serious, he loves her, they love each other. She is determined to call for a taxi, if he doesn't give her the telephone, she will go outside and hail a cab. He will drive her, he says, if she absolutely insists on leaving, but she is overreacting. She carries her suitcase downstairs and out into the car, he drives, but slowly, he tells her that if she leaves him now, he will kill himself.

'I mean it. If you leave me now, I'll kill myself!'

She looks at him.

'I mean it. If you leave me now, I'll kill myself.'

Will he? That is what he says, but will he really do it?

'If you go home now, I'll kill myself,' he says as he stands outside the departure hall looking at her, and he repeats: 'If you leave me now, I'll kill myself.'

She runs inside the airport without her suitcase. She has to talk to someone. She calls a girlfriend, in tears, and asks her.

'Arnold Bush isn't going to kill himself,' her friend says. But if he does, it will be Ida's fault. Ida has to brace herself and follow her own strong impulse for once, and Ida braces herself and follows her own strong impulse. She walks back to the car to fetch her suitcase and flies home to Oslo. She buys wine, changes the bedlinen, goes swimming in the public swimming pool, uses the sunbed, heads into town, to places where she knows she will see familiar faces. She goes home with an old flame and stays over. She spends the morning with him and makes dinner plans with a girl-friend in town, she is out the next evening and night as well so she won't have to go home and be alone, so that Arnold can't reach her.

Arnold understands that he loves Ida, he says on her answering machine. He is sorry, that is the point, and he understands that he loves Ida. They make up. He visits her again. They drink wine in bed again and talk about their problems again and about their great love again. There is tension. An element of tension has arrived. Some issues don't go away just because you decide to move on. They go to the public swimming pool. They sit in her car on their way to the swimming pool. She has questioned him, she can't stop herself. Was he in love with the Danish woman?

'Perhaps a little,' Arnold says, it hurts so much. What did he talk to the Danish woman about? Every reply hurts, yet she can't stop herself. What does the Danish academic write about? The more real she becomes, the worse it is. She keeps asking, she can't help humiliating herself. While they swim, he swims slowly and with his head above the water, she faster and underwater, she works it out. She works out how she feels about it. How she will deal with it.

When they have changed, separately, and they meet outside with wet hair by her car, she says:

'I've worked out what I want to say. I'm going to tell you what it is and then we'll speak no more about it: if you ever do it again, it's over.'

It happens again, one time that she knows about, there are probably many more, but there is this one time that she does find out about and still she doesn't leave him. Due to mitigating circumstances she doesn't leave him because he didn't plan it, he hadn't thought it through, it wasn't a punishment on that occasion, but a slip after a party so she doesn't leave him, she forgives him. But it becomes yet another issue that doesn't go away just because they decide to move on.

There is a party at the Department of German. Arnold is catching the plane to Oslo the day after. He is due to arrive at 11 a.m. but he calls her from Trondheim at noon and says that he overslept. She can hear it in his voice, she knows at once. She picks him up from the airport some hours later, he smells of hangover and beer, he has been drinking on the plane. She has brought her daughter so that she can buy her new shoes on the way back. She can tell from looking at him, his trembling hands, his breath, it is awkward because it is sunny outside and she has her young daughter with her. Everything was ordinary, bright and safe, then he turns up in this state. Ida has seen through him this time and he is scared. She asks him that night when they are in bed, when everything has been done, dinner, homework, children in bed. Then she asks him. He shakes his head. Yet it is still there, unspoken, between their bodies, it exists, in the body of the sinner and in the subconscious, and they start to hate each other. They argue about Japan, they argue in Trondheim the following week and Ida wanders the streets like so many times before and when she comes back, he is sitting by the telephone with a piece of paper on the desk in front of him with someone's initials and a telephone number.

'Whose number is that?' she demands to know.

That is who she has turned into, a nag.

'No idea,' he says.

'No idea?'

'It's not my handwriting.'

'It's not your handwriting? Hah! Then whose is it, may I ask.'

'How would I know?'

'For God's sake, Arnold!'

'It looks like Leif Asnes's handwriting.'

'Leif Asnes?'

'It could be.'

'For God's sake, Arnold!'

He is such an idiot. He self-sabotages everything. For an hour's validation, for a quick fuck, how can she still respect him? Are men like this, no, men are not like this. He is afraid to tell her. And no wonder. She knows what happened, but he can't tell her. Because she said outside the swimming pool: If you ever do it again, it's over.

They go to Spain. She wants to show him northern Spain, he hasn't been there before. She has been looking forward to it, she is looking forward to the scents of northern Spain, the early spring scents in northern Spain. Thyme and rosemary and dry dust on the roads. The smell of squares, old clothing and amber and flowers, roses, flaming orange roses. Show him the sea and the rocks along the shore, the harbour and the white mountains and the path up there which smells of thyme, rosemary, dry dust. They set out. She has stopped asking, she will soon find out anyway. They change planes in Copenhagen, but don't make it any further. There is fog, they wait in Copenhagen airport for an hour, two hours, three hours, they wait and they drink, they can talk about it now, it is ruined anyway.

Yes, this is what happened. A student at a party in the Department of German. Arnold carried on drinking and woke up naked, without his trousers, and by then she had gone. But it wasn't a success, he says, he can barely remember any of it, he says. When he woke up without his trousers the next morning, she had gone, he doesn't think he was able to get it up so there is no reason for her to get angry.

'I knew it. I knew it when you called. I knew it when I saw you.'

'And that's why I'm telling you now. But I felt like such a fool and so I didn't say anything before, I still feel stupid.'

Should she leave him now? They are in Copenhagen, on their way to Spain, but they don't get any further, they are put up at a hotel for the night, they can ask for separate rooms as if they are not travelling together. She asks for her own room. All night she lies awake thinking about it. It is not as bad as before, not as paralysing as the first or the second time, she is toughening up. She has a new insight: it's never going to end. It's going to be like this for ever because he can't say no. So should she leave him now? On her way to northern Spain with her plane ticket in her bag. Dear God, should I leave now because it's never going to stop, it's going to carry on, he is incorrigible.

The movement away from him has begun. Here, in a hotel room in Copenhagen, on her own. On their way to northern Spain, but stopped by fog in Copenhagen, she can feel it. How she has started to edge away from him and there is no turning back. Perhaps she has been travelling in that direction for a long time, she wonders now. She is losing faith. It's not going to get better. And she can't live like this, she can't grow old like this. It will end at some point and that will be a relief. She can't suffer like this for ever, she can't fear this pain for ever. As long as she knows that, as long as she can be sure that she will leave him eventually, then their relationship can carry on, as long as she knows there is a way out, an end to it.

He knocks on her door in the morning and she lets him in. They cry and make love and cry some more. She can't be bothered to ask him if he was in love with the student, what the student is studying, how old she is, what she looks like.

'It meant nothing, it was a mistake,' Arnold says. Yes, yes, I believe you. Poor Arnold. We'll forget all about it. Let's go to Spain.

Close to each other on the plane. Close to each other through the arrivals lounge and out into the air. Close, close to each other through the streets, in cafés, in restaurants. Closer to each other than ever before, we will grow from this, you'll see. We can only grow closer, more intimate, if that is even possible, perhaps he actually believes it? Every cloud has a silver lining. Couples who manage to stick together for better or for worse, tell each other everything, they forgive and accept. Just look at us now! Even better friends than before. Why should an affair make any difference, destroy the precious relationship we have? From now on they will tell each other everything. They are solid. Cheers, Ida!

She doesn't tell him everything. It never crosses her mind to tell him everything. It is out of the question. It is bad enough as it is and if she were to tell him everything . . .

She buys new sunglasses. Back home it is late autumn, here they can still sit outside. They buy beer as usual. Beer helps. Down by the river, watching it flow past. Ducks on the river. Ducks are ducks. The river is a river and Arnold is Arnold. Spain is Spain. They buy postcards and write greetings for those at home: Look at us, we're off travelling again. Having a lovely time. Ida and Arnold.

He struggles with himself. He tries to change. He calms down, he is much nicer for a long period. The inscription in the books he gives her say: To my dearest love. My only friend. My girl, the best in the whole world.

Little gifts, an advent calendar in December, a present every morning, miniature bottles of champagne, boxes of paper clips and chocolate hearts. Yet the old Arnold is still there, she knows what he is like. He is changing, he becomes the protector when all is well, when she is nice, when he is strong and he tries hard. But the other side of him goes deeper, it is fundamental, if he drops his guard for a moment it stirs immediately, if he has doubts, gets angry with her or drinks, it comes out. And so she, too, drops her guard, she stops caring because it's going to happen anyway, they will break up. Not now, not yet, but one day so why should she invest, understand, give in to his wishes. His undermining and destructive qualities gain ground, it is not until now, afterwards, that she can see it. He complains, but she continues to ignore his complaints, she doesn't listen. Doesn't meet his demands like she used to. Why should she give in to him constantly? What thanks does she get? Does he think she wants him just as badly as she used to?

~

He writes notes when he leaves, which she finds in surprising places. In her jewellery box, in her toiletries bag, in the drawer where she keeps the candles: Hello, Ida! Spare a thought for Arnold who loves you. Thank you for last night! With a date and time. Little figures he thinks look like her wrapped in tissue paper or tinfoil, a troll because he thinks she looks like a troll in the morning. The most wonderful one in the whole world. Little things to remind her of something they have experienced, places they have been. Calm mornings under the duvet in the winter. The children have gone to school, they light a fire in the bedroom fireplace, they read newspapers and make love, talk and drink coffee. He makes it and brings it to her. He has brought in firewood and lit the fire. He has cooked a delicious meal, they eat it in the morning and in the evening.

'It's so good to be with you,' he says.

'How pretty you are,' he says.

'Snuggle up to me,' he says.

'Take off your clothes,' he says. 'So I can feel your body. It's so good to feel your body.'

Perhaps he says that to all of them. Perhaps he just knows what works. But thank you anyway. Perhaps he does love her. Thank you anyway. He uses the really big words, thank you. She can't regret that he said them. She learned them from him. Thank you.

The radio play she wrote in London and in Athens is finished. She has discussed it with him, to an extent, cautiously.

He doesn't read it before she submits it. She submits it and gives him a copy at the same time. She is excited to hear his feedback. She is not nervous, she knows that she is good at what she does, but she is excited about which words he will use. He hasn't yet heard, hasn't yet read any of her work before it has been broadcast. She has written this play by his side, in the same room as him, while he translated Brecht's erotic poems, she wrote this.

He says when he calls her later that he read it on the plane home and that he likes it. She has been waiting by the telephone.

'I cried,' he says, later he will always say that whenever he reads her work, he cries over nothing. He has no observations to make, no comments, apart from that.

It is being broadcast tonight. They sit together by the radio to listen to it. She is nervous. It feels like taking off her clothes. As if she is being undressed by strangers. Her words come out of other people's mouths, in their voices. They are in Trondheim, alone. Arnold has cooked, they have had steak with fried potatoes and drunk red wine. They drink some more while they wait. She is tense, but also expectant. It usually goes well. No, that is an understatement. She feels joy, release on hearing her words become voices, sound. Perhaps Arnold senses it, perhaps Arnold can recognise it. He is quiet in order not to disturb her. For a long time before it starts he is quiet, in order not to disturb her in case she wants to be alone with it. He has put a bottle of champagne in the fridge. She stays at the dining table. Arnold tops up their wine glasses and sits down on the sofa. He has turned off the extractor fan. It begins. *Seeing Too Much*, by Ida Heier. It is the first time he hears her work. He looks at her, he nods. He is more nervous than she is, why? Because he has doubts? Ida has no doubts. Because he is scared that it might be a flop and it will show in his face if he thinks it is a flop, and then their relationship is over, he knows that. The damage would be irreparable. If he doesn't like it, if he doesn't respect her work, what she creates. Nothing is as dull as a dull text, nothing is as dull as dull theatre, there is nothing more embarrassing, duller than an actor's voice filled with pathos if the words can't sustain it. It mustn't happen. Isn't he sure that he loves her? This is crunch time. Will the words be strong enough? Arnold is afraid that the words can destroy, her heartfelt words on the page might end up being a conceited philosophy about life, about the sea and that would be embarrassing and people listening to the radio, in their cars, on their way home from work, will be embarrassed on behalf of Ida Heier, who is Arnold Bush's girlfriend.

She doesn't ask for his reaction. It went well. She is happy. She turns off the radio, fetches the champagne and goes to join him on the sofa. They raise their glasses. They smile and clink their glasses: 'You're an artist, Ida,' he says. He didn't know that until now.

~

Arnold is on Ida's side. Her enemies are his enemies and he thinks she ought to have more than she has, she is far too laid-back when it comes to enemies, opponents. He acquires new enemies, opponents for her sake and never forgets what they have done or written, at times Ida forgets and smiles at an old enemy in town, and Arnold will look at her sternly and remind her that the person who just passed them is an enemy.

He doesn't nag her about weeding her garden. He doesn't nag her about washing her car. He doesn't nag her about normalising her relationship with her family. It suits him the way it is, that she hardly ever sees them. He doesn't like normal family relationships. He doesn't like normal families. It is fine. He doesn't like family dinners and family Christmases and Sunday visits, he doesn't like families with young children who pack their car and set off on Easter holidays with screaming kids in the back and skis in the roof box. He doesn't like moderate people and prudent, lower-middle-class aspirational people or conventional people who work in banks and insurance companies.

He likes tramps and rebels and drunks and people who kill themselves. Those who shock the middle class, he likes outsiders and he likes female students. He likes poor people and revolutionaries, mutineers, fighters on barricades, Communists, rabble-rousers, and there are few of those.

However, when her mother has a big birthday and throws a party, he comes with her because she dares not go without him. Her children must see their grandmother, of course, every Christmas her ex-husband takes them to a family Christmas party. But now Ida has Arnold and if Arnold comes with her, perhaps she will have the courage to go to her mother's birthday party and meet her father and siblings whom she hasn't seen for almost three years. Arnold is happy to come with her. Arnold understands the problem and sides with Ida. She is nervous. Her children sit in the back of the car and they are nervous, too. They pick up on Ida's anxiety, it is an anxious car that pulls up at the restaurant where the party is being held. Her children haven't seen their grandparents, uncles, aunts, cousins since last year's Christmas party. They don't know them and they aren't looking forward to this and would prefer not to go, to do something else instead, but Ida insists: they must all be there and stay close to her. Arnold is not to leave her side for a second. Arnold drives. Ida is unable to drive. She staggers inside and says hello, Arnold is with her, right behind her. He holds her arm, her hand, he sits down next to her. Thank you, Arnold. Arnold agrees with her when they discuss the forthcoming EU referendum. It is the two of them against the rest and Ida survives and when they leave, when they have taken the children to their father's, they go out to join the big anti-EU protest, the whole of Youngstorget is teeming with people, as are the surrounding streets. They drink beer at Stortorvets Gjæst-giveri together with people who agree with them and toast them and each other.

'They don't know who you are,' Arnold says. 'They have no idea who you are. Your parents, your siblings, they don't know you.'

Arnold knows her. Arnold sees her. Arnold knows exactly what to do.

Stortorvets Gjæstgiveri on the big No vote evening, they have gone out after surviving the family party with the help of Arnold my sailor, Ida loves him. In the autumn darkness together with other noisy people who share their opinion. On the night of the referendum in the rooms of the No camp they follow the count on the big screen. They feel the same, they experience the same physical tension, the same joy as the results begin to come in. Not almost the same kind of joy, but the exact same joy. They don't agree a bit, they agree wholeheartedly. They don't share a little, they share everything. They hold each other's hands and squeeze them with the exact same strength, constituency after constituency. They hug each other when the result becomes clear. They are each other's party, how lucky the two of them are.

Their first trip to Morocco. Her new play *A Secret Room – Norway in Autumn* has been filmed and will be shown on the television. She dreads it because it is on TV and not hidden away as it is on the radio, for the few true devotees of radio drama who will sit with a cup of coffee as they listen. Not just voices, but faces, bodies moving through space. Her family, will they think the play is about them?

There will be reviews in the newspapers. All kinds of people who pressed the remote control by accident might land in the middle of it. People who know nothing about theatre, who don't understand the concept, but who will still have an opinion like everybody has an opinion about everything on TV and feels entitled to have one. Women in shops, men in banks, the parents of her children's school friends: So that's what goes on in Ida Heier's head.

So they travel to Agadir, Morocco, a cheap package holiday off-season, February. It is warm, they wear summer clothes during the day. At night there are blankets draped over the chairs at outdoor cafés, it is like Easter after a skiing trip.

On the night her play goes out, they sit outside wrapped in café blankets, drinking red wine against the chill that comes with the darkness. They toast, now it is being broadcast. It is strange. To know that so-and-so might have seen it, her family. She doesn't ring home. Her ex-husband rings the hotel the following morning and says the press reviews are positive. That is kind of him. It makes her happy. Arnold buys champagne and they have a champagne breakfast on the balcony, they open the door and the sun shines so they get into bed and carry on drinking. It has gone well, they are together, they have champagne, there is nothing more to wish for, a physical sense of serenity that opens the body to pleasure of the most intensely slow variety. Don't they argue this time, don't they row? Yes. Something makes him angry. He smashes a table he has bought, there is always something to be angry about. It could be a situation, Ida, something she has said or done, it might be the past, money, it might even be him, he calls himself an idiot, a fool, bloody hell, I'm such an idiot! But he is mostly mild, slow, two steps behind her when they are in a hurry. She is the one who orders, runs, jumps, talks. Arnold is two steps behind her with his inscrutable smile. Glances at something and makes up his mind in silence. Ida rents the car, Ida drives the car, Ida says: Sure! Points to Marrakesh and sings, books them into a room at a hotel with a sunken mosaic bath in a thousand colours, Ida haggles. In the restaurant where they are the only two guests, there is belly dancing. Arnold is dragged into the centre, you wouldn't think he was a professor. Small, introverted, his head pale and naked. Skinny legs under his shorts. Speechless and robbed of his manhood. They take him to the floor and dance around him. They shake their breasts over Arnold's immobile face, open their mouths and roll their tongues at him, their bellies, breasts quivering right over Arnold's nose that grows ever paler, he doesn't move a muscle. Ida has never laughed so much, she loves him.

A single car, a yellow 2CV convertible over the red mountains. Ida behind the wheel, the wind in her hair. Arnold with a map and a beer and a kerchief with three knots on his head against the sun. Blue sky, no one knows where they are, where they are going, Ida has a beer as well, soon they will be by the sea.

'My girl,' Arnold says.

Just the two of them, like Jane and Paul Bowles through the desert – if they had been as rich as they were, been childfree as they were, they, too, could have moved to the desert for good, to the slow North African pace of life and live like Jane and Paul Bowles did, on kif, marijuana and majoun, drinking champagne while they wrote.

'Like we're doing now,' Arnold says, he is translating Brecht's drama theories, Ida is writing a play. She wants to be in the yellow 2CV on her way to the sea for ever. They drive from Imintanoute towards the coast, and suddenly they see it. It seems overwhelming so close to the equator. She takes in the panoramic view. The sea arches as if spilling over the curvature of the Earth. Endless in every direction, an awe-inspiring dark blue foaming mass.

They get a hotel room by the beach in Essaouira and head into town. They find Paul Bowles's autobiography in German in a bookshop, Arnold reads out loud while they sit under the awnings in cafés and drink red wine.

Lesbian Jane and homosexual Paul Bowles meet each other in Greenwich Village, New York, in 1939. They marry to escape, they leave to survive, under the big North African white – and towards evening – red sky, they love each other. They make love with other people, but they love each other, it is possible. Paul with young, Arab men, Jane with old Arab women, Paul is scared of them, the women might gossip. But there they are, the two of them working in the same room, joined by fate, for life.

'Cheers!' Arnold says.

'Cheers, Arnold,' Ida says.

Paul is strong and resourceful, Jane is sickly and destructive. Paul smokes kif and eats majoun, biscuits with an intoxicating marmalade, which in the right doses enhances your ability to concentrate for a prolonged period of time, Jane drinks alcohol. Paul is successful, becomes famous and is highly productive. Jane's books are badly received, she produces less and less. But they love each other, they live together until she falls ill and ends up in an institution where she dies at the age of sixty-five. Paul lives to over ninety.

'Cheers!' Arnold says.

'Cheers, Arnold,' Ida says. 'One day we, too, will leave. For good.'

They have entered a good phase. It is summer. The children have gone away, the newspapers are thin, the neighbouring houses are empty. The phone doesn't ring. There is no one in the cafés. Wind in the trees outside when they wake up. The smell of trees and flowers through the window. They make love in the morning, Arnold makes coffee and they drink it in bed. Then they slowly get up. Arnold makes breakfast, they eat and work, he on his, she on hers, until late, until they go running. They walk to the water's edge and they run around the lake, they count the types of animal they meet, dogs, horses, musk oxen, goats, sheep, cows, the occasional cat. They swim in the lake, she is naked, he keeps his underpants on, his undies as he calls them, lifting his legs high in order not to touch the long reeds and the other slimy plants that grow in fresh water. They walk across the rocks, Arnold gingerly because of the thin skin on the soles of his feet. In the car are dressing gowns and a cold beer for whoever isn't driving. Arnold drives, he is kind. Ida drinks beer. Once they get home Arnold cooks dinner, Ida sits on the terrace, Arnold serves her a Campari. They eat on the terrace, they sit outside until the sun goes down, until ten o'clock or later, and when they have drunk too much to focus on their own work, but still have some energy left, Arnold Bush fetches his laptop and they create a new file: Twig.

Seeing as they can talk like this, given they can finish each other's sentences, given they have the same opinion of what they read and hear, they can probably write a play together. They decide to give it a go. A play about the unhappy Professor Twig, who lectures in Greek Drama at the university and whose own life starts to resemble a Greek tragedy more than he would want it to. A comedy in five acts, just for the fun of it.

This must be how partnerships who write sketches for television feel. It has to be. One plus one doesn't make two, but more, many more. They give birth to Professor Twig. In a language that isn't Arnold's, that isn't Ida's. At ten o'clock at night when they go inside, they step outside their own language and into a third one which grows out of their minds through the warm touch of their fingers on the keyboard. They take turns talking and writing, it doesn't matter who does what, they have the same voice, cadence, the same pulse, that is how TV sketch-writer duos must feel, the audience can tell that they must feel like this, how they must have laughed, how they are still laughing to themselves, and from their laughter a dialogue is born and thoughts that give birth to thoughts, one, long, serial delivery.

When they wake up in the morning, the sun is shining as they open the curtains. They make love in the sunlight on the bed. They make love in the sunlight in the forest, they are always alone. They can smell soil and plants being broken and crushed. It smells of sex, they are friskier outside, this is clearly the smell that brings about procreation. They work, they write. Ida a play for the theatre, for the stage. For Nationaltheatret, she hopes, but she doesn't say anything, not even to Arnold. She is going to send it to them, she is, she is happy, that is the most important thing. Summer. Arnold translates Brecht's drama theories, tricky German concepts for which there are no equivalent words in Norwegian. All day until they go running, until they go swimming, until they eat Arnold's food and drink white wine or head to a café with outdoor seating in the evening with Arnold's laptop and continue writing their play about Professor Twig, to which they have given a working title, *The Unlucky Man.*

~

Professor Twig's life has not panned out as he had hoped. In his youth, ever since he read Greek tragedies and became consumed by their majesty, he had hoped that his own life would also be grand. That it would contain great passion and challenges, in love as in work. That he would become an important, indeed a major role model to his children, an ideal. That his old parents would be proud of him. That if he were to encounter unexpected obstacles in his path, as most people do, then he would face them with dignity. Like Oedipus faced his life's big crisis, his incredible fall, with dignity. Yes, Professor Twig had hoped that his life would collapse as tragically as that of Oedipus, that he would have the courage to pluck out his eyes, to blind himself like Oedipus did.

However, as already mentioned, it hasn't worked out quite the way Professor Twig had hoped. True, he has become a professor. And many people might say that someone who becomes a professor at a Norwegian university can't really complain. And Drama might not be a particularly prestigious subject, that's true, but even so. After all, Professor Twig is guarding our cultural heritage, the cradle of our cultural heritage! The Classics, especially the Greeks. And it had meant a great deal to him when he was made a professor. But that was many years ago now. He writes a paper now and then and has it published in a domestic journal, but it never really leads to anything. He is still invited to seminars, not only in other cities, but also abroad, and he always travels when offered the chance. But it has been a while since he was last abroad. Professor Twig spends most of his days in his small, dusty office, in the dimly lit and distant corridor allocated to Drama, or in one of the two small lecture halls which are never full.

Twig fears that his third divorce is imminent. He has slipped, almost imperceptibly, into one marriage after another, and almost as imperceptibly, the women have slipped away from him, one after the other. The most powerful emotion that Professor Twig has managed to stir in his wives, he thinks as he cradles his head glumly in his hands, is anger. Both his ex-wives and his current wife are furious with him. Endless arguments about money, about the child who, incidentally, has chosen to live with his mother in a different part of the country, as a result of which the professor rarely sees him. Twig has been left behind, picked clean, is how he feels, and it is a pretty fair summation of his situation. And now he fears that he is indeed heading for his third divorce. His wife, twenty years his junior – yes, he was once her supervisor – has long wanted children. And though Twig doesn't want any more, he gives in and stops using a condom. But Solvei doesn't get pregnant. Professor Twig's semen quality is no longer what it once was, it says so in black-and-white. Solvei had looked strange when he showed her the test result just a few days ago. And last night when she was nagging him as usual, she ended up walking out in anger. And she hasn't come back.

Is it any wonder that Professor Twig feels glum? He will turn fifty soon, but will anyone throw him a birthday party and who should he invite? His life increasingly resembles a Greek tragedy without a plot. With quivering lip he fetches a bottle of brandy he keeps behind the collected works of Henrik Ibsen on his bookcase, takes a sip, opens his dog-eared copy of *Medea* and reads aloud in a tearful voice:

But you women are all like that. All is well / as long as you can rest safely in the marriage bed./

But if you suffer the indignity of having to give way, / the man you used to worship and adore / becomes the most hated one to you. Men should have children / in another way. Yes, it would be better if women had never been created; / if it were so, there would be no evil on Earth.

Then he breaks into song:

It's not easy to be a professor-man
    He toils and struggles as best he can
    But what's his reward for all his toil
    It has taken him here *(Twig throws up his hands to indicate his small study)*

Wohin soll ich mich wenden? [Where should I turn?]

His wife doesn't understand him
    His female students are ever fewer
    And ever harder to seduce
    What's a professor-man to do?

Wohin soll ich mich wenden? [Where should I turn?]

He has written about the importance of Greek tragedy
  And papers on the application of drama
  And all for what?
  What does he have to show for it?

Wohin soll ich mich wenden? [Where should I turn?]

In a series of flashbacks, we see how Professor Twig has had a literary quote ready for every major moment in his life. *And all that we have lost is ours for evermore,* he says when his first wife leaves him. *The strongest man is he who stands alone,* he tells himself when his third marriage falls apart, but it doesn't get him very far. Citing clever lines doesn't necessarily make you clever. Professor Twig knows a great deal, he has read extensively about the big questions in life, but can he translate his theoretical knowledge into practical application? How much has Professor Twig really understood and to what extent can his literary ballast help him in his own life? Professor Twig shuffles home in the twilight and finds a Dear John letter from his third wife on the kitchen table. She has gone to live with her mother, she writes.

Professor Twig starts to cry. At the age of only sixteen he could boast of having read the four great Norwegian writers. 'Read the four greats!' he said to his sister, who was studying Home Economics and had been taught that the four greats were onion, leeks, potatoes and carrots. It is not until now as he is nearing fifty that Professor Twig begins to have doubts. Perhaps onion, leeks, potatoes and carrots really are more useful than Ibsen, Bjørnson, Lie and Kielland, he muses, then stops himself. What use is literature to Professor Twig now? He no longer knows if he can hope for a miracle.

Professor Twig reaches for the bread knife, but before plunging it into his chest, he calls a student he has slept with a few times. A man, however, answers the phone. Twig hangs up, having now made up his mind that he will definitely kill himself, and goes out to get drunk. He staggers from bar to bar and then, intoxicated and morose, goes to Solvei's mother and begs Solvei, who sits surrounded by her family, to come home. He is completely harmless as he leans against the doorframe, yet the women cower in a corner as they scream and Twig's muscular, builder brother-in-law protects them chivalrously with his broad chest, which seems twice as broad next to that of the small professor. Solvei grabs the telephone, calls the police, she sobs and acts like a victim, but there is no doubt that she is in control of the situation.

The police arrest Professor Twig and in the final scene we see him in a prison cell. He stands craning his neck in order to glimpse the sky through a small, square window, the bars cast shadows over his face. 'Give me the sun,' he says. 'The sun!'

~

Are Ida and Arnold making fun of Professor Twig? Are they sending him up? Yes and no. They present Professor Twig, they ask the question: How do you go on living when you don't want to die? Are we responsible for the thoughts we think? Professor Twig complains that he has been treated unfairly by society, but is he working against that same society? No, on the contrary, he strives to live a life that avoids any conflict with society even if it means that he constrains his personality, his needs. So doesn't he by implication subscribe to the very rules that ultimately trap him and break him?

The Unlucky Man asks, as does its protagonist when he is refused a bank loan:

Twig: But why not?

Bank clerk: Because you're not a successful person.

Twig: Oh?

Bank clerk: You're a hedonist.

Twig *(considers this)*: Yes, I guess you could say so.

Bank clerk: And a hedonist isn't a success.

Twig *(quizzically, to the audience)*: But surely being a hedonist is a form of success?

Arnold and Ida think the same thoughts about Professor Twig that whole summer. Every night when they have finished their own work, they invent him from situation to situation and let him meet his increasingly sad fate with lines from famous plays, and they laugh with growing compassion at him and see themselves in him, see their colleagues and rivals in him and their ex-partners whom they also portray as accurately and as lovingly as Professor Twig's wives, former as well as current, and Twig's colleagues at the university. Arnold knows drama history, Ida can write the dialogue. They get it done. In the final week of summer, they put their own work aside and dedicate themselves to Twig. They are at it together morning, noon and night, and in their dreams. They have created him, he lives in them and he is the same to both of them. Neither of them has experienced this before. They won't experience it again, it is impossible. They share the intoxication of creation when it is almost done and only a few pieces are still missing, which only someone who has been involved from the start can find, one piece after another from their minds and hearts.

They stay up every night during the last week before the children come back, before they have to leave one another, step out of the Twig space and descend to earth to earthly things, children, dinner. At night over the laptop, walking in circles on the living room carpet and thinking out loud, the very last piece falls into place.

They personally go to the head of radio drama to put the play on his desk. Then they go to Theatercaféen and drink champagne and raise their glasses in a toast. Not for one of them. Not for Arnold's new translation. Not for Ida's new radio play. For them. They share equally. They don't live it with the other, they live it together. They hope in the same way. They wait in equal anticipation. Arnold with his son in Trondheim. Ida in Oslo with her children. She wakes them up in the morning and sends them to school. She works on her own projects. She talks to Arnold several times a day.

'Have you heard anything?'

'No.'

'When do you think we might hear something?'

'In a week, in two weeks.'

'What are you doing?'

'Working. Ferrying the children around. Grocery shopping. Laundry. Tidying up. It never ends.'

'What else are you doing?'

'Reading.'

'What?'

'This and that. And you?'

'Reading. This and that. Exam papers.'

There isn't always much to say. But they need the voice on the telephone, one more than the other. One lonelier than the other. One seemingly further away from the other. At times she has enough. She says she is going to bed and wishes him good night so she can have some time to herself.

'Are you sure you're going to bed now?' he says suspiciously, he senses her mood and doesn't like it.

The telephone rings. The head of radio drama would like to produce *The Unlucky Man* this very autumn. He refers to it as a satire and why not. It fits well, he says, because it is light and the other autumn productions are heavy, one classic after another. Arnold and Ida return to Theatercaféen and celebrate again, they raise their glasses again. No one can know how they feel because this is rare. Once the play has been recorded, only four months later, in November, they go to the studio to hear it. Arnold enters the offices where Ida normally comes on her own, that feels strange. Some things can't be shared, they must be as they were, whole, it is essential. They sit down together in the studio to hear it, the studio where Ida normally sits alone and hears her plays for the first time when they have just been recorded, with the same, almost the same tinkling feeling, but smiling now, they smile to each other under their headsets. They look at each other and they laugh, moved and stirred, at Professor Twig to whom they have given birth and who is now about to be launched into the world. It will be fine. For Arnold it is the first time, they walk with their arms around each other, holding each other tight from the studio to Theatercaféen and they drink champagne again and they raise their glasses again and ask each other how they think it will go. How it will be received. What people will think. Their colleagues, the world of theatre, the world of academia. They will probably find it hilarious, they think, but they are about to be proved horribly wrong.

They sit together in front of the radio one evening. It is the start of December. That is apt, Professor Twig shuffles through the many streets of Trondheim, shivering in the frost. They have had a good meal, opened the champagne, they wait, they listen. They have turned off the television. They have only *The Unlucky Man* in their ears.

They have heard it before, yet it is different this time. Sent out into the ether.

'There's nothing new under the sundress,' Professor Twig mumbles to himself, having groped yet another student.

'Cheers!' Arnold says.

Their sleep is restless that night. Early the next morning, Arnold goes to get the newspapers. Most of the critics, many of whom have been chosen from the world of academia for this occasion, appear to be offended and outraged and want to put Ida and Arnold in their place. Who do they think they are? They mock the entire Classics tradition, as if the humanities aren't struggling enough as it is, in terms of prestige, financially, in every way, and then some wannabe professor Arnold Bush decides to inflict the fatal blow on them, for his fifteen minutes of fame, to provoke as is his habit, provocation for provocation's sake. This time aided and abetted by this lightweight woman radio drama playwright, God knows what she has done before, but she certainly has no serious academic credentials.

They sit in bed, speechless. It takes ten minutes before they can speak. They had slept badly, but deep down they had been looking forward to it – go on, be honest – hoped for and looked forward to a little praise. If only for the unusual nature of the project, for its originality. But it was not to be. Not a kind word anywhere. Everyone is negative, aggressive even, out for blood. Slowly their defensive instinct awakens, out of disappointment and betrayal grows an urge to fight. Yes, it feels like a betrayal. It was unexpected, they were ambushed. They thought they were going to a birthday party, but they ended up in a fight. They had prepared themselves for celebration, instead it is a declaration of war. But if they want war, war they shall have, and Ida and Arnold won't spare their powder. The two of them against the world, that is how it is going to be from now on. They shake hands on it. They put their other work aside and get wound up together, punching the duvet, unable to write as quickly as they talk, as they think. One word inspires the next, the words of one inspire the other, just you wait. The two of them go into battle together, bent over their laptops in a state of outrage and euphoria and as the text grows on the screen, their outrage abates, their euphoria soars, finally they write for pleasure, out of happiness and look forward to submitting it, to see it in print and they have to go out and drink in order to sober up after this intoxicating experience.

'I'll drink to that.'

The two of them against the world, surrounded by enemies, together they are strong. Through thick and thin.

They seek out the worst dives in order not to meet people who read newspapers or listen to radio drama, to let off steam among the unemployed, benefit claimants, the divorced, the childless, the lonely, far away from the cultured elite, which has decided to hate them and which they now hate in return.

'I'll drink to that.'

No one can threaten their unity. This increasingly strong bond only they themselves can destroy. Hell is other people, fuck them, the fucking, self-righteous, sanctimonious, pathetic, cultured elite who are so easily shocked, who can't laugh at themselves, who never get drunk.

'I'll drink to that.'

They are nothing like their critics. They are like each other, like no one else. How amazing that there are only two of them in the whole wide world and that they just happen to have found each other. So that neither is forced to languish in a corner, which is what would otherwise have happened. Thank you for being you, Ida. Thank you for being you, Arnold.

They do battle in the newspapers for months. Their number of enemies grows, their number of friends falls, no one comes to their rescue, but they have each other and Professor Twig whom they defend to the death.

~

They book a weekend trip to northern Spain to recover. Arnold misses his plane to Oslo, and Ida can hear why in his voice. He denies it, but when their plane to Spain is delayed in Copenhagen due to fog and they are sitting in the airport, drinking, her fears are confirmed and she thinks: he is never going to change. If he can do that after they have been to war together. If he can do that *now*.

Did he not see their relationship the way she saw it, if he was willing to risk it all to fuck a student? Or, more likely, he thought about it the way she thought about it and moreover he was so sure of it, its rare quality, so confident was he that he didn't think it could ever be at risk, that it might come crashing down.

The dry, Spanish earth. Across the plain, through the wind, black horse, red moon. Alas, death waits for us before we reach Córdoba. People eat, sleep, kiss. They argue, they make up, they try to kill themselves. From time to time they feel tenderness for each other, from time to time they leave each other, they come back, from time to time they talk about something else, they don't cry all the time.

Ida is more light-hearted than Arnold, like the light in Spain, her mind is fundamentally lighter than Arnold's. Ida's attitude is never mind. Ida is June, she is quick, too quick at times. Arnold is slow. Arnold is pensive, Arnold is November. That is what it looks like.

They don't have the same need for closeness. Having the same need for intimacy or distance is important. He wants to be closer than she does. He believes that the person who wants to be the closest, the most intimate, is the person who loves the most, she disagrees, but she can't get her point across to him. She is as close to him as it is possible for one person to be to another without morphing, without losing herself, becoming dependent, although dependency is tempting. But she must have space. He strives for symbiosis and she feels its attraction, but soon needs to get back out, to the others. She needs other people. She loves him, but she looks forward to travelling with other people, without him. It is nice to be with other people when she knows she has him, her beloved in her heart, who is waiting, to have him to return to, to be away in the knowledge that he is there, at home, waiting while she is away. She can travel to another continent and feel her love for him, look forward to coming back to him to tell him what she has been doing in his arms. She has to travel, to go away so that she can come home again.

'I want you with me everywhere,' he says, 'on all my trips,' he says. 'Everywhere,' he says reproachfully as if it makes him better than her, his love greater than hers.

'Yes, but –' she begins.

'So you don't think I should have taken you with me to Sweden, to Denmark, to Germany in the past?' he asks.

'Don't get me wrong, please, Arnold! That's not what I'm saying, Arnold. I've enjoyed travelling with you! It has been brilliant to be away with you, accompany you on your travels! I'm grateful, Arnold! Please don't get me wrong,' she says, but she is unable to explain it to him. They have been together for years by now. She no longer feels the urge to jump on a train, on a plane the moment her children leave the house, to be with him, but she still loves him. And neither does she expect him to jump on the first train, on the first plane whenever he can, to be with her at any price, after all, they are an established couple now. Surely he can be in Trondheim for a day or two on his own, do his own thing, clear out his shed or something, while she is on her own, in Oslo, sorting out laundry. Mundane tasks they never do when they are together because they define the time they spend together as precious, even though this is the seventh year they are together, they define the time they have together as so precious that it wouldn't cross her mind to clear out the attic or do some gardening or clean the gutter or do the ironing when Arnold is with her even though they have been together for seven years, because Arnold wouldn't like it if she did the ironing on one of the evenings he is with her or started clearing out the attic when he is finally there after a week alone with his son in Trondheim and he will soon have to leave again, in only three days, and so Ida can't start raking up leaves in the garden because what would Arnold do in the meantime, he hasn't paid all this money to visit Ida just to sit on her sofa and twiddle his thumbs, has he?

'So shall I come?'

'Yes.'

'Sure?'

'I thought that was what we agreed?'

'Yes.'

'Sure?'

'It'll be quite hard. It'll be quite stressful.'

'There's no rush.'

'What do you mean?'

'That you don't have to get stressed on my account.'

'What do you mean?'

'No. I'm just saying. Take all the time you need, don't get stressed on my account, if it's stressing you out. You should do what you want to do, what you think is best.'

'Hm. [Pause] So what are you doing then?'

'Me?'

'Yes.'

'Tidying up. Sorting things out.'

'So you don't want me to come? Because you have other plans?'

'Of course not. Of course I want you to come.'

'It doesn't sound like it.'

'What do you mean?'

'Well, you're busy with all sorts of other things.'

'I'm just saying don't stress yourself out. You said yourself you'll have to hurry if you want to catch that train.'

'And what are you going to do tonight if I don't come.'

'Pardon?'

'Are you going out with your writer friends tonight?'

'Of course not.'

'I know you. That's what you'll end up doing.'

'What are you saying?'

'You'll find someone to go out with and then you'll stay out all night, I know what you're like.'

True, she increasingly wants to find someone she can go out with, stay out with all night, to escape, the urge gets stronger and stronger the longer they talk, the conversation has been going on for too long.

'Arnold!'

'So what are you going to do then?'

'Tidy up, I've already told you. In the garage, perhaps. But please come. I prefer you to come.'

'Are you sure?'

'Yes, I'll put a bottle of champagne in the freezer. I'll cook us a nice meal.'

'Do you mean it?'

'Of course I mean it.'

'So shall I try to make it?'

'Yes! I'll put the champagne on ice. Please come, Arnold!'

'Do you really want me to?'

'Yes! I can't wait to see you!'

He comes. She picks him up from the station. He comes, he is with her so intensely that it never crosses her mind to clear out the attic, do the ironing, to read a book in a different room. Perhaps it is not him, perhaps it is them, it is just how they are together. Perhaps he can't help it, perhaps she is oversensitive to his presence. She is reluctant to go to the laundry room and put on a load of washing, she will do so only if he is on the phone or bent over a saucepan, busy with something else, because any second he will call out: 'Ida! Where are you?'

When she isn't near him or close to him, her heart is in her throat.

She doesn't sit down to write unless he sits with his work next to her on the sofa. She doesn't sit down with a book unless he sits down with his books next to her, close to her on the sofa. It feels as if he is hoovering her brain, hoovering up her energy, commanding her attention so that she is constantly tuned to him, circling him, hypersensitive to his presence, perhaps he is unaware of it, perhaps he can't help it, it may well be her fault, something about her, her own damage. He is not doing anything, it is just the way it is. Her thoughts can't take flight when he is there. If they sit quietly talking about themselves, her thoughts can't take flight unless they take flight with his, in the same direction, they don't fly, they don't have wings of their own when he is close.

'What are you thinking?' he will ask. And she will say: 'I'm thinking about you!' And it is true.

'Where are you?' he wants to know and she scurries back to him, it is nothing he does, it is just the way it is. Not even in the car, it is in the car that she feels it the most, it is in the car that she misses it, that she can't daydream even during their long drives from Oslo to Trondheim, from Trondheim to Oslo, where they don't talk, where they sit in silence, her thoughts still can't take flight. They don't soar. It is impossible while he sits next to her, it is as if he can catch her thoughts before she has thought them, as if he has hung flypaper over her head. She doesn't thump her hands against her knees or the dashboard no matter what song plays on the radio because she can't surrender to the music, carefree like she used to be, because she is no longer her old, complete, whole self, but one half of a couple.

When they sit in bed together in the morning, drinking coffee, they tell each other that they feel sorry for ordinary people who have to go to work every day, commute by car to work, sit in a traffic jam, wear suits, an ironed shirt or a skirt suit and tights and polished shoes. They don't have to do that, how lucky are they. He hates it when someone calls her while they sit in bed, working. It disturbs him, she can feel it, even though she keeps her voice as low as she can, says as little as she can, she is aware that it ruins the mood that existed when the two of them were alone in bed. She senses his resistance. She senses his opposition so strongly that she whispers in order to end the conversation and be able to ring off. And the person she is talking to picks up on her anxiety and becomes anxious in turn and changes their voice and winds up the conversation sooner than he or she had intended, and if the caller is a man, Arnold's hostility increases and she becomes curt and dismissive and the man she is talking to senses it and brings the conversation to a close, a premature end, before he has managed to say what he called to say and learns to call Ida when Arnold isn't there. She gets scared when the telephone rings, she is startled when it rings in case she has to be curt with someone. She doesn't want to be curt or dismissive towards someone she doesn't want to reject, whom Arnold thinks she ought to reject, the chairman of the Dramatists' Association or other people he regards as enemies. Even before the telephone has rung she is scared that it might ring and that Arnold will freeze her out with his coldness and fall silent and punish her with his silence for hours afterwards and complain about how many people are forever calling her and about nothing, your telephone never stops ringing, he says when they are in Oslo, it is always ringing in Ida's house. He hates it, he says, that whoever rings always takes priority. That someone can ring and start to talk as if it is totally acceptable, without considering whether it is convenient for the person they have called.

'No one ever calls me at home,' he says as if that is a good thing. Sometimes he will fling aside the duvet theatrically, get up and dress to make it clear to her that she is ruining their morning with her unnecessary telephone conversations, he has an opinion about how necessary her conversations are and how long they ought to be.

'Was that call really necessary?' he says.

258

'She seemed to be doing most of the talking,' he says.

'You were just talking about rubbish,' he says. 'Nothing but gossip,' he says.

Sometimes he will time her: 'Twenty minutes,' he will say, checking his watch, 'you've been talking for twenty minutes about nothing at all!'

If they make love afterwards, then all is well again. If he hasn't got dressed and is sitting on a chair, sulking, they can make love and all will be well again. Even if he has got dressed and is sitting on a chair, sulking, all can be well again provided they make love. It just takes more time. She has to tiptoe up to him and undress him, warm him up, make him laugh, turn him on, entice him back into bed and make love to him, that usually does the trick.

When she is out running on her own, she listens to her Walkman. If she is running with Arnold, she doesn't, he gets annoyed if she does. Even though they don't talk while they run, she can't listen to it because it takes her to a place where he isn't, where she can lose herself in something he can't hear and she disappears to him. He will race ahead of her to demonstrate what he thinks of her Walkman, and she will turn it off and accelerate to catch up with him and she will shout:

'I'm not listening to it anymore! Look, Arnold!' she will call out, showing him her earphones hanging loose around her neck. She experiences a silent, undefined failure to thrive. Thoughts are stirring, thoughts are stirring inside Ida.

~

Her term as deputy chair of the Dramatists' Association comes to an end and she invites the board to a farewell dinner at her house. Arnold does the cooking; while she attends the board meeting, he cooks in her house, then he heads out into town with a friend. When the board meeting is over and they go back to her house, the food is ready and waiting in the kitchen, legs of lamb in the oven and home-made rosemary potato mash in a saucepan on the cooker. Arnold has gone out with a friend and will be back around midnight when her dinner party has finished. The next day they are flying to Istanbul to get married again.

The food is good. The board members praise the food. Ida says that Arnold cooked it. Silence. They have mixed feelings about Arnold. Ida is not the person she was before she met Arnold, irrespective of whose fault it is. When Arnold comes back around midnight, most of the guests have gone. The two who are still there are drunk. Arnold, too, has been drinking. A brawl breaks out. She doesn't remember the details, who says what, who starts it, who throws the first punch or who gets hit first, but they end up fighting, people rolling around the floor. Ida runs to her garage where she hides until it is over, until the guests leave, their taxi arrives and Arnold throws their coats, their umbrellas after them.

'Get the hell out of here!'

'You're mental! What the hell's wrong with you!'

'Bastards! Wankers.'

'Fuck you! I'm going to smash your fucking face in!'

'Arsehole!'

She is so tired of it. She is so, so tired. They get up at five o'clock in the morning, she has remembered to set her alarm clock, but only just. Arnold has slept on the sofa, he was furious and stayed up in the living room, drinking. The alarm clock wakes them and they get up, they try to get organised, money, passports, tickets, laptops, without talking, without saying anything. They call for a taxi and make it to the airport at the last minute, still without talking. They smell of alcohol, they doze on the plane from Oslo to Munich, without saying a single word, they don't speak. She is so tired. She finds a café where they can wait, they have to wait for an hour in Munich airport, by now it is ten o'clock, they order beer, once he has had his first beer, his mood will improve.

'Arnold!'

'Yes?'

'Arnold!'

'Yes?'

'Cheers, Arnold.'

He lifts his glass, drinks, then sets it down.

'Arnold!'

He lifts his glass, drinks, sets it down again.

'Arnold!'

He is smiling now, thank God, thank you Arnold, so she smiles as well.

'Why don't we just laugh it off?'

'Laugh it off? Do you know what they said! Morons!'

'We're not going to talk about it. We're going to forget all about it. We're going to have a nice time now. That beer hits the spot, doesn't it, Arnold?'

'Do you know what they said? Did you hear what they said?'

'No?'

'Didn't you? Did you hear what they said? Did you?'

'What, Arnold?'

'Did you hear what they called you?'

'Called me?'

'He had his hands on your tits when I came in.'

'No, Arnold.'

'He had his fucking hands on your tits, down your bra when I came in.'

'No, Arnold.'

'No? No? No?'

'I don't remember that.'

'Because you were drunk. As usual.'

'No, I wasn't.'

'That only makes it worse. Jesus Christ.'

He drinks. He just needs to keep drinking, order another round.

'Can't we just forget all about it? After all, it doesn't matter.'

'It fucking does. Twats. And those are the kind of people you work with.'

'Not anymore. I won't be working with them anymore, it's over now.'

'Thank Christ for that!'

'Let's drink to that.'

'Yes, let's drink to that.'

They drink to it. They order more beer and drink to it once more. They kiss each other to celebrate, they caress each other's arms and the back of their head to celebrate. Now it is over. Now it is back to being just the two of them again. Thank God. Abroad. Where nobody can disturb them. Where nobody knows them, where nobody calls. Just the two of them, thank God. Through the streets of Istanbul down to the harbour on the Galata side with a view of the Strait of Bosporus where they order champagne and say that they have just got married. The waiters bring flowers and a photographer takes a picture of them, that picture still exists. They are wearing sunglasses, they smile as they lean towards each other, interlacing fingers, sniffing each other's hair, the back of each other's ears. There is champagne on the table, champagne flutes, a bouquet of flowers, the books they are reading, the small diary she had back then, she can look up the entries. It says: But I still love him although he is a little mad. Then again, I'm a little mad too and we are most definitely mad when we are together. At a café now. Must work. Have had so many orgasms. Arnold has asked me to write that, so I do. My period is starting.

But some days earlier, before this trip, before the board members came round for the dinner party that turned into a brawl, one evening when she was on her own, while he was in Trondheim and she was reflecting on what he did in Denmark, what he did before the trip to Spain, she wrote: I can't force him to be only with me. I know that I'm the one he wants, so why does he keep jeopardising it? Perhaps he thinks about other women in a romantic or erotic context, which he wouldn't do if he had been able to live out all his fantasies, got it out of his system, except I can't say: Just do it! I'm so angry. I'm starting to detach from him. I can feel it, I can't relax with him. I have to compete, I have to win him over again and again, maintain my distance, which means that I, too, become just another fantasy. I want something else in my life. I believe in a third option. Perhaps there is a third option where we can be together as equals?

Their manuscripts lie on the table, they work even though they have just got married, they work on their wedding day. He writes about the process of translation, an essay which will be published along with his translation. She writes her stage play, when they get home she needs to finish it in order to get paid. Postcards and stamps lie on the table. They write postcards to people they know and they sign each other's postcards so everyone gets a greeting from Arnold and Ida. And Arnold tells Ida to write a postcard to the Dramatists' Association with the wording: In Turkey they arrest too many playwrights. In Norway they don't arrest enough.

When he is with her and her children are with her, when she has them all at the same time, sometimes it goes well, at other times not. When everything runs smoothly, when it is just the two of them, everything is fine, they go for walks, they shop, they go skiing or swimming and drink beer afterwards, but it doesn't lead to trouble as long as everyone is calm, and he cooks and there is a wonderful aroma in the house and the children look forward to coming home to dinner, hot food every night when Arnold is there and everything is quiet and the house is tidy and there is a log fire in the fireplace, the smell of logs burning in the winter, the smoke from the chimney as they walk up through the deep snow on the drive, just like when they stay in a cabin at Easter.

However, if they have meetings in town or on the rare occasions when they are invited to a dinner party or arts event where people might flirt with her, with whom she can flirt, he gets angry and they argue, and sometimes they don't stop arguing, they carry on after they have come home and he can't control himself, he screams that she is humiliating him and making him a laughing stock.

'You can't treat me like that,' he screams, he yells at her and pushes her, he grabs her by the shoulders and shakes her, he is out of his mind, he doesn't know what he is doing. He slams her against the wall and her children wake up and come downstairs and they are frightened and angry with him, and at times her children have shoved him outside and locked the door and told him that they won't let him back in. Then they lie in her bed with her and eventually they manage to fall asleep, but she can't sleep, what is he doing now, is he wandering around the garden?

At times he will leave of his own volition.

'I'm leaving! I'm not staying here a minute longer! Fuck you! You'll never see me again!' He takes his suitcase and his rucksack and tucks his laptop under his arm and staggers down the drive, scattering socks and underpants and razors behind him in the snow or on the grass, depending on the season. At times her children have pushed him outside and locked the door and called a taxi, at times he has taken it and at other times he hasn't, and she doesn't know where he is or what he might do next. Sometimes her children, who are now teenagers, have called the police because Arnold is slamming Ida against the wall and the police have turned up and taken him away and her children lie in her bed and sleep in her bed, but Ida can't sleep for guilt, towards the children, towards Arnold, towards everyone.

She doesn't dare let him come back for a while. Her children have said that they never want to see him again, that they hate him. Things have to calm down, everyone has to calm down first. He understands, he is not stupid, he has messed up, he understands.

If he comes to Oslo to work now, he will stay in a hotel, and she will tell her children that she is off to see a girlfriend and then meet him in secret, just like they did at the start. Forbidden and tantalising sex in hotel beds which are newly made with clean sheets. Dressed in a suit, he will meet her in the hotel lobby and they have a drink in the bar before they go upstairs and make love, and she calls her children and says she is staying over at a girlfriend's and asks if they have had dinner and if everything is OK. And if it is, which it usually is, they can relax and make love again; the next morning he has to work before he goes back home, to Trondheim, and she will travel up to stay with him as soon as her children go to stay with their father. They have been together for a long time, but there is always something new because they don't live like other people, that is for sure. Ida has finished her play, she gives it to him and he reads it and they discuss aspects she thinks are tricky, the catalyst. He reads the articles she writes for *The Journal* and discusses them with her, he helps her with the titles with which she often struggles. And she reads his translations and helps him with tricky words, and she reads his essay on translation and makes corrections with a pencil in his draft just like he edits and puts question marks in her texts. After Professor Twig they know what they are good at, the other's individual strengths and their differences, their differences are fewer than what they have in common, they agree, they agree on most things and they trust each other. If one of them gets a good review, the other is delighted even though it is best if they both get good reviews at the same time, that happens occasionally and that is the best. If one of them gets a bad review, the other is furious and hurt, as if the criticism, the panning, was directed just as much at one as at the other. Because they are a couple, they can't come to each other's rescue in public, they can't reference each other, promote each other in public, in print or verbally, but at home under the duvet, they compose their many defence speeches, what's mine is yours and vice versa, and if anyone touches even a single strand of hair on your head . . .

His translation has been published along with his introductory essay about the process. They go abroad so as to be away when the reviews come out, their second trip to Morocco. They sit close together in the taxi to the airport. They hold hands as they walk to the airport restaurant, order beer and slowly start to decompress, individually and with each other. Passports, foreign currency, bills paid, letters posted, houses locked up. Do you love me? Yes. They leave everything behind. Cheers me dears. Side by side in the taxi from the airport to the hotel. Twenty-four hours a day in the same room except when one of them needs the lavatory. Brecht's drama theories as translated and introduced by Arnold is out. They have gone abroad so as to be away when the critics have their say. Air Maroc from Copenhagen to get away from the sound of Scandinavian languages as quickly as possible, to where they can feel free, which they do when they are abroad, like Jane and Paul Bowles, in the North African desert. They have been there before. He stands on the hotel balcony and watches her cross the large, dusty square, make her way through the crowds to the phone box. She calls his publishers to gauge the reactions while he waits on the balcony. He doesn't want to do it himself. Ida isn't scared of calling, of asking. Thank God he has Ida. Thank you, Ida.

The book has been well-received. Well-received is good enough. After the Professor Twig furore, they can never be sure, they have many enemies in the old country, Arnold has made a list, it numbers more than fifty people. North Africa is the place to be, they will move here one day; when their children have grown up and don't need them anymore, they will move here like Paul and Jane, to eat majoun, which when consumed in substantial quantities will heighten your concentration for long periods of time, in order to work under parasols and in the evening when the sun goes down, they will drink gin and tonic on the sand by the sea and write new radio plays.

'Deal?'

'Deal!'

A new trip, a new project, always an element of surprise, an element of discovery to keep the infatuation alive. A sudden turn down a new road to see a completely different view, always an element of chance, an element of uncertainty: Hold my hand or I won't dare! An element of revelation: Look at us now! We're doing it!

No big newspaper features, but it was well-received, says his publisher. And so they buy champagne. Let's drink to that. They sit on the balcony in the evening when they have stopped working and watch the medina. Children run around the streets until midnight, a few yellow lamps are lit. There are people everywhere, they stand in dark alleyways, smoking. They can see the orange tips, how they breathe with the smokers. Men enter secret bars where they serve alcohol. Across the street stalls sell big, grilled chickens that glow as they turn on spits. One evening they will buy one. They have red wine and bread, now Arnold goes down amongst the Arabs in the twilight to buy one of the golden chickens on the spit. Ida sits on the balcony. The door slams. Now she is alone. Ninety seconds pass before she sees him down below, crossing the street. Her man. In his white shirt and khaki shorts, a little nervous of the strange Arabs in the darkness, but it is usually fine. Now he is at the stall, now he buys the chicken, now he turns, now he comes back, relieved that his mission has been accomplished. Arnold! In his white shirt, and his crumpled khaki shorts she has mended so many times. Does he still have them? Does he still wear them? Does he ever think of them?

They eat in the darkness on the balcony. The yellow lamps cast a golden, reddish glow across the medina. They throw whatever they can't eat over the edge, there is probably someone down there who wants it. Swallows fly. A black, changeable sky makes a sound like the wind. They don't write. It is too dark, the power socket is too far from the balcony and they have drunk too much. The next morning they walk down to the sea because the sea is beautiful to look at, it is necessary. Not down to the harbour, but to the sea, the endless sea, hand in hand, underneath the sun, in the heat to find a place where they can gaze at the sea, be outside while they work, the horizon arches so that they can see that the Earth is round, how the ships appear with their funnels, with their masts first, how water is held in place by gravity. They always lean their heads together after a while and become one head. They will bend over their work, shoulder to shoulder for a while, by the sea on which they rest their gaze while they think for hours before they lean their heads together. They told each other everything a long time ago, now they experience only the same things. They order the same, they eat and drink the same, there is nothing unfulfilled, no longing. When she comes home, when they part, she always throws up to rid her body of the shock of this sudden separation.

Is it my body or yours, your leg or mine? Where does your body end, where does mine begin and how can I desire you when you have merged with me. I rub myself against you or against myself or something, I touch you or me, whose fingers are where and what is the difference, your sweat, mine, your smell, mine or ours, whose orgasm, now that we have seen everything. We have looked as far as is possible, there is nothing left to discover. Magazines, films with ideas for expansion. Expand the bedroom, the hotel room, it can grow. It hurts a little to begin with. Then it gets better. When she thinks about it now, she still feels stirrings of desire. Perhaps it is sick, perhaps it is harmful. But they are not like other people. They are pioneers, rule-breakers. A club? One is mentioned in a magazine. Who says no? Ida doesn't say no. The word no doesn't exist in Ida's mouth. She forgets about it. He doesn't. One time when they visit the foreign city where the club is, he brings it up, does she fancy going. If you want to. She isn't scared. What is there to be scared of? If it doesn't kill you, it will teach you something. Nothing of human experience should be alien to her and so on, but she feels a knot in her stomach.

'But we don't know where it is,' she says, but he does.

'But we don't have the address,' she says, but he does. He has brought the magazine. He has thought of everything. He is serious. Something happens, doesn't he realise? Something happens, but does he not realise or does he not care? She hopes they won't be able to find it, but they do. The taxi takes them downtown, it is easy to find. It is closed, thank God. But it opens in one hour, all they have to do is wait. Arnold is excited. Ida traipses after him. Why not, if you absolutely insist. Ida isn't a prude. A glass of wine would be nice while they wait, they go to the nearest bar and drink. She keeps on drinking. Ladies get in for free. Men have to pay. There are red lamps in the reception, like in a small hotel, there is a naked woman behind the counter and condoms everywhere and in every room. They have to take off their clothes, they get numbered keys, everyone has to take off their clothes and be naked. They store their clothes in small lockers like at a railway station. Dimly lit, red rooms where men stand masturbating around a mattress where two people are fucking. Every single room has big mattresses where a couple is fucking, one or several couples are fucking or jerking each other off, and around them men are wanking, limp penises in their hands, the tried and tested movement with their right hand, back and forth, what are Ida and Arnold doing there? They lie down on a mattress and they fuck next to another couple who is fucking, they reach out their hands for other bodies. Then they watch porn in a kind of cinema, behind them single men are wanking as they watch the screen where people are fucking people in every possible orifice, if you squint all you can see is the rhythm, in and out, something moving in and out, the old tried and tested rhythm, slightly faster every now and then before it stops for a moment with a moan and then more of the old tried and tested movement onwards, onwards. Prominent, hairy pussies or proud, hairless pussies, pink and dark red, almost blue pussies, plain buttocks with pimples and lips sucking bulging, purple cocks, teeth with black fillings and costume jewellery, rings in ears, in nipples, labia, the state of their teeth suggest they are East European. The men jerk off. Arnold is touching a woman, he touches Ida and Ida is touched and touches Arnold, while the men jerk off, well, we're here now, but get me a drink first. They fuck on a mattress next to other couples and reach out their hands for other bodies, Arnold touches someone else. Arnold touches another woman's breast, the breast of the woman lying next to him, in the way he touches Ida's breast, in the exact same way, with the exact same hand. He touches the other woman's pussy, the pussy of the woman lying next to him, with the hand with which he usually touches Ida's pussy, in the exact same way he touches Ida, he may be choosing to touch her, the other woman, rather than Ida, for the sake of variety, yet he still does it in the exact same way, which makes it worse, it is why they are here, to touch, to be touched, by others, she hates it, she is sinking, she doesn't say anything, but she is sinking. This is where it starts. If it hadn't already started, then this is where it starts. He touches the other woman's breast, the other woman's pussy in the same way he touches Ida, Ida's breast, Ida's pussy, Ida is right there and yet he touches the other woman, but in the same way, which makes it worse. Love is only possible where there is innocence, a tiny little bit of innocence, a little bit of trust. The knowledge that you can't be substituted, that you are not replaceable or interchangeable, that the hands of the beloved and a stranger can't be the same, that they can't touch a stranger in the same way they touch someone familiar and loved, that hands, when they can choose, will always choose the beloved. They are quiet in the taxi on their way home. The experience turns them on. They have sex all night and in the morning, it turns them on, but makes them sick, they can't go to the seminar they are meant to attend. Arnold can, Ida can't, she is unable to get up, Ida is sick, they have to call and say so: Ida is sick, it is true, she can't get out of bed. Turned on by it all night, perhaps he thinks they both are, but she is alone.

They try to understand it. Afterwards, at the airport, on their way home. They abandon the seminar, they go home and try to understand it, why Ida feels so outside. Arnold is sad because Ida feels outside. She isn't so interchangeable after all that he doesn't get sad or worried and tries to talk about it, to reason it out. Ida's breast or the breast of another woman, they are both the same and yet completely different. He can come with any woman and it will feel pretty much the same, she already knows that. It is like that for everyone, she already knows that too. Except it is not like that for Ida, but she doesn't say so. No one must know what it is like for her. He must not know how alone she is. They drink. That helps. Soon they laugh it off. We learn, we grow, they tell each other. We're pioneers, rule-breakers, we embrace the darkness and we learn, we grow, they tell themselves and each other, we seek knowledge all the time. Anyone afraid to tremble is a coward, they say. But they are not cowards and that is why they are trembling now.

Do you feel freer now? No. More intimate? Perhaps it glues them together. They suture their bodies together with a sharp needle. They get to know each other's bodies better, each other's desires and responses. They look deeply into each other, they learn as much as is possible, they watch each other with strangers, in ever new situations, anything you can imagine, isn't that a good thing? His

275

hand cupping another woman's breast. As it has cupped countless women's breasts, also while they have been together. That is just how real life is. It is just the real world.

She is unable to get out of bed. It makes her ill. It turns her on. They have a lot of sex. She can never get enough, she will never be sated, never satisfied, never completely filled up. She is distraught, but if they could start over, they would have done exactly the same. Do you ever have a choice? You can't regret yourself. When they come home, drunk, he calls the editor of the magazine and asks if there are such clubs here as well which can make her feel like that.

Keep drinking to avoid the hangover. So they do it again, expand their limitless world. It is impossible to understand it fully. The truth is always wrong, even if it is one hundred per cent the truth. They buy magazines and try out suggestions in them. They read them while they fuck. They stare at other dicks going in and out of other pussies and mouths and bums, fresh stimuli, fresh excitement. They seek out new clubs. They undress among strangers in the glow of red lamps, they have sex among strangers in the glow of red lamps. They touch strangers and are touched in the glow of red lamps. They stick their fingers into other bums, others touch them, they are rarely fully awake, although they seldom sleep. The novelty wears off quickly and they soon get bored. They are always on the lookout for something more. Perhaps it is not surprising, but they don't talk about it. Neither of them does, and they are people who normally talk about everything.

So that I can say that I have tried everything, she tells herself. So that I have experienced every kind of feeling. To see what it does to her, what it does to him, if anything happens, if they survive or possibly trigger their breakup – she tells herself. In order to have experienced it before it happens, so that it won't ambush her, a river she doesn't know, hasn't prepared for and might end up drowning in. There he is having sex with someone else. Look!

They have a system. One week Ida is alone with her children in Oslo, the following week Arnold is in Oslo with Ida and Ida's children, the week after that Ida is in Trondheim with Arnold and his son, the week after that, the fourth week, they are alone, they mostly go abroad if they can, it is not easy to explain to others. They don't feature in any statistics. They don't exist for the authorities, they love each other, but there is no official record of them being a couple. When they are apart, they deal with practicalities so that nothing needs doing when they next meet, they go through the non-weeks on autopilot, with half a brain, only half present, until they can be together again.

They have a system. Skiing across Nordmarka in the darkness, near the floodlit track. Quietly in the darkest place after the downhill slope. Just the two of them. Afterwards to the nearest restaurant with a licence, the Chinese, two beers and then an illegal drive home. Two beers in their skiwear before they go home and cook dinner and read the newspapers. Hello you. Are you in there somewhere? Look at me.

'Are you in there?' he asks.

'I think so.'

'There's someone in there who is watching me,' he says. 'Isn't there?'

'I think so. It feels like it.'

They go running around the lakes in the summer and swim in them afterwards. She swims naked, they are always alone, it is like an old photograph. He keeps his underpants on, they are grey, she remembers how he looked. Beloved Arnold. He lifts his thin-skinned, bare feet from the rocks and sets them down gingerly. She goes in first, he follows. Her heavy breasts float in the water. They kiss each other in the water. More frequently in the early years than in the later ones. They don't kiss each other as much in the later years as they used to, as they did during the early years. But they make love every day. In new ways or in the same old, quick way. From behind, she touches herself, it takes them less than five minutes.

'When do you want to make love?' he asks in the morning while the children are at school. Before they come home from school or tonight when they are in bed? They check the time and decide. At times they put it off until the evening, but then they drink too much and fall asleep.

'We didn't make love yesterday,' he says sternly the next morning.

They have a system, summers are spent in a cabin by the coast, his child and her children, sausages on the barbecue. They manage it, they see it through. He cooks, barbecues with a drink on a rock, in shorts and wearing a Panama hat against the sun. His child with his friends and her children with their friends, ten or twelve of them, scrambling over the rocks, hollering, towards the sea.

In Casablanca, Morocco – because they are starting to look like a married couple, people ask them:

'How many children do you have?'

And Arnold raises his hands and proudly displays three fingers.

Why don't they make a baby, have a child together? They could have one. If they want to, they can, it's that simple. They have never loved anyone like this. They will never love anyone like this, why don't the two of them make a baby?

'Would you have a child with me?'

He cries again, no one has ever said that to him before. What would their child look like? A dark, petite girl with olive eyes. But it is probably not such a good idea after all. With Slavic features, after my slave, she says and he smiles. My dumb waiter, who isn't dumb. Yes, from time to time he is, especially with the children. He helps her shop for groceries, carries them inside, puts them away in cupboards, he cooks, chops wood. Dumb, mute, but present in his muteness. He hoovers the house in silence, he lets the silence flow.

In the spring they go to the cabin by the coast, just the two of them, in order to work, in order to run under the white sky. While other people go about their nine-to-five lives. If it is warm, they swim in the sea. If it is cold, they pack red wine and glasses, walk to the furthest rock and watch the sea turn red as the sun sets. It is windy, but they have blankets and fleeces over their knees and they sit close together. Wind in their faces, wine in their mouths, why can't they stay there for ever, away from everything.

They travel as soon, as often as they can. They write down, then circle all the places they have been together. It is a long list and it grows steadily. They hope to write a book about their trips, about what happened there, in Trondheim, in Oslo, in Copenhagen and Paris where they have been many times.

One time they are running late and don't get seated next to each other on the plane. Arnold is cross. Ida is a slowcoach, the one who says: Never mind! It'll be fine! Who leaves things to the last minute, optimistic, who must always check, for the umpteenth time, that the cooker is turned off.

'It'll be fine,' she says, 'we'll make it.'

And they do, but they don't get seats next to each other. Which was what he had feared. Which was why he wanted them to hurry. Now does she see that he was right? They have to sit apart, it represents a change. He doesn't want to ask if they can swap seats. He doesn't want to cause any trouble. Arnold never steps forward to demand something. Arnold never makes a scene. Which is ultimately a good thing. Arnold stays in the background and doesn't make a fuss in public offices, in airports, in hotel lobbies. You could forget Arnold was there, given how quietly, how modestly he stands in a corner. Ida asks, Ida steps forward and shouts, and usually solves the problem.

'It'll be fine!' Ida says and pats Arnold on the head, but it isn't fine this time. She inquires if they can swap seats so they can sit together, but they can't, so this time it is not going to be fine. Arnold is cross, Arnold shuts down so she has to mollify him. As soon as they turn up with the drinks trolley, with the wine, as soon as he gets a drink, things will improve.

She turns to smile and wave, he doesn't smile, he doesn't wave back. She passes him on her way to the lavatory, bends down and kisses him on the head, it is no good, he has shut down, it is her fault that he has to sit on his own. But once the drinks trolley has been and he has had a few bottles of wine, a flight attendant brings Ida a folded piece of paper, a note from Arnold:

Darling Ida. I miss you terribly! I look forward to seeing you again when we finally meet! The most beautiful woman and my best friend in the whole world!

Kisses to my migrating bird. Love from the man at the back of the plane.

She writes back, drinks wine and looks out into the blue void, she loves him, the two of them will be together for ever, anything else is unthinkable, you can only be this close to one person, and when you realise that, then that person becomes indispensable and you become hooked on them. They write notes to each other all the way to Paris and when they meet at the luggage belt, they hug as if they haven't seen each other for ages, two hours alone among strangers is a long time when it happens unexpectedly.

They are so engrossed in each other, so outside the world that occasionally they will arrive at the airport a day too early, they think it is the eighth, but it is the seventh, or a day too late, that has also happened, they arrive at the airport on the thirteenth when their tickets are for the twelfth so they have to buy new tickets to get home. They lose track of morning and evening, day and night, themselves and the other, everything blurs, there is only space, no time anymore, just mass, body, the only thing that is missing is them taking drugs – had anyone offered some, they would probably have said yes.

Early on he writes her postcards from the places they visit together, he will buy a postcard without her knowing and also write it without her knowing, when she goes to the lavatory or out on an errand, on the back of a restaurant bill or on a beer mat, put it in an envelope and post it without her knowing so it is in her mailbox when she gets home or a day or two later, a greeting from the place where they have just been. He doesn't stint his words, he uses only the grandest. She wonders about other couples. How can the others be happy when they don't have what we have?

A wagtail lives behind her garden wall. It flies around, constantly busy, but they never see another one, no mate, no chicks.

'A divorced wagtail,' Arnold says and tilts his head. 'Poor thing. Never leave me. I'll kill you. I'll kill myself!'

No matter how open he pretends to be, he is never entirely open. No matter how vulnerably he presents, he is never completely vulnerable. No matter how desperate he seems, he is never truly desperate. He calls to say that he is going to kill himself, but he is one of those people who never will. He might appear needy, but he has his own campfire, he can survive anything. She is the one who might perish.

'I'm coming to get you,' he whispers, lying behind her, talking into her hair. 'I'm going to fucking get you. I want all of you just for me! I fucking love you, you're mine, hit me!'

She tries to, but she can't do it.

'You're such a flirt! You're flirting! Why do you need to have people looking at you, you want them to look at you, don't you?'

Yes. Perhaps she does. She seduces, he seduces, they are seducers, they pose, they are poseurs, but from different starting points, they have different objectives. Language is their means but to different ends. He, the man, needs to get it right in, that is the test, that a woman drops her knickers. For her, the woman, it is enough to know that she could if she wanted to. A look is enough for her. The seminars, when he lectures, that is where he scores, otherwise nothing, no lectures no sex. To watch him lecture, command the room in his unique, quiet way doesn't make her proud of him, it drives her crazy with desire, an aggressive desire, just like he feels angry rather than proud of her whenever she makes someone laugh and he immediately wants to destroy them, kill anything that threatens their love, which might cause them to break up one day, so they drink each other ugly, they drink each other fat and wrinkled, they drink each other poor, they beat each other until the blood flows, they give each other terrifying scars, they bring about mutual destruction.

If only it wasn't a pattern. If only she hadn't seen how much he needs it. If only she didn't know that every time he is away on his own there is a real danger that it could happen again, if only she didn't know that every time he is cross with her, feels offended, which he often does, it could happen again. Pre-emptive anxiety, exhausting scenes during discovery, exposure, the never-ending arguments, it can always be brought up again and recycled. It would be a relief to let it go and be free of it, when you have experienced something else, when you know that it could be different.

There is something she doesn't know. There is something he hasn't told her, she knows that much. Though she hasn't worked out what he did, it exists, it is in the air.

'Did something happen in Switzerland?' she asks. 'Did something happen in Århus? Did something happen in Seljord that time when you didn't call me?'

'You're definitely wrong about Seljord,' he says, so does that mean that she was less wrong when she asked about Switzerland, about Århus?

Who doesn't want an adventure? Familiarity is all well and good, but predictable and humdrum in the long run. Who doesn't dream about a life with no bills, no laundry, no mortgages or kids? Arnold does! A purely erotic space with a postgraduate or an undergraduate who admires him, her tutor, her professor, to be irresistible for a few hours, wise, fiery, invent yourself and present yourself at your most advantageous to this semi-stranger who swallows you raw. Who doesn't need to be worshipped and admired like that? Arnold does! He needs that and she knows it and fears it and on the rare occasions she stops by his office, she dreads finding something revealing, a woman's knickers between the sofa cushions, a used condom in the waste bin, so she doesn't look in his waste bin while he is there, she doesn't look at his screen while he is there in order not to see the name of a woman she doesn't know and lose face while he is watching, a handwritten note in his in-tray, an earring under his desk, if only she could have his office to herself for an hour! She never looks his colleagues in the eye in order not to see that they know something she doesn't, perhaps a half-naked student ran out of Professor Bush's office half an hour ago with the flames of orgasm on her chest. When she drinks, she can't stop herself from asking about the women she fears he might have been with, about the women she knows he has been with, she digs and probes for details in order not to live in uncertainty, but the more she learns, the more distraught she becomes. How many times did you have sex that night? How old is she? Twenty-eight, he says, if you absolutely must know. What does she look like, is she pretty. She can't help humiliating herself with her growing list of questions. When he is out, she rifles through his flat like a lunatic, turning out pockets, sniffing clothes, looking for smears of lipstick. She fine-combs papers, receipts, the bin for anything compromising, hoping to find something. If she finds something, she will kill him. If he calls to say he will be late, her imagination spins out of control, she rings his former mistresses to hear their voices and everything becomes fuel on the fire, which burns and crackles so hot in her chest that she can't breathe. She screams and wants to hit him because of what he has done, but nothing helps, she is furious but impotent, obsessed by unbearable images of hotel beds.

He denies it and she can't prove it. She knows, she is sure, she has every reason to be angry, but she lacks proof.

She never gets the evidence to justify being as angry as she is and it's driving her insane.

No, she isn't in love with him, not like she used to be. And he knows it, that she isn't on her knees as before, no one can be after so many years, but he doesn't like it, he doesn't accept it, he has grown accustomed to her being on her knees, he has become dependent on her being on her knees, he picks up a butter knife far away and she reacts as if he was right next to her with an axe. He is losing, that is probably what it feels like to him, it feels like a defeat, as if he is teetering, that he is losing control, her attention, what if she starts to look elsewhere?

She loves him and wants to be with him, she writes that to him. I love you and I want to be with you. I'm sorry I didn't ring you the other day and I'm sorry that I came back later than I had said I would. It was mostly because of the children, but possibly also because of you. But I don't think it is such a big deal and I think it's unfair for you to draw such extreme conclusions about our relationship based on my transgression. It is also hard for me when you don't accept my apology. I can't get a word in. The moment I start a sentence, you just talk over me and milk it grotesquely in a never-ending rant, dismayed, offended, irreconcilable. You accuse me of lying, you don't believe me when I say I'm sorry, you go on and on: So you would rather go drinking with your writer friends than have a real relationship with me? Answer me! Do you? You prefer to go drinking with your writer friends! Yes! You do! You're talking crap! I don't want to listen to your crap any longer. It's just bullshit! Your kids are home alone, you're out getting drunk, you don't give a toss about me, I don't exist for you, you can't even be bothered to call. You keep telling me that you're bored with your writer friends, but that's nonsense, I have to stop listening to your bullshit! You want to get drunk with your writer friends, you don't give a damn about me and from now on I'm not going to be so readily available! And so on, and so on and so forth.

And it goes on and on and never ends. It is humiliating to hear you say over and over that I lie, that I'm drunk, that I don't care and so on and so on and so forth, I'm trying to go to sleep, I have work in the morning, meetings, but my adrenaline is spiking. I try to make you switch off the light, I try to make you stop drinking, I say – when you have been raving for almost two hours – that if you don't stop, then I'll sleep in another room. Because I haven't got the energy to listen to you any longer. You don't stop and I get ready to go to another room. You tell me that if I do that, you are leaving. So I stay put, but you go on and on, the same complaints over and over until finally I go to another room, and you leave.

Arnold! You get yourself into a state where the dimensions of my 'transgression' are exaggerated, while at the same time you force me to defend myself through your distorted lens though you refuse to listen to anything I have to say. There is no conversation, no exchange, it is purely your endless frustration, in which you are completely caught up, it seems almost as if it becomes meaningful in itself, to you, while at the same time it is essential for you that I am present and take it. If I try to extricate myself, you threaten to leave, which gives you power over me, you force me to stay, to listen to your grievances, which I don't think are justified. Why should I put up with it? Yesterday you broke me. You threatened to leave so I stayed where I was, but you went on and on and I felt so trapped, so controlled, so crushed by your narrative that I broke.

If he does X or Y, it can go back to being the way it was. If he does something that upsets her, which isn't hard, she gets needy and clings and says she can't live without him, only him, and then their relationship is more like the way it once was, the way it is supposed to be. She thinks now, long afterwards, that he subjected her to things from which he should have shielded her. Whenever she surrendered like a child, their relationship would once more be like the way it used to be, the way he wanted it to be. Perhaps he didn't do it deliberately, perhaps he didn't do it consciously, but that was what happened.

They have been invited to a wedding. She is the matron of honour and is due to give a speech. A spring wedding, and no, they are not the ones getting married.

'You don't want to marry me!' he says.

'Of course I do, we're going to get married.'

'When?'

'Next year perhaps, like we decided on that first beer-for-breakfast day.'

'You don't want to.'

'Of course I do.'

She is invited to the wedding at the registry office, to drink champagne with the nearest family afterwards because she is the matron of honour. She stands on the terrace with her champagne flute in the sun, in a fine dress, with a fine speech in her handbag, it could be a very nice day. Arnold is the external examiner at Oslo University, they will meet at the party later, she needs to be composed, she is about to give a speech, he has finished his week of being the external examiner and he can relax, chill out, can't he? Warm summer in Oslo, all the bars are open, chairs and tables on the pavements. The wedding party, a blushing, infatuated bride with flowers in her hair and bare, innocent shoulders. A proud and slightly agitated groom. Both of them said so clearly: I do! When they were asked by the registrar dressed in black.

'How lovely you look,' Arnold says. Yes, she does look lovely. Her speech is entertaining, she pulls it off, yes, she is clever, the guests are laughing, now she, too, can raise her glass, job done, relieved she chats exuberantly to the bride's seventy-six-year-old uncle and after dinner she dances with him, while Arnold feels ignored on a sofa, it becomes apparent when he knocks over a table, a bottle breaks and

Ida knows what comes next so she runs, grabs her handbag and runs, takes a taxi home and doesn't know if he will come back to her house while hoping that he won't because her children are there, and Arnold is angry drunk.

She has work the next morning, a debate about theatre and values in Studenterlunden, he knows about it and turns up there, crestfallen and anguished. He is tearful. It is a vicious cycle, the more he breaks and destroys, the more frightened he is of losing and his fear takes over when he drinks, it makes him turn nasty. She has rarely seen him tremble so much. They find a bench and sit down, he shakes and sobs, how can she help him?

His finances are a mess, disaster is looming, he is still arguing with Kjersti about custody arrangements for their son, she is threatening to take him to court, Ida's children hate him, everything is miserable, he feels miserable, what is she going to do? Leave him. Let him suffer the consequences. It is impossible, it becomes increasingly impossible or so it feels. Their lives and work are so interwoven that she feels she is suffocating, but then again when he is not there, she still struggles to breathe as if she shared a single lung with him.

They show each other how they masturbate. They tell each other how they were with other people, what they did and how they did it with other people. They tell each other their fantasies and they live them out. They read porn magazines and do the things described in them. They use kitchen utensils and carrots, French batons which slowly go soggy. They might go to bed with a toolbox, they drink and urinate on each other and cause havoc and are scared to go down to the hotel lobby in case anyone has heard how they yelled and hit each other and went mental all night. In Paris she dances in the street while he plays his accordion and people drop money in Arnold's Stetson, they make 300 francs in a few hours that night, they are drunk, of course.

It is hot, a summer heatwave. In Copenhagen windows and doors are left open, even at night. A columnist in the Danish newspaper, *Politiken,* writes about it. His wife is heavily pregnant and can't sleep, she keeps tossing and turning at night. In addition, he writes, an infatuated couple is having loud sex in the flat across the street. When they are finally done, the rest of the neighbourhood is so inspired by them that everyone starts to have sex in their own bedrooms. He writes about it, a funny little column which they read on the plane going there. They pick Danish newspapers rather than Norwegian ones. A long weekend in Copenhagen, she doesn't remember why, what the occasion is, perhaps it is just because they feel like it and they have money and want to go away, and as previously mentioned it is summer and hot, no other reason for going away other than wanting to, no excuse necessary. They take a room at the Hotel Ibsen and head out into the city in light summer clothes to eat Japanese food, she can't remember how it kicks off, not that it matters, it is probably the usual story. They quarrel, she can't take any more, throws herself into a passing taxi and finds another hotel where she can sleep in order not to argue with him all night. The next morning she goes to the Hotel Ibsen to pick him up, hoping that he has calmed down so that the rest of their weekend can be nice, so that they can do something together. She finds him in bed. All her things are scattered across the floor, toiletries, their duty-free bottles, everything that can be broken has been broken.

She lies down beside him in the bed, he is exhausted, semi-conscious. At seven o'clock the hotel reception rings to tell them to leave. They are no longer welcome guests at the Hotel Ibsen. So they leave. Two days later, they read in *Politiken* a piece by the writer whose column they read on the plane going there, who wrote about the heat and his pregnant wife who couldn't sleep, he writes that after the lovemaking and the heatwave, they were then kept awake half the night by a Norwegian man standing in a window calling for his girlfriend: Ida! Ida! Where are you?

They are tired of working. They are tired of newspapers, tired of books, of theatre, of reviews. They are tired of each other, but too tired to break up, dependency makes people miserable. They are tired of being parents. They are tired of getting up in the morning, of the thought of having to get up in the morning, of the thought of all the years they have to live, the thought of maybe living to eighty, autumn is looking at them.

'We're just going for a walk,' they say to the children and escape out into the November darkness to the nearest café with an alcohol licence, the Chinese restaurant if they are in Oslo, the shopping centre café if they are in Trondheim. Out into the rain through wet streets, without talking, their hair and their shoulders get wet. They take off their coats and stagger to their regular table in the furthest corner.

'The usual?' says the bartender in a compassionate tone of voice and they nod and he brings two beers which they down immediately and they gesture to him and he brings them two more.

'I'm off for a wank,' he says and takes a porn magazine with him to a bedroom, they have rented a holiday cabin in Denmark in order to write.

'You're welcome to watch,' he says and she does, he likes her watching him, and he asks if he can watch her and she takes off her trousers and shows herself to him and touches herself and he comes and then she comes, she touches herself while he caresses her buttocks. It is starting to feel more and more like doing the dishes or mopping the floor. From the front, from the back, from everywhere, if there is something we haven't done yet then let's give it a go, why not, it makes no difference. They urinate on each other, it is just a warm sensation across their face and chest, like a caress, and it doesn't smell. Why remain in ignorance about anything they can experience, the scale of surprise, jealousy, joy, nostalgia, anger, everything they are capable of feeling, why not? Or is it dangerous to live out your secret dreams, are they really acting out their deepest fears?

There is a regional event to celebrate the anniversary of a late dramatist. The guests are staying in a B&B in the middle of nowhere. Do they think it might happen, is it something they have considered trying, seeing as they decide to go? A woman approaches Ida early in the evening, she says her name is Ida, two Idas at the same event is unusual. Arnold sits with his arm across her knees, there is a photo of it, it really is her. Ida is resting her legs on the chair next to her and Arnold has his arm draped over her knees, she belongs to him. The short, fat Ida approaches Ida and something happens, afterwards it is difficult to explain how it could happen, how it started, how both of them suddenly knew what was going to happen, without anyone saying anything, suddenly they are in the same room. It has to do with the mood. In their bedroom. Ida and the much shorter, fat Ida, small, fat Ida's husband and Arnold, with wine and vodka, they undress, they haven't tried this so it must be tried. One step closer. Strike out normality in yourself, it is a fake normality, a societal construct, they think – if they think, that is. It can't be reconstructed. Four naked people. Ida with the other Ida's husband on top of her on one bed, Arnold with the other Ida on the other. Their bodies are so similar. As are the shoulders over which hands glide, as are penises that rise when touched, back and forth in the same old way. The hairs at the back of the neck and on the chest. The hand between the legs, searching in the same old way, finding the moist hole and navigating from there. She can do it in her sleep, she can do it no matter how drunk she is. The same movement with the hips like dogs do. Some people like having their ears kissed, so kiss their ears. Some like a finger up their bum, so stick a finger up their bum. When he comes, Arnold says: I love you! It works. Arnold says as he caresses breasts, a waist: How pretty you are! And it works. She always says it now, I love you, when she comes, how handsome you are, while she caresses him, he has taught her well. She is having sex with the other man when suddenly Arnold gets angry. He screams and goes crazy. He hits her, then runs out and slams the door, wails, disappears. They get up, they come to their senses, so it wasn't a good idea after all. It wasn't what they thought it would be. He can't handle it. No wonder. Ida can't handle it either, but she has lost the ability to say no. Arnold has gone. Arnold runs screaming and swearing down the corridor, he wakes people up, they come outside and grab hold of him.

'She's fucking another man! Kill her!' Fat, little Ida and her husband leave the room. Ida stays in the bed. Arnold comes back, someone has grabbed his shoulders and steered him back to the room where they are staying. He attacks her. He is not big, she isn't afraid of him, just tired. Tired from deep inside and all the way out. He shakes her, he seizes her shoulders and shakes her, slamming her against the wall, she is so tired, so almost dead that he can do whatever he wants to her.

They don't have breakfast the next morning, they don't take part in the celebration. They leave as soon as they wake up, they pack their things and throw away anything that isn't theirs, empty vodka bottles and two unfamiliar pairs of pants, one female, one male, so it wasn't just a bad dream. They tiptoe outside when the place seems deserted, when no one is likely to see them, as quietly as they can, scratched, upset, broken. They leave and they don't talk all the way back. The children are waiting. This can't really be written down, it can't be thought, it can only be lived.

They soldier on. As if it is a virtue. They plan trips abroad as if it is an external problem, other people they need to get away from. They book hotel rooms, they go out drinking and return to their hotel room to drink and then go out again. It is madness, but they can't help themselves. What they are seeking, what they are drowning in, is never mentioned. Every now and then they feel scared, they exist in a state of profound grief. They cry. But they don't talk. They are mourning that they no longer love each other. They know nothing more than that, that is what they are saying without saying anything, they can no longer speak. They drink. They can't get close to each other without fear, without trembling.

They spill out of the train at Kongsberg for the jazz festival, they have been drinking, they are still drinking, hanging on each other's arms, but they both know: it can't go on. They buy tickets, they listen to the music, she dances with another man, he doesn't like it, but he doesn't have the energy not to like it, he is drained of strength so nothing happens, they no longer fight, they no longer kiss, they just lie down and turn to the wall, separate walls, back to back, they no longer make love or they do it the old way, in five minutes or less, in four and a half minutes or three, he on top of her, behind her, she touches herself and she dreams herself away, there has to be something better than this.

A dingy hotel, a dingy café, they stay there half the night, until the morning and in the morning, late morning, before the train leaves, all they want to know is: Where can we get a beer at this time? At Andy's, and they go there, but on entering they discover to their horror that someone is reciting poetry inside and beat a hasty retreat.

It is unthinkable that the two of them won't be together for ever, and that thought is what drains them, exhausts them.

Arnold arranges a trip to Berlin with his students. He is their tutor, Ida comes with them as the professor's other half. Ida starts it, it is Ida's fault, if blame must be apportioned. She sets it in motion. She tells Arnold's colleague, an unhappily married, sexually frustrated man, as soon as they are at the airport or on the plane or at the hotel terrace on the night they arrive in the hot Berlin air, that they have done it many times, her and Arnold, with other people, when she has been drinking she brags about it. When they have gone to bed, there is a knock on the door: Arnold's colleague is outside with an undergraduate and a bottle of spirits.

Nothing happens that night, but it does on the following. On the roof terrace in the darkness when the others have gone to bed, she stays up chatting to the undergraduate, who is drunk, she confides in Ida, she is crying, and all Ida can think is: Be kind to her. How can I help her? She strokes her hair and lets her rest her head against her chest and the undergraduate cups her breast. She cups Ida's breast and presses her face, her mouth against the other breast as if she wants to kiss it, and Ida kisses her hair and the undergraduate turns her face towards hers and they kiss each other on the lips. Ida touches her, her large, available breasts, the large, very pink nipples that contract and harden in her mouth. The fat white stomach, a source of shame, Ida kisses it as if to say: You're good enough. You're so pretty. Behind the big air-conditioning plant on the roof garden, they are alone, it will be morning soon, it is already dawning, she kisses the big white belly, the belly button, she places the palms of her hands on the inside of the undergraduate's thighs, prising them apart, and says again: You're so pretty! She kisses the brown hair. She kisses the small, red bud that grows as she kisses it, sucks it, kisses the opening from where moisture is running, sticks her tongue into the wet opening as if she were a man, kissing around it, the blue, dripping pussy, waits until it is almost unbearable, like she knows it can be, and then she sucks it, slurping noises, sighs, the rhythmic breathing she recognises from herself, she knows what it feels like, now, and now, and now, just before, now she comes, the wet pussy trembles. The swollen, wet pussy trembles, the big white belly trembles. Then they go their separate ways, each to their room. Arnold is asleep. He will be getting up in a few hours to take his students on an excursion.

She is alone. Is it the alcohol, the sex, the drama or is it everything at once, it is too much. The undergraduate is young, perhaps she doesn't know what she is doing. It is madness. Ida can't stay inside, she can't be outside, she can't sit, she can't walk. She is distraught, all she can do is pray, except that doesn't help either. Dear God! I'm not praying not to suffer. I'm not praying to escape the pain. I will take my pain like other people take theirs. I know there is an infinity of pain out there, but this particular pain that you are inflicting on me right now is unbearable.

She calls her children to hear their bright voices after school, she is standing by the telephone in the hotel lobby when she walks past, the woman from the roof, the undergraduate, she hasn't gone on the excursion with the others but stayed at the hotel, she must be as upset, Ida thinks, as Ida is. She happens to walk by while Ida is standing by the telephone in the lobby.

'Hello,' she says, she looks lost.

Has Ida hurt her? She has to talk to her, ask her. The student has sat down in the hotel garden with a beer. Ida also orders beer and downs half of it at the bar before she goes outside, to the young woman from the roof, from last night, the unreal night, and asks if she can join her and the young woman smiles and looks happy, Ida thinks, sits down next to her and asks cautiously. The young woman smiles. She has done this before, she says. Ida mustn't worry.

When Arnold and the students come back, when they have had dinner and been drinking, she tells him. He doesn't think it matters.

Ida issues the invitation. Ida says: You can join us. Why does she do that? Does she know what she is doing? And she joins them, she joins them in their bed, Ida kisses her first, Ida touches her, she touches Ida, Ida is in the middle. Is this how they will reinvent themselves from now on and in future, or is it how Ida unpicks their relationship, step by step, with increasingly extreme actions, and does she in fact know exactly what she is doing? The next day she is beside herself, just like after the club in Copenhagen, completely beside herself and clings to Arnold and loves Arnold, only Arnold, and can't bear to look at the other woman, this stupid woman who intrudes on their life, who comes over to them in broad daylight and tries to talk to them as if nothing has happened. Ida wants to have sex with Arnold, she lusts after Arnold, caressing and squeezing and clinging to Arnold, putting her legs on top of his in the bus, and she is wanton and beside herself and erotically obsessed by Arnold. At night the plump young woman knocks on their door and they let her in and Ida lies in the middle, but Arnold also touches her now, he wants to join in, he says, he has sex with Ida, he is on top of Ida, but while he is having sex with Ida, is on top of Ida, his hands caress the other woman's body, the other woman's breasts which he sucks and her pussy which he licks while he is having sex with Ida. The very last night she turns up again, again she knocks on the door when everyone is in bed, again they let her in and allow her into their bed and they touch her and Arnold has sex with Ida and when Ida has come, but Arnold hasn't and is still going, Ida needs the loo and she says she needs the loo and pulls away from underneath him, pushing him off, and says, as she is going to the bathroom, that he can have sex with her, with the other woman, and then she goes to the bathroom. Now he is having sex with another woman, his arms are around the waist of another woman, his arm, which is around Ida's waist most mornings, is moving now and it is moving down there. Ida stands with her toothbrush in her hand and imagines it. It hurts so much. His hand moving downwards. The other woman sighs and his hand becomes eager, she sees it. Ida stands in the doorway and sees it. His eager hand over the pussy, the dark pussy, the blue pussy, the small animal. He bends over the other woman, kisses her nipples and feels them harden in his mouth as they did in Ida's mouth, soon he will enter her – he doesn't know that Ida is watching – how similar it is, what he likes, how he likes it, he is with the other woman as he is with her, why is she doing this to herself? It is going to happen soon. He is going to come soon, it feels so good. It feels so good for him to be inside the other woman that he comes. Ida returns to the bathroom and locks the door. So it is true, so it is possible, the impossibility that she can't live with. She can't bear it. She is in the bathroom, now he is thrusting against the other, now he comes, now he moans, now he feels amazing. It is unbearable. She can't bear it.

In order to have tried everything. In order to experience the split before it happens. If they don't break up, they will die. If you are going to leave me, leave me slowly, please, little by little so I will barely notice, so that when it happens it has happened already and is over. Leave me early on before we get to know each other, let me meet someone other than you if you are going to leave me anyway, you have already left me, you left me in my childhood.

She doesn't come back out.

'Ida, come out,' they call, but she won't. They can lie there in the bed and fuck and manage without her. She sits down on the floor, she is unable to get up, she covers her head with a towel, the pain is searing.

'Ida, come out!'

She unlocks the door and opens it a crack for Arnold, she isn't going to come out until the other woman has left.

'Make her leave!' she whispers, she hisses. 'She has to go! Make her go away. I'm not coming out until she has gone, I don't want to see her, I hate her, tell her to go.'

'All right, all right.'

'Get rid of her, I say,' she whispers, she hisses. 'I can't stand that she is here, I hate her, get her out of here!'

'Ida!'

'Or I will scream. I'll scream, I'll howl, do you hear, at the top of my voice, I'm just about to do it and once I start I can't stop, I know it, are you listening to me, get her out of here!'

Arnold goes back and some minutes pass. Perhaps the other woman gets dressed, yes, she gets dressed, and he watches her get dressed and perhaps he helps find her knickers or her bra, which is under the bedspread some-where or in a corner, he watches her body, her naked, half-dressed body, which he has just made love to, yes, pre-cisely, made love to, perhaps they talk, intimately, perhaps he kisses her. Perhaps he says that Ida is crazy, perhaps he winks at the undergraduate and says that once they are back in Trondheim and Ida is out of the way, they can have a beer and talk about it, she can come to his office, but right now she needs to leave, for Ida's sake, regardless of what Arnold thinks, Arnold is happy for her to stay, but she, Ida, is being difficult.

Then he knocks on the bathroom door and says that she has gone and Ida comes out and they go to bed and make love, desperately.

'Be rough with me!' he says. And: 'Hurt me!'

'Punish me!' he says, 'be rough with me!'

'No, not that rough!' he says. 'Be gentle!'

'Hit me! Hit me!' he says.

'No, not as hard as that. No, ouch!' he says.

'I love you,' she says. 'Enter me, split me! Let me hear the angels sing!'

'I'm going to hit you!'

'Yes! That feels good. Let me die!'

'I'll tear you to pieces!'

'Burn me! Send electric current through my nipples, let me bleed!'

'You'll never be the same again!'

'I'm different already! Use your fist, darling! Just be rough with me. Yes, that's good, keep going until I die!'

'Don't die!'

'Thank you, thank you! Humiliate me even more, let me feel the humiliation!'

When she first met him, he was light. He came from the main entrance to Frogner Park down towards Herregårdskroen where she sat on the low wall, waiting. His hair was downy, fair, almost transparent. Years later he was dark like her, he had grown darker, heavier and more compact, more masculine in order to suit her better. When she met him he drank black coffee, now he drinks coffee with milk, like her. He asks: Are you wearing a coat, and if she puts on a coat, he puts on a coat. If she puts on a hat, he puts on a hat. He had a broken toenail when she first met him, a fat woman had stepped on his toe when he was young, when he played at a dance, and it never recovered. The last year he was with Ida, the last summer, it slowly improved, it finally healed. But then Ida dropped a plate on her big toe that same summer when she was washing up and her toenail turned blue and fell off, and slowly a new nail grew out and it looked like the toenail Arnold used to have. On the night that he was unfaithful to her for the last time, the first time with the last woman, of the women she knows about, the glass on her wristwatch broke and the hands fell off.

Another friend of hers is getting married and asks Ida if she will be her matron of honour. They are getting married in Skagen, in Denmark, far away from her family with whom she doesn't get on, it is understandable, that is how they would have done it if they were getting married, as indeed they will be, next year, her and Arnold.

'You have never proposed to me!'

Back when I could, I couldn't. Now that I can, I can't.

Just the happy couple, their best man and their matron of honour, catching the ferry Thursday night, on Friday they will arrive at Skagen, a quiet wedding on the Saturday and then home again on the Sunday, that is the plan. The happy couple is paying. Is she free?

Yes, she has no plans for the weekend. It suits her fine. But she doesn't voice her immediate reaction which makes her stomach lurch: But what about Arnold? Has no one thought of Arnold? Arnold will be furious. He is invited to the couple's big party the following week, but he hasn't been invited to Skagen.

'That's a bit excessive, isn't it? Three days? After all, they're having a big party next week. That's enough, surely? Is her wedding going to require your presence for a fortnight? It's rather rude to demand so much of your time, isn't it? And you've already said yes. Without checking with me first. If we had been married, they would have included me in the invitation. Your friends don't take our relationship seriously. They never have done. I'd been thinking that we should go to Denmark that weekend. I'm due to give a lecture in Århus and I was thinking that you could come with me, that we could spend the rest of the week in Denmark and work, I mentioned this to you a long time ago, but you just go ahead and make plans with your girlfriends and don't even think to tell me, you take me for granted.'

Now they have to talk about it every night and every day until she leaves. Three weeks before and three weeks after, and every time since whenever they argue. Sometimes she will cancel or turn down invitations because she hasn't got the energy for the quarrelling in advance, the quarrelling afterwards, the arguments. He gets so angry, so disappointed, so offended that he goes upstairs to lie on the sofa and she has to go after him and cajole him back

307

downstairs, or he goes to bed during the day and closes his eyes and says he is depressed so that she has to go down and talk him out of it and cuddle and pat him, make love to him, to cheer him up again. There's only you, Arnold, no one else matters. How did he get such power over her? What is she afraid of? That he will leave her, be unfaithful to her, inflict pain on her, he holds the instruments of torture: Mercy!

Sometimes she will cry off, but she can't pull out of her friend's wedding. An important day, a big event, a close friend, an honour, but it is no use explaining and deep down she has given up trying. So she just goes. He hates her for it. That she leaves apparently without a second thought. She makes a point of seeming a little troubled for his sake, but she has no real doubts, she never seriously considers cancelling and instead going with Arnold to Århus where he is due to give a lecture. She and Arnold will spend the following week together in Denmark, that is the plan. That has to be enough, a whole week. And that is not the problem, the problem is that he hasn't been invited, that he isn't included, that he doesn't count, that is how he sees it, that she is slipping through his fingers, that is how he sees it. She travels to Skagen. He travels to Århus, later they can meet halfway, rent a place where they can work, just the two of them, for a week. It will be fine. But they could have travelled together and been away together for longer. Just like Arnold had planned a long time ago. Except for this Skagen event which came out of nowhere and to which Arnold isn't invited. That represents a slight and something is bound to go wrong. She knows it. She has bought a foreign SIM card for her new mobile so that Arnold can call her, but something will go wrong all the same. He feels insulted, something is bound to happen and she can't help but worry. The bride and groom stand on the quay waiting, the best man is there, they smile. They are going to have a lovely time. Why is Ida's smile so stiff? They can tell from looking at her. That something is wrong, that she is dreading something. Her mobile is in her bag. Arnold calls and she tells him she is on the ferry, that they are going to have dinner shortly. He is distant, he is disappointed, surly. Well, you go and enjoy yourself while I sit here all alone.

She is worn out. She calls him to say good night when she is in bed. He says good night, he is alone and has to travel on his own the next day, the two of them could have travelled together, but that is her choice. She scratches the small bumps on her back and upper arms until they bleed. She can never relax. Why should she wish that he was here when she doesn't, she is so tired. She has to come up with a plan so that nothing can go wrong: Arnold can join them after his lecture, she has to persuade the couple to invite him to the wedding dinner, she has already assured him that it won't be a problem. She is dreading it, everything is an issue, pressure from all sides. If only it was over, if only it was all over and she was home again, in a kind of peace. In her own home and at peace. She can't handle any more stress, any more pressure, it's got to stop.

She calls his hotel Saturday morning, his tone is dismissive and he tells her to call back in five minutes. Why? What is it this time? A woman in his room he needs to get rid of, after all, he was angry and she knows what he is like and what he does when he gets angry, she knew that something would happen. She calls him back five minutes later, he is calmer now, oh yes, he is on his way, he has done well, he says, he gave a great lecture, he says, and many people praised him, he says, he is hung over, she can hear. He is on his way.

Then he calls her mobile while they are walking along the beach, on Grenen, picking up pebbles. He is at the station, about to catch his train, it arrives at six o'clock, he says, she can hear that he has been drinking. He misses her, he says, because he has been drinking and he isn't angry anymore, perhaps he spent the night with another woman, perhaps that is why. He says he is looking forward to seeing her.

'Please don't turn up drunk,' she says, she shouldn't have said that, he slams down the phone. It kicks off now, it has already kicked off, what is she going to do, her friends are getting married in an hour. She finally plucks up the courage to ask her friend if Arnold can join them. Arnold is in Århus and he and Ida are practically married, Ida says, and it is fine although the mood changes because her anxiety infects them, there are just four of them, but Ida thinks that everything will be all right now. They change the dinner reservation after the wedding to include Arnold who will arrive at six o'clock, and as long as everything goes smoothly until then, as long as they get married, they are happy, Ida will pour all her efforts into that so that they are happy, contented, then Arnold will come and they won't even notice her, they will have had enough of Ida, no one will mind that she gives Arnold her full attention then, which is what she will have to do once he arrives.

Her friends get married, they sing in the nearly empty church, there is just the four of them, the vicar and the bell ringer. They walk up the aisle, very seriously, and pledge their troth to each other. She doesn't think of Arnold as they do so. She doesn't miss Arnold as they do so. She just dreads what might happen next. Please let it be all right! But when they sing *Love Divine, All Loves Excelling*, her voice cracks on the high notes, she could burst into tears at any moment, she longs to collapse. They take pictures, they smile, they walk across the sand dunes. The bride with her black hair and green eyes, the glow you have when you are in love. Her body so light that the groom lifts her up as if she weighed nothing at all. By the sea, by a boulder, next to a brick wall.

'To us,' he says and raises his glass. They drink champagne on the lawn in front of the hotel where they are staying, Danish flags are stuck into the ground. Sunshine. Arnold is coming soon. She is picking him up.

'To us,' the bridegroom says and raises his glass. He speaks softly because they are the only ones there, the four of them, on the lawn in front of the hotel. He is emotional, it is wondrous to see. The bride raises her glass to his. He looks at her, he is very serious, and he says, and his voice breaks, that they have now marked an important event in their lives, which is that the two of them met. Ida goes to pick up Arnold, but he isn't at the railway station. The station is closed, Ida runs to the nearby shops and asks about Saturday trains, there are no more trains today, they say. Arnold isn't there. He doesn't have a mobile, she can't call him. She goes back, he rings her on her way back. He is drunk. Because she told him not to turn up drunk. He got off the train, he says, he is in a neighbouring town, drinking. So what does he want, what does he want to tell her now? Why is he calling now, what is she meant to do with this information?

'So what am I supposed to do?' she screams, she loses her temper, she can no longer control herself, this is the last straw. He hangs up. She can't call him back, he doesn't have a mobile, she can't reach him. He doesn't call. What should she do now? Go back, drink champagne with the others who have reserved a table for five, not four, raise a toast to the happy couple on their wedding day!

'He wasn't there,' she says. Well, he wouldn't be, would he?

'Let's just go ahead and eat,' she says. There is no reason to wait. Arnold isn't there, but Arnold's ghost haunts Ida.

They go to the restaurant, Brøndums in Skagen. Nothing but the best today for the happy couple! Oysters with the champagne. Her mobile lies on the table, but it doesn't ring. Suddenly he appears in the doorway, plastered. Ida leaps up. He is absolutely wasted, he can barely stand. He wants to have a row with her, she herds him outside. He is angry because of what she said, because she told him not to turn up drunk. Angry because of what she has done, but mostly because of what she hasn't done. She asks if he is capable of behaving himself until it is time for them to go, until the dinner is over and they can go to bed.

'You're not pleased to see me!'

The oysters are waiting, the champagne is waiting, the newly married couple is waiting.

'Of course I am. Now are you able to behave yourself until we can go to bed?'

'And here I am having given a bloody fine lecture on Brecht and been a bloody great big success, but you're not happy to see me!'

'Of course I am. Now will you be able to behave until it's time for us to go? They got married today. We have to join them. The food has arrived.'

'You're not pleased to see me.'

'Of course I am. Now can we join the others?'

'I might as well leave. I should never have come.'

'Of course you should be here. Now can we join the others?'

'You're not pleased to see me.'

313

'Of course I am. NOW CAN WE JOIN THE OTHERS?'

'I might as well leave. You don't want me here!'

'Of course I do!'

Oh, it is sad to write, it must be sad to read, how long does it go on? Ten minutes, fifteen or more before they join the others. Arnold talks about his success, his Brecht lecture. He doesn't want any food, he smokes cigars.

'Keep your voice down,' Ida says because his voice is loud, it dominates.

'Keep your voice down,' he then starts to mimic every time she speaks.

I can't do this anymore, she thinks. It has to end, she thinks. It can't go on, I can't live the rest of my life like this, she thinks.

Arnold talks loudly about his amazing Brecht lecture. He might have spent the night with someone, is that why he is so drunk, he slept with a woman at the seminar and feels guilty and needs to be drunk to find the courage to turn up, is that it?

Arnold talks about his brilliant audience.

'Åshild and Rune were married today,' Ida says.

'Keep your voice down,' Arnold says. Ida goes to the ladies. She is crying, she can't help it. The bride comes after her because she has noticed, she understands, she follows her and strokes her hair to comfort her.

'It's fine,' she says. 'Don't worry about us. We don't mind. Just relax, we're having a very nice time,' she says. 'We're fine. Just let him be, don't worry about it, Ida.'

They rejoin the others and Arnold goes to the gents, the best man looks gravely at Ida and asks in a slow voice: 'What's going on here?'

He means: Why are you with this man? This small, balding man with a pot belly who is being a bore. Whose Brecht lecture might have been a success, but he has no manners, he doesn't know how to behave. A stranger, who has known Ida for only two days, wonders who Arnold, her German professor boyfriend is, and he is shocked.

'What's going on here, Ida?'

Ida is scared of Arnold. She walks on eggshells around Arnold. The bride is scared too on Ida's behalf, and the bridegroom is scared for the bride, but the best man isn't scared.

'Now shall I tell you what the theology students thought of my Brecht lecture,' Arnold says rhetorically, lights his cigar and is about to continue.

'No,' says the best man and turns away from Arnold, faces the newlyweds, changes the subject and Arnold shuts up. That is how to handle him. It is actually possible. It beggars belief that she has never managed it. Arnold has some brandy with his coffee, that helps. The others want to go out after dinner, Ida goes back to the hotel and gets Arnold into bed and once he is snoring, she sits there watching him. Naturally he sleeps in her bed, a single bed, which they will have to share because her hosts were not expecting him. Naturally he makes himself comfortable, he spreads out and snores. She doesn't go to bed, she hears the others come back and retire, she sleeps in a chair. Her sense of being responsible for him hasn't gone in the morning, it is as if he were a child, she is ashamed, she dreads leaving the room, seeing the others, looking them in the eye. If only it was over, if only the two of them were alone in the car, their luggage in the boot and on their way, if only they had found a place to stay and could sit down with a beer. They get dressed in silence. They don't speak. They pack their things and carry them to the car, hoping they won't meet anyone and they don't meet anyone and they knock on the doors to the others before they leave and the doors are opened and everyone pretends that nothing has happened. Arnold acts as if nothing has happened, is he ashamed or isn't he? They ask if they fancy a cup of coffee before they leave and Ida says yes please and they each have a cup of coffee, they sit down and Ida tries to be light-hearted, she asks about last night, where did they go after the restaurant, did they have a good time. Arnold stares at his coffee. Then Ida gets up and says that they really have to be on their way now. They say thank you for the coffee, they set the cups down on the table. They say thank you and they leave. Ida drives. Southbound to the place they visited in the summer. Four or five hours later they arrive at the town where they spent the summer, by the sea, Arnold has yet to say something, he is depressed. They park by the seafront and go to the restaurant where they have been before, right down by the water's edge and order beer, food. Arnold hangs his head.

'Arnold,' she says, reaching her hands across the table. He shakes his head.

'Arnold,' she says, he just about looks up.

'I should never have come.'

He has finished his beer, she orders him another one. 'Well, at least we're here. Can't we just forget about last night? Now it's just the two of us here. We have a whole week to ourselves.' She clinks his glass with hers. 'Cheers, Arnold.'

He drinks, sets down his glass and stares into it, continues to hold it, then he looks up at her and smiles tentatively.

'Arnold!' she beams.

They have rented a holiday cabin. They work, they sit at the same table with their laptops. They go for walks by the sea, they find strange stones and seashells. They go to cafés, eat out, eat at home, their standard routine. There is no double bed in the cabin but two single beds in two different rooms, which can't be moved. Sometimes she will move from the bed where they have gone to sleep that night to the bed in the other room in the middle of the night. To get a better night's sleep, to have a bit more space. The man, whom some years ago she couldn't get close enough to, keeps breathing down her neck. How are they? Heavy, they are heavy, their heads are heavy, their bodies are heavy, they no longer run, time passes slowly. She

317

doesn't like herself, she doesn't like her face in the mirror. They are quieter than usual and slow, they don't even argue until their last day, they can't even manage that. Arnold accuses her of showing too much cleavage, so at least they manage one argument before they leave. What is she trying to achieve with her deep cleavage. They sit in the bar on the ferry home and they get drunk as usual. If anyone is watching them, can be bothered to watch them and can be bothered to think about them, they will be thinking that there is a couple of tired old drunks arguing about crap. And then: We never want to turn into them.

They stagger through corridors to their cabin, fall asleep in separate berths and wake up in the morning as silent as when they went to bed, exhausted and hung over and desperate to get away from each other, he to Trondheim, her to Oslo, they don't say a loving goodbye to each other. But just fifteen minutes after their separation, he to Trondheim, her to Oslo, they feel a hint of pain and a mere hint is enough for them to call each other and reassure each other that they will never break up, that they love each other. They are so terrified of the pain that they call out of sheer terror to assure each other that they will never break up. They can't leave each other now, they are unable, they are too weak. It is just as agonising to break up as it is to soldier on with life as they know it. They have travelled together, but arrived at separate destinations as it turns out.

~

Rune and Åshild hold their big wedding party for friends and family. Arnold has been invited, but doesn't show up, he is in Trondheim, but he wouldn't have come anyway, given how they insulted him in Skagen. There is seemingly no end to how much this marriage must be celebrated, he remarks. She doesn't read him the speech she will give for Åshild and he doesn't ask to hear it. He rings her on her mobile just before she is about to go to the function room, there is a party at the German Department, he says, he's going to it and that makes them even. She gives her speech, she makes conversation, she dances and stays out late. When she wakes up in her own bed the next morning, the glass on her wristwatch has smashed and the hands have fallen off. Arnold is in a state. He has been calling her mobile all evening and all night, but she didn't take it with her in order to avoid him. He gave up at five-thirty in the morning, he says. So what did he do then? When she calls him that night, they usually call each other at night, at midnight to say good night, his line is busy for a long time. When she asks him who he was talking to, he says: 'No one.'

'No one? But the line was busy.'

'How is that my fault?'

He comes to Oslo. They sit on her bed and drink sparkling wine, then she asks him again who he was talking to late last Saturday night, and he smiles mischievously and says it was an undergraduate he met at the party at the German

319

Department while she was celebrating Rune and Åshild's wedding for the umpteenth time.

What is her name? How old is she, she asks, now he has got her going again. But don't tighten the screws now, Arnold, you can never know which straw is the final one.

'Everyone tells me how good I look,' Arnold says. He has grown a moustache and bought himself a new jacket. It suits him, people have told him so, the undergraduate told him so, at the party at the German Department he was complimented on his moustache and his jacket. Just so that Ida knows it. Twentysomething-year-old undergraduates think he is a handsome guy. Just so you know, Ida, so perhaps you should make more of an effort.

'You never make the first move these days,' he complains. When he is due to travel back to Trondheim, she says in terror, out of pure, actual fear:

'Please don't sleep with anyone else from now on, Arnold.'

'We'll see,' he replies.

She sees it happen, but she can't stop it. If it happens, it is because Arnold is Arnold and can't be any different, and then it might as well happen sooner rather than later, besides, it is too late now, he isn't going to change and she can't live with it, she can't keep pleading with him not to do it again.

She goes to Trondheim to visit him while her children are with their father as she usually does. But she doesn't leave on the Monday as she usually does, as they have previously arranged, because she has been invited to meet with the artistic director of a theatre in Bergen who has read her most recent play. So she will come to Trondheim, to Arnold, a day later, she will spend a night in Bergen at the theatre's expense, she has been invited out to dinner after the meeting with the artistic director and the theatre's dramaturg. She accepts the invitation, of course, she is very excited about it, but Arnold gets cross. He personally gives up so many things for Ida, has she any idea how much he neglects his work at the German Department to be with Ida, how angry his colleagues are with him because he goes to see Ida and wants to be with Ida as much as possible? Ida takes their relationship for granted, it may just be a single meeting to her, but it is a twenty-four-hour delay to Arnold, so Arnold has to sit alone in Trondheim.

The meeting goes well, they will probably want to stage her play if she makes a few minor changes, she is so happy, she is so excited, she can barely eat during the dinner which doesn't last very long, she runs back to her hotel room to call Arnold and tell him all about it, but he doesn't pick up. She knows immediately. She recognises the familiar pattern. She calls back, he doesn't pick up, but then he does and she can hear Chet Baker in the background. He didn't expect her to call this early in the evening, that her dinner would finish so soon, that is why he picks up the phone because he doesn't think it is her, there is someone with him, that is what is going on. She realises it immediately, intuitively, the old routine, he is curt and doesn't want to be disturbed, he wants to go back to what he was doing, to the woman who is with him.

'I think I might go down to the bar,' Ida says, this is a test.

'Yes, I absolutely think you should do that,' Arnold says. 'Go to the bar and have some fun,' Arnold says and hangs up. She is certain now. She knows him. Arnold has never ever suggested that Ida should go down to a bar to have some fun. She waits ten minutes, then she calls him again, he doesn't answer. He doesn't pick up for the rest of the evening or at any point during the night, he has pulled out the plug so that he can do it in peace. She knows it. She lies in her hotel room and knows it. He doesn't pick up in the morning either, she calls him from 7 a.m. onwards, but she doesn't get through to him until she tries the Department of German three minutes before his twelve o'clock meeting.

This is the end. There is no mistaking it. But I'm not going to milk it, wallow in it, it bores me already, it seems so infantile, so banal, that even the pain it caused seems infantile, banal, embarrassing, a source of shame; with the little bit of common sense still active in her brain Ida realises how banal it is, yet still it hurts, perhaps it hurts even more because even the most stupid, most infantile action can cause pain, but I won't wallow in it because I, too, know shame, even now as I sit here writing down only the most important insight: the pain was so all-consuming that only one remedy would do. End it so it can't happen again. The only remedy that will help: making that decision. She has no choice, her entire body is telling her that it is over, it is enough, now it is just a question of survival, she will never, ever sleep with him again.

She catches him at his office, three minutes before he is going to a departmental meeting at noon. She knows it and she can hear it in his voice, but still he lies to her. She screams that she can't take any more.

'Sweetheart,' he says, but still doesn't confess, he doesn't dare confess because he can hear that she is going completely out of her mind.

'I won't talk to you until you tell me the truth,' she says and leaves Bergen, she doesn't go on to Trondheim as they had agreed, but travels back to Oslo. She can't sit still, this is unbearable. She calls a friend and tells her, and her friend says: 'Don't talk to him. Please don't talk to him. Ignore him, cut contact with him for a while, it might help a bit, that way you'll transfer some of your pain to him.' It is over. She leaves Bergen. It is over. It hurts like hell. It is over. Her children call, she tells them that she has broken up with Arnold. Her ex-husband calls, she tells him that she has broken up with Arnold. Her parents call, she tells them that she has broken up with Arnold. For good this time. Arnold calls her. She says that she won't talk to him until he tells her the truth.

'Why are you so being angry and suspicious?'

'You bastard. I refuse to talk to you until you tell me.'

He doesn't ring until later, at night when he is drunk.

'I refuse to talk to you until you tell me.'

'Tell you what?'

'You know what I mean.'

'What do you mean?'

'YOU KNOW WHAT I MEAN!'

'My phone was out of order. Ask Berthold. My phone was out of order.'

She gets hysterical, she loses her temper, a primal scream erupts from her, she has never screamed like this: 'I CAN'T TAKE ANYMORE! I DON'T WANT TO BE WITH A MAN WHO LIES!' She hurls her mobile against the wall and tries to breathe slowly, to calm her pounding heart. Then he doesn't call, then they don't speak for days, she borrows library books about grief in the hope of finding help, in order to cope. Stick to her guns in order to survive, until she can't take any more and calls him because it is excruciating and unbearable and it doesn't get any better, only worse. She calls him Saturday morning to tell him how unbearable it is for her and he can't bear it either, they cry and say that they love each other, and she isn't angry, only desperate, and he asks if she thinks they can be together again, and she falls silent. She asks what really happened that night. And Arnold, too, falls silent, then he says that he feels like an idiot.

She waits, he doesn't add anything so she asks if he was with the undergraduate, and he says: 'Yes.'

She knew it all along, but it still hurts, she feels worse even though she was sure that it couldn't get any worse, as if deep down she has harboured a tiny hope that there might be some other explanation so that she wouldn't have to do this. He doesn't have the energy to talk about it, he says.

'It's up to you to decide what you think about it,' he says and rings off, but there is nothing to think about. There is no alternative. He calls her ten minutes later and asks what conclusion she has come to and she tells him that it is over. She can't take anymore, he is never going to change, it is the end.

An avalanche has started where she is. She is caught up in an avalanche.

It is over. From now on it is a question of getting through it. Exist in it and survive. Rest, at times she finds it impossible to get up. Trust those who say that it will pass. It is impossible to believe, but some people say that the same thing happened to them and that time really is a great healer. Though that seems inconceivable right now. When she is able to get out of bed, she goes to another library to find better books about the grieving process, which could help her, surely there must be something. What can you do to accelerate it? Can you do anything at all to speed it up? Acknowledge your loss and mourn it. She lies on the sofa, acknowledges her loss and mourns it, screams over it, if it doesn't ease she will kill herself, except he isn't worth so great a sacrifice.

'It will pass!' says everyone she asks, she asks everyone, she asks the librarians, women in shops, the off-licence where she buys wine, shoppers in the queue at the supermarket, taxi drivers, they all say that it will pass, but can she trust them? How can it hurt so much now and not hurt in a few months, what if it goes on for ever? She calls the Samaritans at night and sobs. It's all right, they say, just let it out, your calling us is a good sign. She starts to believe that it will pass. That it really is a matter of getting through it.

It is unfair that he has a shoulder to cry on. He goes to his undergraduate with his sadness or perhaps he doesn't feel sad, how can she know what he feels. Perhaps he doesn't know what he feels, perhaps he is a little bit in love, confused, like he was when he broke up with Kjersti. He goes to his undergraduate so as not to be alone with his confusion and she welcomes him so he doesn't have to be alone at night. Ida has no one, she is alone. It is better that way, people tell her. She tracks down the undergraduate's number and calls her and asks about Arnold and screams and shouts and afterwards she is ashamed and she calls her back and promises not to do it again, and almost keeps her promise. Let it all out, feel your feelings, have a good cry. Keep walking through the snow. Drink beer, it helps. Have a beer, her friend says, it helps. She takes off the ring he gave her. She takes down photos of him, of the two of them together from the walls. She packs his things, his books, his clothes, his shoes, stuffs them in a bin liner and drives it to his brother, who lives in Oslo, and leaves it on his doorstep. She makes it final this time, seizes the chance to do it properly, complete it. The undergraduate, she tells herself, is ultimately a gift to me. Her body aches at the thought that he is doing it with another woman, in the bed where they used to do it, they will never do it again. But it was bound to end. Now it has ended. She will never go there again, never set foot in that bedroom. Never sleep with him again, never, ever. She feels no desire, only pain, she will never desire him again, when she thinks about them having sex, she feels only pain, only hurt.

She travels to Røros, to the hotel by the railway station where she stays occasionally in order to work because she gets restless at home when the children are with their father, but she is also restless in Røros, she stands in the window, watching the trains pull into the station and remembers one time she was there, alone, before she started seeing Arnold, but after she had met him. She waited by the window, hoping he would step out of one of the carriages and come upstairs to her, if he did that then she would be happy; that was all it would take. She stands at the same window and watches the trains arrive at the platform. It is evening and dark as it was back then. It is winter and cold as it was back then, but she doesn't think that Arnold will be getting off the train. She has lost faith. If Arnold were to step off the train now, she can't be sure that she would let him in. There is no rest, no consolation in Arnold's arms, there is nothing he can do which can take away her pain.

If life were a movie, she tells herself when it is bad and she fears the pain will never end, she has now reached the dramatic peak, that's something to be grateful for, one of the more exciting sequences, at least it is not dull, and the audience watching is now wondering: What will happen next? How will this end? That is how she needs to think of it when it hurts the most, as if it were a film, to wonder what will happen next. Just like her daughter said after they had been to see *Titanic*: 'Nothing exciting ever happens to me!'

'You're not fighting for our relationship,' he says on her answering machine. He had thought, perhaps he had expected her to fight, is that why he did it in the first place? To trigger her competitive instinct, to ensnare her? A rival, an undergraduate, now let's see who ends up with Arnold Bush! Did he think that that would be her response, to fight to win him back and then gloat over the undergraduate: Look, I won! And while the battle is ongoing, the feted and desired Arnold Bush can stroll through the university corridors with a hard-on. Is that what he thought?

He hadn't expected her to be capable of what she is doing now. He doesn't believe that she can do what she is doing now. He regards it as a crisis, an episode before she calms down, starts missing him and comes crawling back like she always does, so that they can make up yet again because she can't live without him. Can she live without him now?

'You may think you loved me,' he says on her answering machine, 'but you never loved me, you never loved me as I really *am*.'

Should she love his infidelity? Would hers not be a true love unless she also loved his infidelity and his need to control? Is it a weakness of her love that she can't endure everything?

'Tove Ditlevsen,' he says on her answering machine, 'could cope with much more than you. You're a poor imitation of Tove Ditlevsen,' he says. 'What I have done is nothing compared to what Victor Andreasen did to Tove Ditlevsen.' The Danish author Tove Ditlevsen and Victor Andreasen, the editor-in-chief of *Ekstra Bladet*, stayed together their whole lives, almost, no matter what one did to the other. Because they loved each other. 'We love each other, Ida! You know that!'

Tove Ditlevsen, she answers in their imagined conversations, ended up killing herself. Tove Ditlevsen was admitted to a psychiatric hospital and Victor Andreasen couldn't take any more and left her, she reminds herself. Perhaps Tove Ditlevsen should have left Victor Andreasen much sooner. Then she might not have ended up in a psychiatric hospital, she might not have killed herself, who knows. Tove Ditlevsen planned to write a book about her life with

Victor Andreasen, whom she referred to as a highly intelligent psychopath, did you know that, the title of which would be *The Woman Who Put Up With Everything*, a bittersweet title, if you ask me, as if she might well have many regrets and would have done things differently had she had the chance, she tells herself quietly in their imagined conversations.

'You should be careful about being so pushy, fighting so hard to get a man you don't really want,' he says on her answering machine, she doesn't answer her phone when his number comes up.

'You never put me first,' he says. 'You never wanted to come to Trondheim. Well, perhaps you did to begin with,' he says, 'but not in the last few years. You put your friends and your fellow writers first the whole time.'

Not a single one of my friends or my fellow writers have felt I put them first, she responds to him in their imagined conversations. Go on, ask them, she responds to him in their imagined conversations, they all think I put you first, always, and made allowances for you far beyond what was reasonable.

He tries not calling, to see if that works. She asks when she comes home in the evening, during the day or in the morning: Has anyone called, in the hope that he has called, that he has left another message on her answering machine. Even an *I fucking hate you* would be better than nothing, better than silence. Because she is aware of how she does the same to him, silence is a most effective weapon. She doesn't want to be the only one in pain. The knowledge that he is hurting and is expressing his pain is almost the only thing that helps her.

He tries letters, but he writes the way he speaks and she can't answer him. It would take a novel to explain to him what it was like for her, a completely different story to the one he would have written, she can feel it the few times she talks to him on the phone, before she gives up. He gets irritated, he says that she is wrong, that if she had changed then they could have made it work, whereas she believes that he was the one who had to change, but she no longer believes in change, she has lost her faith.

'You never listened,' he says on her answering machine. 'You never took on board the things I struggled with in our relationship, which I tried to discuss with you repeatedly, but you just carried on doing what you always did.'

Does he mean that she should have stopped travelling, stopped spending time with other people because he had told her how anxious it made him feel? Should she have called him more often, done fewer of the many things he didn't like her doing, would that have been to listen to him, to follow his prescriptions, put herself in a cage so that he would feel safer? Assume his contempt for everything he despised, his enemies and his points of view because not doing so would lead to sanctions and pain? She reads his letters and argues with them in the evenings, lies awake at night and argues with them, there is so much she wants to say, but even thinking about it is exhausting.

But what if he is right? What if their narrative is the way he tells it? What if his truth is closer to the truth, if such a thing exists, than hers is?

'Have you any idea of how you are with men when you're drunk?' he asks. What can she say, after all, she doesn't know. She thought she was gentle and happy, but perhaps there is more, something she is unaware of. Perhaps her behaviour gave him cause to react, perhaps all men would react as Arnold did, how can she know? Perhaps it is the way he says it is on her answering machine and writes in his letters, that no man can cope with being with Ida, given how she is, given how she behaves in public.

She has been invited to a first-night party and is looking forward to it. It has been a long time since the last one. She has lost a lot of weight and wants to show the world that she is fine, that she is surviving, six weeks have passed since her trip to Bergen and since she caught him with the undergraduate, at times it feels as if she is over it. Her son has got his driving licence and gives her a lift, everyone feels sorry for her and they are kind. She sits in the back of the car, drinking champagne. Stupid Arnold who cheats on her with his students, ha! If only he could see her now, smiling, drinking champagne and wearing her best dress. If what you said on my answering machine is true, Arnold, that I'm the only woman in the world for you, if I really am the only one who understands you and has truly seen you, as you said on my answering machine, the only woman you can confide in, the only woman you can talk to, how could you throw it all away just to fuck a student! Eh? You should see Ida now, Arnold, in the back of a car on her way to a first-night party, she already feels like the belle of the ball, and that is a dangerous feeling with which to go to a ball. She knows it, but she has forgotten it on this occasion, here comes a woman in charge of her life, who is on top of things. Smiles to right and left, and are there any handsome men here and yes please to champagne!

She remembers the table. She remembers who was sitting either side of her and who she had coffee with afterwards, Trond, her wise, old, lovely flame, who has found himself a nice wife and had three children in the meantime. Then only fragments, queueing for some venue, a bar, she hangs on the arm of a man in a coat and remembers running from a hotel room out into the November darkness in the middle of the night and flagging down a taxi and waking up in the morning in her own house, but without her handbag, her purse, her shoes and her mobile. Her children are with their father, thank God, she lies in bed, trembling. Perhaps she can't cope on her own, without him. She must write to her psychoanalyst, she stopped seeing him because he didn't believe in her love, it turns out he was right after all, she should have gone four times a week back then rather than three. Arnold, why are you doing this to me!

It is Saturday, there is a Christmas meeting at the Dramatists' Association, she had accepted the invitation and was going to go, but doesn't have the energy now. Instead she calls a fellow writer who doesn't have the energy to go either, they arrange to meet in town for a beer while the meeting happens and then just go to the party afterwards. She needs someone to talk to, who can listen to her and tell her that everything is going to be all right, someone who has been through hard times themselves. On her way she stops by any hotels she thinks might be likely candidates, places she might have run out from last night, to ask if they have found her handbag, her purse, her shoes and her mobile. She visits one lobby after another and asks if they have found them.

'What was the room number?' they say.

'I don't know,' she replies.

'Who paid for the room?' they say.

'I don't know,' she replies.

'Are you quite sure you were at this hotel?' they say.

'No,' she replies.

No one has seen her handbag, her purse, her shoes or her mobile. She meets her writer friend at a café, he hugs her tightly when she arrives, anyone can see from her eyes and the shadows underneath them, from the way she drinks her first beer, that she is grieving. She pours out her heart and he listens, then they go to the Christmas party at the Dramatists' Association and she says to the first people she meets there:

'I'm no longer with Arnold!'

'Yes, we know.'

'How?'

Because they saw him at Kafé Celsius where they have just been, with a woman. At Kafé Celsius where Ida would have been with her fellow writers, if she had gone to the Dramatists' Association Christmas meeting. She would have gone to Kafé Celsius afterwards because they always do, which Arnold knows they always do. Which is why he went there with a woman in leather trousers to drink beer and just happened to meet Ida's friends but not – and purely by chance – Ida herself.

Beer won't do now, she orders tequila. A double, then two more doubles and then she passes out on the floor.

Someone calls a taxi to take her home, but then discovers that she doesn't appear to be breathing and takes her to casualty instead. There she wakes up hours later in a bed with a doctor holding her hand, asking her what happened and the name of her next of kin. She gives him the name of her ex-husband, who else? The doctor calls him, he is in Paris but he answers his mobile and the doctor explains the situation, and Ida tries to talk to him, but can only cry. They keep her in for observation while her friends, who are still waiting in the corridor, go home and some hours later Ida gets to leave as well, they have decided that she isn't going to kill herself once she is discharged. She reads Gunnar Ekelöf, it is the only thing that helps. When you are in pain, when you can't take any more, go to the shore and throw pebbles into the sea. One after the other and feel how you slowly become unburdened. She goes to the shore and throws pebbles into the sea, one after the other, it helps a little, she picks them up and she throws them. She sits on the shore with a sheep's fleece around her shoulders as darkness falls on this already dark Sunday in November. When she thinks about it now, afterwards, it is still a good memory. A moment frozen in time while everything else rushes past and disappears. An awareness of the human condition, her common sense and sensibility asking the same question: How will I get through it? How will I cope? What am I going to do with myself? She lies down and feels the chill of the earth, the warmth of her body and her wish for warmth, to be carried, the promise of the rocks. This is another way of knowing that we are alive.

Look, he dances with another, Tove Ditlevsen wrote. And yet I don't leave. Because suffering is a link that brings the magical pleasure happiness can never deliver.

And it is also like this: Love yourself happy and love yourself sad. Gunnar Ekelöf: You ask why we have words for genitals, why cock and pussy? Because we have no words for pain. The most exquisite, the hardest to describe. The most exquisite pain, the dark sibling, is passion for the young and warm memories for the old.

~

When she returns to her house, a paper bag from Paris is hanging from her door handle. In it is a T-shirt with the following caption across the chest: One tequila, two tequila, three tequila, floor! A present from her ex-husband.

On the Monday she calls Trond to ask him if he saw the man she left with on Friday night. He didn't. She had been on great form, he says, when people started making their way home. Then she disappeared for about ten minutes, came back to collect her handbag and announced that she had found a man with whom to leave the party since he, Trond, was now married and a father of three. He didn't know who the man was.

She calls the party organisers and asks about the guest list, wonders about some of the names and asks to have the men described to her, where they work and takes a chance on a man she reckons to be the most likely candidate and looks up his number and wonders whether to ask him a strange question, that is to say, maybe it is not strange, it depends: Did you and I go to a nightclub last Friday? So that she won't have to ask if she spent the night with him in a hotel room.

'Hello. It's Ida Heier,' she says tentatively.

'Hellloooo!' replies a deep, knowingly erotic voice, so it is the right man. He can tell her which hotel they went to, but he doesn't know anything about her handbag. He fell asleep and couldn't find one of his socks when he woke up and didn't think he could go home to his wife with just one sock and so he had to wait until the shops opened. But he had searched the room for his sock and he hadn't come across a handbag.

Even so she is relieved to be able to put a name to the face, to hear his voice, it sounds sympathetic.

'What a shame,' she says, 'that when I finally manage to chat up such an attractive man I was too drunk to enjoy it.'

'Well, I wouldn't say that,' he says, 'you came three times.'

She imagines herself rolling around the bed, moaning and groaning, she is good at masking her absence as presence, she can experience her body as completely separate from her mind, she can numb out during the act, her thoughts a thousand miles away, cut off and inaccessible.

She happens to see him, the man from the nightclub, some weeks later, on a plane back from Stockholm where she has been visiting a friend to get away for a bit. She has been in a brilliant mood for four days, but the reaction comes now as she sits quietly and alone, with wine on the plane. He enters with his wife and children and takes a seat right behind her. She starts to cry and tries to explain herself to the young man seated next to her: I'm heartbroken, you see. It feels as if someone is pulling pieces of flesh off my body with a pair of pliers.

He looks at her, horrified; is it really like that?

~

Arnold leaves a message on her answering machine saying that he misses her. 'Don't you miss me?' He says that he has told his son that they have broken up and that it made him very sad. Ida is making his son sad. He says that he misses her children. Then why did you do it, she asks him in their imagined conversations, if they mean so much to you, if your son is so fond of me, why did you do it? You called the undergraduate and arranged to meet her, you took her back to your flat, you put on the Chet Baker CD and unplugged your telephone when I called, and you fucked her in our bed where we usually fuck, WHY THE HELL DID YOU DO THAT? Didn't I tell you: If you ever do it again, it's over. Why are you so surprised? Did you really think we were strong enough to argue over yet another infidelity? If you are into extreme sports, playing Russian roulette, then you can't be surprised when it goes wrong.

'As I see it –' she begins when she picks up the phone once when he calls, but he says that it is not a matter of opinion, it is a matter of facts, and he proceeds to state the facts only she doesn't recognise them. She says that she never said the things he says she said, and he says that he remembers them clearly. 'I was there,' he says and she says: 'I was there too,' but what is the point, they are never going to agree. If she could get a word in, if she had the opportunity to speak calmly without being interrupted, she might say: Yes. I love you, but it's no use because you're never going to change and nor do you want to change because you don't think anything about you needs changing, you just want me to change. I'm complicit because I let it happen, I exposed you to my damage which you manipulated subconsciously, my lack of boundaries, my sense of guilt. Did you ever ask yourself: Is this good for Ida?

Whenever you felt uncomfortable, you let your discomfort rain down on me in the form of aggression and recriminations, you poured it over me rather than hold back, as if every uncomfortable feeling which my behaviour produced in you was my fault and my problem, never yours. And I let it happen, that was my fault, our tragedy. I love you, but we can't be together because nothing is going to change, and everything that has happened, the things we did to take revenge, to survive, which bought us temporary relief, will tear us apart if we were to meet and talk, so it is the end, it really is over. I'm trying to understand it, not to be angry – not to hate you because you ruined it – you ruined it!

Am I being unfair? Of course. In the throes of emotion, I feel hate and I want to be rid of my hate, you selfish bastard, I will never sleep with you again, never, I can't. Our history, our conversations and our promises, what we said to each other in the past is no longer valid, it lies in ruins, it is over, my body tells me so unequivocally. The ring I gave you no longer means anything, take it off. Not because I don't love you, but possibly because I do. Never again, my darling, you inside me, never again. Never again my sounds in your ear or yours in mine, I no longer know what they mean. Never again: Come lie with me. Never again in the same bed, it is over, ruined, like when a vase is broken and you see that the pieces can't be glued back together, you can break it and glue it back together three times, but finally it lies pulverised on the floor and you can see immediately that this time it can't be mended, it is lost. It is heart-breaking, yes, my heart is breaking as I write this.

She wishes he had stabbed her in public, stabbed her four times in the back so she lost consciousness and collapsed, so pools of blood grew on her back. This is how it feels, exactly like that, it would have been easier and the people around her would have been able to see how brutal it is. What has he done to her? Is this how she will die, from loss of blood because of him?

Will she ever love again? Do you love only once? Or is it the case that love for one person can lead to love of another, like writing grows from reading, a book from books, it has to be so!

It has been sixty-eight days and I don't know what you are doing. If you are grieving like I am, it is like mourning a death, if you are crying or if you are happy, carefree and in love. Are you moaning: Oh, I'm coming now, inside another woman and creating a new love language with her? Holding hands around the city like you always wanted to back when we were happily in love while Kjersti was depressed in Trondheim? It means nothing, Arnold. I want to be a kind and decent human being and I force myself to write: I hope you're all right. I wish you only well, while I feel an exquisite, masochistic pleasure in trashing one of the most wonderful memories I could have had in my life.

It has been one hundred and fourteen days and I am hoping that you won't call me because the man who should call me has to be someone other than you and talk in a way other than the way you talk. Am I in love with the person you could have been – if you had gone to therapy and changed, no, probably not, it is more likely that I am in love with the worst parts of you and which, for that reason, I need to free myself from. And the feeling of loving you, which always came back to me when I saw you again after an absence, will it be gone when I meet you, if I meet you again, if I see you and if I get close enough to recognise your smell? My beloved happiness and pain. Your footsteps, your voice, far away, what have I left of it? Why, why, why?

Perhaps in time, say the wise and there is no one I speak to now more than them, I will finally stop loving and finally stop hating and, at some point, I might even think: How could I ever have been with that man?

It has been one hundred and sixty-two days, and I still wake up with a sense of emptiness at times. You can teach yourself to seduce, but not to love. Sometimes I stay up at night, drinking and smoking. Do I feel it now, I ask myself. Or now, as I breathe in, as I inhale, as I draw the smoke down through my throat and into my lungs. Or now, when I breathe out or when I return the filter to my lips. When was it, when exactly was it, the moment of love?

I went to the railway station the other day and I sat down with myself, twenty years too late. I unpack everything in order to look at it again, again and again before I put it back and carry on, I still carry it like a sack over my shoulder, I will carry it for ever. I set it down, I open it, I unpack it and I look at it again now that I am no longer so anxious. I unpack it with care and I repack it just as carefully and I gently tie the sack and continue to carry it, I will carry it with me for ever. It has left a wound. It is not until now that I realise how deep it is. I can feel the pain gather there as I write and I wonder if instead of burying them, I am reopening old wounds.

If only there was a cure, a cure for love. Did he open up an old wound so that the infection could pour out, be released at last, so that the wound could be cleaned, rinsed repeatedly with disinfectant, with stinging fluid, right down to the bloody, open sore, the pus drained, no matter how much it hurt so that love could finally die? Because love dies like books die, they are created and live their lives, short or long, and then they die as all living things must die; doomed to die because without death, there is no life and without death, no love either.